# Christmas on Inishmore

## KC McCormick Çiftçi

*For anyone who is in the process of remembering that work does not equal life.*

# One

Some days, Emma wondered if working in the cutting edge field of social media app development was *really* making the world a better place. Scratch that, she knew it was actually a dumpster fire of addiction and FOMO, but the paychecks and the prestige of being a founder? Well, those were some pretty great perks of the job.

Still, at a moment like this, as she clapped for the non-profit founder exiting the stage, the same stage she was about to go out on, it was hard not to take a second look at the career she had chosen for herself. She surreptitiously checked the program in her hand to make sure she had his name right. Tom Conley...he'd invented some sort of water filtration system that was revolutionizing development work all over the globe. Good for him. Her social media app SLICE was revolutionizing things too, even if it was just how much time people spent on their phones every day.

"Tom," she said, holding out her hand to shake his. "That was really inspiring. I'm Emma Kells, founder of SLICE. It's nice to meet you."

"Nice to meet you too, Emma," he responded. "Though of course I knew who you were already. SLICE is a huge deal. Congrats on all your success."

Emma smiled. "Thank you. And thanks for warming up the stage for me, though it's going to be tough to follow you out there."

Tom dismissed the compliment. "I'm looking forward to learning from you. Break a leg."

Emma turned back to the stage to hear the end of the emcee's introduction. "Please join me in welcoming Emma Kells to the stage. Emma is the founder of SLICE, a social media app that has transformed the way we connect with each other all over the globe by capturing the power of live, real-time video. But I don't have to tell you that—I'm sure half of you are SLICEing this right now! Emma is frequently the youngest founder in the room, as well as the rare female founder in an industry that is largely male-dominated. We're honored to welcome her to the Southwestern Innovation Conference today as our keynote speaker. Put your hands together for Emma Kells!"

As the crowd erupted in applause, Emma took one last deep breath, closing her eyes to ground herself. There was a time when making a speech like this would have had her breaking out in a cold sweat. But after five years of keynote speeches and live on-air interviews, she had become something of a pro at charming a crowd while wowing them with her technical knowledge. She barely even registered the size of the audience anymore—whether she was speaking to a group of people standing around a table at a cocktail party or inspiring the entire student body at a high school, it didn't make a difference to her. She could give a speech like this in her sleep. And the best part was, even if she was kind of phoning it in, that wouldn't translate to her audience. No matter how much—or how little—genuine enthusiasm Emma brought to the stage, people would be inspired. The work she had done spoke for itself.

"Thank you for that warm welcome," she intoned to the crowd. "And thank you all for being here! Austin, Texas—what a great city! Let's give it up for our host city and for everyone involved in making SIC a success. I know I've been inspired here...have you been inspired? Let's hear how inspired you've been in your applause..."

While the crowd clapped and cheered, Emma smiled. She was like Tinkerbell—applause like this brought her back to life. No matter how tired she got or how frustrating a challenge was, a room full of people cheering—even if they were cheering for Austin and not necessarily for her—brought some pep back to her step and made her stand just a little bit straighter.

"In the spirit of the Southwestern Innovation Conference, I'm here to share my own story of inspiration and innovation in the hopes that it will ignite something within you. Who knows what inventions, apps, and businesses are going to be born out of the collective brainpower in this room? So, as we get started, I'll invite you to leave your imposter syndrome, your doubts, and your insecurities at the door. Ideas are going to pop up in your mind, and before you can squash them down with reasons they won't work...don't. Let them breathe. Let them live. And who knows...you just might be the one taking this stage one day."

Emma knew it was important to bring the audience along on her journey like this, to make them feel like everything she had achieved they could, too. She knew—alas, from experience—that leaning in to the idea that she was a tech genius and most people couldn't do what she had done garnered negative reviews. Harsh ones, too. Definitely harsher than the reviews that her male counterparts got when they were a little too ego-driven, but that was the nature of living in a man's world, she supposed.

"Is anyone in this room old enough to remember living in a world before social media? Put your hands up if that's you. Don't be shy. I'll put my hand up, too...I'm not ashamed to admit I may not be as young as I look. Where are my fellow 90s kids? There you go!" Emma continued to stall as sporadic hands went up around the room.

"For all the rest of you, I know it can be hard to remember a world without social media. Or without smartphones, even. But those of us who put our hands up remember a world with a lot less connection. Oh, sure, we were connected to our families, to the friends we saw at school...but I'm convinced that the relationships with the people closest to us tend to be the ones with the least depth in the connection. For me, it wasn't until I started making my first batch of internet friends that I realized how much easier it was to connect, to share, to be *seen* by another human without all that shared history and potential baggage."

Emma knew she'd found the right crowd when she saw the nods around the room. A few times, she'd given this speech to a crowd who couldn't relate to the idea of making a real friend on the internet—not to generalize, but those crowds had tended to be from a different generation—and that had created a bit of awkwardness. They hadn't been able to imagine making a close friendship with someone you'd never met in person, and she couldn't relate to them and their super close families. After a few speeches like that, she'd gotten a bit more selective about the events she accepted invitations from, and it was rare that happened anymore.

"With the increasing access that we had to each other at our fingertips, thanks to the advent of smartphones, we saw relationships, businesses, and culture shift at an exponential rate. And of course, the media that we used shifted through that time as well—from long-form text to short-form text to photos, videos, and of course livestreams."

She always paused there for the audible murmur that traveled across the room. SLICE was the king of livestreaming apps, and Emma was the queen for having invented it. Or...a different metaphor. Because she definitely wasn't married to SLICE. True, it took all of her time and energy, their finances were commingled, and there wasn't anyone else in her life who meant more to her. But SLICE wasn't much for cuddling or companionship, and she certainly wasn't getting her *ahem* physical needs met by it.

"SLICE was born when an idea floated into my window just a millisecond before it floated to anyone else. That, right there, is why I encouraged you to leave your doubts at the door—because I didn't *create* this idea, I just received it. And if you can listen and be ready, a similar idea might just perch itself on your shoulder one of these days."

Emma took a strategic pause as she saw a few members of the audience scribbling notes on the pads of paper in front of them. "Listening, paying attention, and being ready with the skills and motivation to take action were my secret weapons. They are the reason I was able to see that live video was the next big thing coming and to pivot from the app I had been working on at the time. They are the reason SLICE exists and certainly the reason I'm here today. And in fact, SIC is the perfect place to announce the next big innovation in the SLICE world. Are you all ready for this?"

Emma reached into her pocket and pulled out her own phone while the crowd cheered. She synced her phone with the projector screen behind her so that everyone could see what was on the screen, and then she opened the SLICE app.

"Everyone knows our collective attention span has gotten shorter and shorter, aided no doubt by these devices right here." She wiggled her phone at the audience. "Now, you usually hear that as a detriment, focusing only on the negative aspects and what we might be losing with these short attention spans. But I don't believe in only focusing on the negative, and therefore neither does SLICE. The idea that a few seconds of content can entertain us opens up a world of possibility, both for creators of content and for consumers of it." In the SLICE app, Emma began to scroll through a selection of videos—art being created, clips of beautiful songs, skits, jokes, dances. With every swipe of her finger, there was something new and entertaining popping up on the screen for her and everyone else in the room to see.

"Now I know you can see the value as a consumer already. Didn't we all just enjoy that a whole lot?" She paused to let the audience cheer. "But I know this crowd. I know the kind of people that come to the Southwestern Innovation Conference year after year. And you, my friends, are not content merely to consume. You are here because you are on this earth to create something of value for other people. You're here today to get some inspiration for your Big Idea. The thing you're going to do that's going to have an impact on the world around you. If you're anything like Tom Conley, the wonderful speaker who was out here just before me, it's going to make the world a better place, whatever you do." Another pause for the people who remembered Tom and his water filtration device and clapped for him.

"But that's a big project. That's years of dedication and refining. And a lot of us take that same attitude to every creative endeavor—I can't publish a book or a blog or a long-form video because it's not perfect. But with this new iteration of SLICE, guess what? There's no room for perfection. It's about what you can create right now, in this moment. Tell a joke, do a silly dance...whatever your thing is, you can publish your first SLICE in a minute or less. In fact, there's a timer in the creation mode that won't let you take longer than that. It won't let you upload something perfect, only capture a real moment, a real glimpse of your life."

There were oohs and aahs as the audience absorbed this new concept.

"It's the first approach to social media that truly doesn't let you create a highlight reel, a curated perfect life that only makes us all suffer from comparisonitis. And do you want to hear the best part?"

The cheers let her know they did, in fact, want to hear the best part.

"Because you're here today, and because I'm the founder of SLICE and know stuff like this...I'll tell you the secret of how the algorithm works. The more you create, the more your posts get seen. Therefore, the more your account can grow. We've been testing it out with a group of beta users, and the ones who publish videos hourly have seen their accounts grow to five and six figure followings in just the two months of our trial."

Another well-planned pause. "Now, who wants to get started? If you open the sharing mode on your phones, I'll send you the exclusive link to download it right now." While the cheers grew and grew, Emma tapped a few buttons on her phone to use the near field technology her team had set up to drop the app link directly in the phones of everyone in the room. She could feel the shifting energy around her, and knew with confidence that this was going to be huge.

# Two

Emma knew there was a problem before she was even back in her hotel room near the airport. Her phone hadn't stopped buzzing in her purse, but she wasn't about to pull it out and check just yet. Seated in the backseat of a taxi, Emma had to keep her eyes on the road to keep her terrible motion sickness at bay. Otherwise, the driver was liable to pull over on the side of the street and force her to get out.

They pulled up in front of the Plaza Hotel ten minutes later. The streets leaving the city had been relatively empty for a Thursday night in Austin. Emma supposed that was largely due to SIC. The annual conference was always a major pull for people to come to the city, and she had heard rumors it was a real boon for the local nightlife as well. She wouldn't know anything about that, though—Emma had an early flight back to New York tomorrow morning, so she was staying near the airport to maximize the amount of sleep she'd be able to get before her departure.

It wasn't until she was in her hotel room that she let herself look at her phone to find out what she was dealing with. The sheer volume of notifications on her lock screen made her suck in a breath. Had every single stakeholder in SLICE texted her in the hours since her speech had gone live? While one hand scrolled, the other cradled her head, massaging absentmindedly at the headache that had reappeared once the excitement of the stage faded. She noted the names of at least three investors, her parents, and her assistant, and answered her own question. Yes, every single person whose livelihood was in any way attached to SLICE had sent her a message, with varying levels of urgency. This couldn't be good.

Emma opened the first message from Dean Fischer, the first person to invest in SLICE. "Did you really say that SLICE wasn't your idea? That it came from the ether? You'd better have a look at this." He had followed the message with a link, which Emma tapped to open in her browser. It expanded on her screen and her eyes widened as she absorbed its meaning.

### CHAD BRADLEY, ESTONIAN APP DEVELOPER, CLAIMS HE HAD THE IDEA FOR SLICE FIRST.

"What in the world…?" Emma said out loud as she continued reading.

In an exclusive interview this evening, Chad Bradley, an American expat based in Estonia, shared files and email communications pre-dating Emma Kells' initial announcement of SLICE. Bradley said he had been holding on to this material on the chance that one day the world would be open to hearing about it. According to him, he first reached out to the media to share his story seven years ago and was met with nothing but ridicule.

"It all changed tonight," says Mr. Bradley. "I heard Emma speaking at that Texas technology conference, and she practically admitted that SLICE wasn't her idea. She said it came from the air, or something like that. Well, I'm here to tell Ms. Kells that she can't get away with it anymore. Ideas don't just come from the air, they originate in the hardworking mind of someone who's a hell of a lot smarter than you. SLICE was my idea first, and I don't know how you stole it from me...only that you did. I'll be making these documents and the email communications I had about my invention

**public, and Ms. Kells can expect to hear from my lawyer in the near future."**

Emma scoffed to herself. "Who is actually going to believe this guy?" she asked. "I've never even heard of him, so I highly doubt he's some kind of 'giant in the tech industry.' And who's to say he didn't just predate his communications? Make the whole thing up? How is this even worth our time?" She tapped back over to Dean's message and sent him a response saying just that.

While she waited for Dean to write her back, she opened the other messages from her investors. Carol had complimented her on a magnificent speech and then sent a similar message to Dean's, expressing her concern about the Estonian app developer. Mark had merely shared the link to a similar article with no questions or comments of his own.

The message from Emma's assistant wasn't good news, either. "I'm getting a lot of calls for you about this Estonian guy, Emma. What do you want me to tell them?"

Emma wrote her back. "What kinds of questions are they asking? I don't know anything about this guy, but I don't want to say anything that will make it sound suspicious either. 'No comment' is generally a good way to go."

Emma rubbed her forehead, her throbbing temples. This night had taken a turn, hadn't it? It hadn't been that long ago that she was standing on stage, basking in applause, and feeling on top of the world. Now, she was suddenly getting more media attention than she had in quite a while, and from the sound of it, it wasn't the attention she wanted.

The messages from her parents were still waiting, so Emma opened up the group chat the three of them shared. *Please let this be something good,* she thought to herself. *I could use the pick-me-up...*

"That was a wonderful speech, Emma," her dad had written. "Very inspiring indeed. You've got me looking and listening for any great ideas that want to come my way."

"Agreed," read her mom's message. "Emma, we are so proud of you."

As much as Emma appreciated the words of encouragement, she had a sinking feeling that she knew what was coming next. Scrolling through the message, her suspicions were confirmed.

"What is this?" The message from her mom read, attached to a link about Chad Bradley and his claims. "Emma, this is a mess. Call me when you get this."

Emma sighed. Even her own mom's words sounded foreboding, suspicious. Why did news and rumors have to travel so quickly on the internet?

Emma flopped down onto the hotel room bed, letting out a groan as she landed. Now that she knew how disappointed and/or concerned everyone in her contact list was, perhaps it was time to think about how *she* felt.

The first sensation that she became aware of was anger. How dare Chad Bradley stake a claim in the work she'd given her whole life to for more than half a decade? The sacrifices she'd made...well, she'd been more than happy to do it if it meant SLICE had a fighting chance in the tech industry. But she hadn't exactly had a personal life, a healthy sleep schedule, or any privacy to speak of since SLICE got its first media feature. Part of being a pioneer in the social media field meant you were expected to use your product constantly, to be its best advocate to the general public. Since SLICE had first become available as a beta app, Emma had been using it every day. Multiple times a day, in fact. She checked her watch and groaned again. It had been three hours since her speech had finished at SIC and, therefore, three hours since her last post on SLICE. On a normal day, it would be time to post again. Only, she wasn't sure anymore if that was what she was supposed to do.

That uncertainty made Emma aware of the next feeling that was settling over her like a heavy blanket: fear. She was in uncharted territory right now. She'd been attacked in the media, sure. What woman in the spotlight, especially in the tech industry spotlight, hadn't? But those attacks had never garnered this much attention. They'd certainly never made her own mother doubt whether she had, in fact, invented her own app and not stolen the idea from someone in a country she'd never even been to. The fear was closing around her throat, making her panic for her next breath. Was she about to lose everything? Would this just blow over, or would it be the end of her? The end of SLICE?

Emma had had a panic attack before, so she recognized the signs before it was too late. She wished she wasn't alone in this room, that there was someone here to hold her and help keep her grounded. The best she could do was to get someone "in the room" with her on a video call. Checking the time again, it was clear it was too late to call almost anyone back in New York. But thankfully, Emma's best friend, Claire, was a night owl. At two o'clock in the morning, she was probably sitting on her couch, laptop open, putting down the words in her latest novel. Yes, it was always good to have a writer friend, but it was especially good to have a writer friend when you needed a "middle of the night" emotional support call.

Opening up her contact list, Emma started a video call to Claire while simultaneously trying to remember the breathing exercises her therapist had taught her. *Was it in through the nose, out through the mouth, or the other way around? Did it matter?* She was still trying to get her breathing right when Claire answered the call.

"Emma? Is everything okay?" Claire's deep brown eyes peered at Emma through the thick frames of her blue light glasses. The room was dark behind her, but Emma could tell her suspicions had been accurate—her friend was indeed sitting in the dark in the living room, the only light on her face coming from the computer on her lap.

"Not...really..." Emma gasped out between breaths of air. "I...think...I'm having...a...panic attack."

Claire's worried expression cleared, replaced by a down-to-business determination. "You've got this, Emma. Breathe in...breathe out... Keep those breaths slow and deep. In...and out... Focus on the breath. Notice how it feels, how your stomach expands with each breath in, how your shoulders drop with each breath out."

The guided breathing continued for a few minutes until Emma felt her heart rate return to normal. As the panic cleared, she wiped her hand across her forehead, realizing to her surprise it was wet with sweat. This had been an intense bout, but it didn't surprise her, considering what was going on. The anxious feeling threatened to rise again as the memory of everything that was waiting on her cell phone returned.

"Hey, stay with me," said Claire. "What's going on?"

"You didn't hear? You must be the only person who hasn't."

"Are you talking about that Chad Bradley clown? I saw the article online, but I didn't read it. It seemed like more of the usual nonsense, not an airtight case by any stretch of the imagination."

Emma shook her head. "People seem to be taking this one seriously, for some unknown and terrible reason. It probably didn't help that I gave my entire speech tonight about how inspiration doesn't belong to anyone and just floats in the air, waiting for someone to bring it to life."

Claire looked incredulous. "So that gives him the right to claim it for himself? Unbelievable."

"I know, it doesn't make any sense. But you know how the outfits reporting on this are. They're certainly not going to try to tell the full story. They'll take some out-of-context quote and run with it, making me the villain and him the hero. People will be outraged about it for a day or two, and then they'll forget about it and move on with their lives."

"Uh huh...and what about you?"

Emma sighed. "Well, I'm guessing the impact for me is going to last a little longer than a few days. I...I haven't really had a chance to think about the long-term impacts yet.

We could lose market share. Our stock could plummet. We could lose users. My reputation could suffer, like it isn't already hard enough to control the narrative of what people are saying about me."

"I'm sorry, Em." Claire's eyebrows pulled together, the picture of concern. "I really am. I think I understand why that panic attack came on."

"Not helping. You're supposed to help ground me, remember? Not tell me I had the right idea having a panic attack. Not unless you'd like to talk me down from another one. What the hell am I supposed to do?"

"I appreciate that I'm your go-to person for advice, I do." Claire was shaking her head. "But I don't think you need me to tell you what my gut says you should do. I think you need to talk with your team—your investors, for sure, and the people who work with you. I mean, don't you have someone whose entire job is public relations?"

Emma nodded.

"Uh huh, then why in the world aren't you talking to her?"

Emma sighed. "Probably because I'm not ready to accept that this is real. And also because it's two o'clock in the morning in New York and you're the only person I'd dare call at this hour."

"So I guess your options are to either get over that and call her—because this is definitely the kind of crisis that warrants letting your PR manager in on it sooner than later—or to sleep on it and deal with it in the morning. Question is, are you going to be able to sleep?"

A groan slipped out of Emma's lips. "No. Definitely not. I'm bone tired and I *need* the sleep...but if I climbed in my nice cozy bed right now, I'd toss and turn and write rebuttals to Mr. Bradley in my head."

"Ah yes, that old chestnut. Having conversations in your own mind with someone you'll probably never talk to face-to-face in real life. That sounds like a great use of your precious brainpower."

"Har har," sneered Emma. "You've made your point with all the snark...message received. I'll call Beth after we hang up. As much as I hate the idea of calling an employee in the middle of the night, I think she'd be pretty upset if I didn't give her a head-start on dealing with this."

"You're right. If there's any chance of getting ahead of this, she needs to be aware of it sooner than later. Waking up to this kind of news tomorrow morning would be a terrible way to start the day. Don't be that boss."

"I won't. I'll stop procrastinating and call her now. Good luck with your words," said Emma.

"Thanks," said Claire. "You gave me some inspiration for the scene I'm writing, so I think I can get back to it now."

"I'm glad I could help."

As much as Emma reassured herself that Beth Kent would thank her someday for the middle of the night call, it was unlikely that day was coming anytime soon. Beth had answered the phone with such a garbled reply that Emma was sure she had startled her right out of the deepest sleep cycle. It didn't take long for Beth to return to her normal down-to-business demeanor, though—news like Emma had to share had a great way of sobering one up and quick-ly.

Once Beth was sounding coherent again, Emma asked the question that had been burning in the back of her mind since this all began. "How bad is it? This isn't going to be a big deal, right? I mean...this kind of thing happens all the time..."

"It does," Beth agreed. "Or rather, some form of it happens all the time. That's why intellectual property lawyers exist. Hang on a second, let me finish..." Emma heard a mouse clicking and fell silent while waiting for Beth's attention to return to her.

"Okay, so this is a little different," Beth continued. "It's not just the media blitz we're confronting right now. It looks like Chad Bradley has already contacted a lawyer, and we've received an official communication from them."

"Already? What kind of communication?" Emma asked, feeling her stomach twist once again, becoming even more constricted than it already was.

Beth groaned. "He didn't waste any time. It's a cease and desist letter. They're claiming that Chad Bradley's prototype predates yours. This thing is pages and pages long, Emma. It's going to take me at least a couple of hours to get through it. Can I take some time to do that?"

"Of course. Whatever you need."

"Get some rest if you can," said Beth, "And call me when you're back in the city. I'll be up."

"Thank you, Beth. I don't know what I'd do without you."

Beth laughed humorlessly. "I haven't saved you yet, Emma. I hope I can."

"No pressure, but I do, too."

Emma hung up the phone, then spent the next few hours lying on her back, staring at the ceiling. Sleep wasn't coming for her this night, not with all that was on her mind, but she still set a few alarms on her phone, just in case. The last thing she needed right now was to oversleep and miss her flight, adding yet another source of stress to her life.

At five o'clock, she sat up and exhaled a deep breath. "I guess it's time then," she said to the hints of sun peeking over the horizon out her window. "Can't keep living in the delusion that this morning is never coming, I suppose."

Emma washed her face, brushed her teeth, and changed her clothes. She selected the closest thing she had to a power suit from the selection of clothes she had brought with her to Austin. If she was going to face any media scrutiny on her journey today—and there was a very good chance that she was—then she should at least be dressed in something that gave her a little extra confidence. She put makeup on after that, taking care to cover the evidence of a sleepless night and lack of hydration as best she could.

By the time Emma was ready to leave in the taxi she had ordered the night before, she had steeled herself for what awaited. With dark sunglasses and a hat, the standard "don't see me even though I'm well aware this isn't a good disguise" look favored by people in the spotlight, she was ready to walk through the airport. What could go wrong?

But as she exited the lobby of the hotel, a figure moved in front of her quickly—more quickly than anyone had a right to move at this early hour. Her suspicions were confirmed when a camera flash blasted in her eyes, making her see a lingering blob of light every time she blinked. Who in the world?

"Miss Kells, is there anything you'd like to say about Chad Bradley's accusations?" The paparazzo wasn't backing down, blocking Emma's way as she tried to get to the taxi. "I'm selling these photos this morning. I'm sure they'd like a quote with it."

"You've got to be kidding me," Emma grumbled, still seeing spots. "This is ridiculous. What do you think I'm going to say? 'Wow, you just asked the right question at the right time. Now let me admit to you that I stole the idea for SLICE so you can make a bundle off it.' Give me a break." She pushed past the photographer and into the backseat of the taxi.

It was only after the signs for the airport came into view that Emma felt the weight of how she had spoken to the photographer. An anxious feeling gripped her stomach—had her frustration at being bothered this early in the morning made her careless with what she said? Even worse, what she said to someone who was eager to sell a story of scandal and intrigue? Emma put her head in her hands and massaged her temples. It was going to be okay. It had to be...right? Things were already bad enough; she couldn't bear to imagine that she could have made them worse.

# Three

As it turned out, Emma's imagination was incredibly limited. If she thought things had already reached the pinnacle of how hairy they were going to be for SLICE, she had been naïve. Far more naïve than the founder of a massively popular app had any right to be.

Emma had arrived back in New York to find Beth waiting for her at the airport. Considering that she had been expecting to call her PR manager only after she had arrived back at her apartment or made her way into the office, the fact that Beth was sitting in the backseat of Emma's town car couldn't be a good sign.

"Beth! What are you doing here?" Emma asked as she slid into the seat next to her employee.

Beth handed her a tablet with a video open on the home screen. "Sorry, Emma. I know we both thought we had more time to get ahead of this, but we were wrong. Keep in mind that in Estonia it's already the end of the workday.

Chad Bradley has been busy, from the looks of it." She gestured to the tablet in Emma's hands, nodding to her to press play on it.

As the video began to play, the feeling that had taken up residence in Emma's stomach the night before burrowed in even deeper, causing her physical pain. On the screen, there was Chad Bradley, a man she had never seen before but who was identified by the text on the screen. He had a gaunt face and silver hair, though from the looks of it, she placed him in his early forties. He was being interviewed on a news program, and where the clip began he was explaining to the interviewer how he had first come up with the idea for SLICE.

"I studied app development as a hobby and worked on projects in my free time. I don't have the luxury of devoting my full-time efforts to this project, but it's my passion, and I spent every evening and weekend for years learning the code and practicing making different apps come to life. That's why it was such an affront to see this Emma Kells come out of nowhere with her app, the same on all counts except for the name. It was such a blow, the kind that's almost impossible to come back from. After all, if all those years of work could disappear just because some pretty girl is claiming it as her own, what hope is there for anything else I could ever set my mind to?"

The interviewer nodded. "And why come forth now?"

"SLICE is going public now. It's everywhere in the news. Before, it was just me and Ms. Kells, my word against hers. But now it's in the spotlight. The app is getting attention, Ms. Kells is getting attention, and, with any luck, the real story will get attention soon."

Emma tapped on the screen to pause the video. "Is he totally making this up, making it sound like he was in contact with me before this all went public? I have never seen this guy or heard of him before...did he reach out, or is that a lie, too?"

Beth looked down and shook her head. "He's not making it up. I dug through the archive of old emails, the ones we received at the generic SLICE address. Sure enough, there are emails from Mr. Bradley. No one ever responded to him, and from the looks of it, the messages were just lost in a sea of cold email marketing messages."

"It doesn't look good that he reached out and we ignored him," said Emma. "It proves nothing, but it doesn't look good."

"No, it doesn't," agreed Beth. "There's more, too, I'm sorry to say."

"What? More in this interview, or...?"

"Something else. Some video from this morning of you leaving the hotel."

"Oh right, the paparazzo." Emma rubbed her forehead. "I was frustrated, and I think I said something dumb."

Beth grimaced. "The video was on SLICE, unfortunately. The worst possible place for it to be, since the media is going to have a field day about the irony of being taken down by your own app. It's only a few seconds long, but it's bad."

Beth reached for the tablet on Emma's lap and opened the SLICE app. There, Emma saw the video of herself and the photographer from this morning, and she heard herself tell him, "I stole the idea for SLICE" over and over again.

No doubt there would be an auto-tuned techno remix of it before the day was finished.

"Oh, this is bad," Emma moaned. "This is really, *really* bad." She reached over to close the SLICE app, hoping the nausea the video was causing her would subside once the video was gone.

It didn't.

"It's not good," admitted Beth. "The internet loves this kind of thing, especially if it becomes a meme. On the bright side, someone else is bound to take the spotlight from you in a few days, maybe a few weeks."

Emma was shaking her head. "A few weeks is a long time in the tech world. If I just put my head down for a month, everything could change by the time I resurface. Will SLICE even still be relevant if I go off grid for a while? Will *I* still be relevant?"

"I know it isn't ideal to go radio silent in the middle of a big launch like this," said Beth. "And I'm sure there are some PR managers who would tell you to run with this—'any publicity is good publicity' and all that. We can certainly try that tactic. But I'm worried about you, Emma. This launch was already hard on you, with the constant travel, and I just *know* you haven't been sleeping well."

"Good catch," smiled Emma. "I thought I was hiding it pretty well, but yeah. The past few months haven't exactly been good for my health."

"I just think it wouldn't be a bad idea for you to take this as an opportunity to get some rest. To recuperate your energy for the next big thing, the next big media press, which you know is going to be never-ending."

Emma shook her head. "I like the thought of disappearing while all this is going down as much as the next disgraced CEO would, but I just don't think it's possible. SLICE needs to keep moving forward. Pulling back could be a death sentence. It could give this Chad Bradley guy the exact opportunity he's wanting to steal the whole thing for himself."

"SLICE *does* need to keep moving forward." Beth was nodding, with a tight-lipped smile on her face. "We'll come up with a more solid plan, but my initial thoughts are that I can keep dealing with the press and we can have someone else—maybe Dean?—talking up the app in an interview. What do you think?"

"I know you're good at your job, Beth," said Emma. "I'm not worried about that. It just seems like a lot of pressure for the two of you and a pretty terrible example of leadership from me if I fade into the background."

"Not at all," Beth shook her head. "Whatever you end up doing is going to be what's best for the company. You're not running away; we're *all* making a decision together. Why don't we get Dean and the other stakeholders on a conference call this afternoon to talk it out?"

"Absolutely," Emma agreed. "Before that, I need a shower and a hefty dose of caffeine. Are you coming with me to my apartment?"

Beth nodded. "I am. I can do some work there while you get cleaned up, if that's alright with you. And I can make you coffee, assuming your coffee machine isn't too space agey."

•❤•❤•❤•❤•❤•

At one o'clock, Emma was logged into the online conference call platform, waiting for the others to join. She had showered to wash the restless evening and hours of travel off of her and was drinking the second oat milk latte of the day. Beth had figured out how to use her espresso machine and milk foamer like a natural, and the beverage was as comforting as it was caffeinating.

Emma took another sip as SLICE's investors made small talk with each other. She had been fortunate as a young founder to stumble on these three individuals who had helped make her dream a reality, and even more fortunate that they'd all taken an interest in the app and continued to share their business expertise with her. They had become friendly with each other over the last few years, too, and these types of calls always had the vague feeling of a family reunion. Dean Fischer was a retired CEO of an obsolete personal computer company. He was Emma's go-to source of answers for all the unique challenges that her work brought up, the head of the virtual table. Carol Calloway and Mark Aimes were both new to the tech field, SLICE being the first app they had invested in. All of them were experienced investors, and they each brought a hands-on approach to the work they did with SLICE.

"How are you doing, Emma?" Mark asked. "Beth sent us a memo, and she mentioned the possibility of having you lie low for a while."

"That's right." Emma nodded to Beth, who was sitting next to her, sharing the computer screen. "And I'm doing...alright. This has been a lot to process, and it's all a bit overwhelming."

"We can only imagine." Carol's smile was warm. "If there's anything we can do to be of service, anything at all, we're here for you. We're all in this together, truly." She looked concerned, and why shouldn't she? Her investment had helped make SLICE possible, and if it tanked now before it could have its chance in the marketplace, that investment was as good as gone.

"I'm taking the suggestion of going off-grid for a bit very seriously," said Emma. "I think if people can separate me from SLICE, it has a better chance. But we can't risk SLICE losing its spotlight. Beth will, of course, continue fielding my inbox and receiving any phone calls from the media. But we're also going to need someone to be willing to go on camera, to downplay what Chad Bradley is claiming and to advocate for SLICE. Dean, I was thinking—"

Dean Fischer interjected before Emma could finish her sentence. "I'll do it," he said, a finality to his tone. "Of course I will. I can answer any questions they may have, and my history may help lend some credibility to the company. Beth and I can work together to present a united front. SLICE is in good hands, Emma, I promise."

"What are you going to do, Emma?" Mark asked. "Where are you going to go?"

Emma shrugged her shoulders. "I'm not actually sure yet. This isn't a vacation, you know? I feel guilty thinking of it that way in the least. It's not so much about where I would like to go as it is about where I'll attract the least attention."

"Don't let guilt make this decision for you," advised Carol. "As a recovering guilt tripper myself—just ask my kids, I was the worst—all that does is turn you into a martyr. You're having a hard enough time already. There's no need to make it any harder."

Dean shook his head. "I agree with Carol. Two things can be true, Emma. A place can be on your bucket list of destinations and it can also be a relatively obscure location where the media isn't likely to find you. There's no need to hole up in a basement apartment in some suburb just to punish yourself."

"Ooh, I have an idea!" exclaimed Beth, grabbing Emma's arm in excitement. "Haven't you always wanted to go to Ireland? Wouldn't it be just perfect and magical and festive to spend the holiday season there?"

"It does sound nice..." Despite the stress of the moment, Emma felt the faintest glimmer of excitement. "Though Dublin isn't off the radar. There's a pretty sizable tech community there."

"Good thing there's more to Ireland than just Dublin then," said Dean. "My sister and her family spent their summer vacation in Galway, exploring all the sites around there. There are even some islands...the Aran Islands, I think they're called...very rustic, very *very* off the grid."

"That sounds like it's worth looking into, Emma," said Carol. Mark was nodding along with her.

Emma shrugged. "Okay, then. I guess that settles it. I'm going to Ireland!"

•❤•❤•❤•❤•❤•

"You're *what*?" Claire was incredulous.

Emma had invited her over to update her on what was happening...and ask for her advice on packing. Emma had already booked a flight, leaving at the end of the week, and she had a lot to get done between now and then.

First and foremost, she had to get her best friend on board with her plans.

"I'm going to Ireland...to Galway, actually. I'm going to stay there for two weeks, and then I'll fly back in time for Christmas. I've already started planning the days there. I'm going to explore Galway, of course, take a day or two each to go to Sligo, Donegal, Connemara...oh! And have you heard of the Aran Islands? They're otherworldly, Claire. Like going back in time. So rustic, so remote...I think there are even people there who speak Irish on a day-to-day basis. This is going to be really good, Claire."

"If you say so." Claire didn't look like she believed Emma's assessment of the situation, and Emma was running out of time and patience to convince her.

"Look, Claire. Here's the deal. The investors, Beth, basically everyone at SLICE, decided it would be for the best if I disappeared for a while. Not forever...just for a while. Just until things settle down a bit. I don't want to go someplace where I'll be spotted or attract any attention, and I've always wanted to go to Ireland."

"Yeah, I mean, it sounds like it makes sense, at face value at least. Are you sure this is what you want to do? Can't you just go on some morning shows and dismiss this whole thing?"

Emma shook her head. "I mean, I probably could. It's not like I *must* leave in order for this to blow over. But the team and I, well, it made sense to all of us to just take this as a warning, essentially. It's a warning that I need a break before I burn out. And if I'm the one staying behind and cleaning up this mess, then that burnout is right around the corner. If I take a little time away and let Beth do the job that I pay her to do...well, I'm pretty sure she can handle this better than I can."

"Then what's the problem?" Claire asked.

Emma groaned. "I don't know, Claire. I'm probably just overreacting, because all of this is so damn weird. I'm leaving SLICE in capable hands with Beth and Dean. I think they'll make a good team, and I know the company can survive without me." She groaned. "I just feel like a new parent leaving my baby with a sitter for the first time. What if something goes wrong? What if they need my help but they can't reach me?"

Claire smiled. "That's an interesting metaphor, Em. In what ways does the social media app you invented resemble a defenseless newborn who can't walk, feed itself, or survive without assistance? Please, tell me more...I'm very curious about this."

"You know what I mean. It's not like everything is going to fall apart without me...but what if everything falls apart without me?"

Claire scoffed. "If your company can't survive without you, you've got a real problem, friend. You're just talking about two weeks right now, sure, but...if you have to be involved day to day in every single decision...well, I hate to tell you this, but you're going to be a terrible boss. When you hire people to work for you—like you've already done with Beth, if I may remind you—you've got to trust them. Otherwise, if you're standing over them, breathing down their necks, you're not going to be keeping your employees for very long."

"Am I really in danger of becoming a Mr. Miller?" Emma's eyes widened with terror.

When she and Claire had first met, they had both been working in the same office on Wall Street. Their supervisor, Mr. Miller, had been a master micromanager, to the point where his hovering bordered on bullying behavior. Neither Emma nor Claire had lasted long in that role, Emma doubling up on classes to finish her computer engineering degree as quickly as she could and Claire spending her evenings honing her craft as a writer. After Emma graduated and Claire sold her first manuscript, the two had celebrated with mimosas over the classifieds. Neither one had been able to launch straight into their dream job after that, but they'd at least been able to find part-time jobs that didn't make them want to pull their hair out.

"If you're not careful," said Claire. "Don't take it personally. We all have that tendency in us, I'm pretty sure. I'm just warning you before it gets too late or you go too far down that path."

"Thanks." Emma exhaled with relief... The last thing she needed to do was subject her work relationships to the same brutal beating her circadian rhythm and overall health were taking. "So I guess that means you're convinced I need to take this trip to Ireland."

Claire nodded. "I am. You just better be back by Christmas. If you miss our Christmas Eve Eve movie marathon, you'll be in the doghouse for sure."

Emma laughed. "I wouldn't dream of it. Anyway, I already booked my flight. I'm coming back on December 22nd—also known as Christmas Eve Eve *Eve*, if you're into that kind of thing. I'll be rested and ready for the cheesy movie marathon, don't you worry."

"Good," said Claire. "Then you have my blessing."

Emma hugged her friend, feeling happier than she had since she got off the stage in Austin. "Now that we've settled that, do you think you can help me pack? I keep looking at the forecast for Galway, but somehow it's not translating into what I actually need to bring. Is it going to be the same weather there as here? Colder? Warmer? Wetter? I don't even know. Can you tell I've never traveled internationally? Is it obvious?" She laughed at herself, shaking her head.

"It's a little obvious, but it's very charming," said Claire. "I think the key to a good packing job is always layers. Now let's get you ready for your Irish adventure..."

# Four

E mma's flight left from JFK airport in the early afternoon, and Claire had been kind enough to drive her. Outside the departures area, Claire got out of the car just long enough to hug her friend and wish her well—any longer than that and the overly attentive security guards were bound to send her away for dawdling too long in the unloading zone.

"Have a safe flight, Em," said Claire. "I'm glad you're getting to have a little adventure in your life, even if it's under these circumstances."

Emma agreed and hugged Claire back, thanking her for the ride. The circumstances had continued to be bizarre, indeed. Chad Bradley was riding the wave of media appearances, it seemed, his story getting more dramatic with every retelling. As far as Emma could tell, Beth and Dean were playing things cool, presenting a front of composure and being unbothered by Chad Bradley's claims. The goal was to take all the air out of his case by showing how little credence they gave it, but it didn't seem to be working yet.

"Oh, there's one last thing," said Claire, reaching into her purse. She pulled out an old flip phone and a disposable camera and handed them to Emma. "Take these and give me your phone."

"What?" asked Emma, gripping more tightly onto the phone in her hand. "Why?"

"You don't need to be following what's going on with SLICE every minute of the day. This phone doesn't have internet access, but it has international calling. And the camera, well...I figured you'd still want to take a few photos, even if you can't take a thousand. You can talk to me anytime you want—though please keep the time difference in mind. And if you absolutely must, you can call Beth and Dean. But if you bring that smartphone with you, I guarantee you'll be spending way more time scrolling through the news—or through your SLICE feed—than you should. Take a proper vacation, Emma. It'll do you some good."

Emma laughed humorlessly. "A proper vacation? Don't you mean a proper banishment from this mess of my own creation?"

Claire glanced over her shoulder at the security guard who'd been eyeballing her since she put her car in park. "We don't have time to do this whole dance, Emma. Just give me your phone, take this one, and be on your way. Okay?"

Emma's sigh was exasperated. "Fine. I don't like it, but I'll do it. Are you at least going to give this number to the people who need to reach me?"

"I will," Claire nodded. "By which I mean I'll give it to your parents and no one else. I'll hang onto your phone in case there's any other kind of emergency, though I can't imagine what that could be."

"Can I still check my email, or is that forbidden?"

Claire laughed. "This isn't some kind of challenge I'm assigning you, Em. You can do anything you want. You'll just have to go to an internet cafe to do it. Or borrow a stranger's phone. Or go to a library. Heck, I don't know how public internet access works in Ireland. But if you can't handle being disconnected, I'm sure you'll figure it out."

"This is cruel and unusual punishment, Claire," said Emma, her chin dropping in horror. "You know that, right? I work in tech, for crying out loud!"

"Like I could ever forget that," Claire responded. "This is going to be good for you. When was the last time you spent even a day without your phone, anyway? Yeah, that's about what I thought."

Emma groaned. "I wish I had known you were going to pull a stunt like this."

"Then what? You would have snuck a tablet or a laptop into your carry-on, I'm pretty sure. No, this is the way it had to be. And...I've got to go. I've been parked here long enough that the security guard over there is getting close to yelling at me or arresting me. Either way, I don't want to find out. Have a great trip, text me when you land. I'll see you when you're back." Claire pulled Emma in for a quick hug, then turned on her heel and marched back to her car. "And have some fun in the meantime!"

Emma found herself abruptly alone, standing in front of the airport with a suitcase in each hand and an ancient flip phone jammed into her back pocket. This trip had just gotten a lot more interesting, and she didn't know whether to thank Claire for her intervention or try to hex her using her brain power and complete lack of knowledge of how to put a hex on a person. Opting to make the best of the situation, Emma slid on her sunglasses, adjusted her baseball cap, and made her way into the airport and towards the check-in desk.

Cashing in the airline miles she'd been saving up for ages had paid off—Emma was seated in first class for the first time in her life. The plane hadn't even finished boarding yet, and she was already convinced this was the best flight she'd ever been on. She watched the rest of the passengers file onto the plane while sipping a mimosa—complimentary, of course—and reading the first few pages of the chick lit novel she'd picked up at the airport bookstore.

She was about to check her email one last time—she was a religious believer in switching off your cell phone during the flight, no matter how many times the flight attendants told her it only needed to be off during takeoff and landing—when she pulled the phone out of her back pocket and groaned. This wasn't her phone at all. This was an ancient piece of outdated technology, and it was some sort of terrible miracle that Claire had even found it.

Thinking of Claire, Emma sent her one last message before the plane doors closed. "This phone is a hunk of junk, but I still love you. Thanks for the ride, and I'll text you from the other side of the ocean."

"Love you back. Have a wonderful, sexy time on the Emerald Isle," was Claire's response. There were a series of boxes with question marks in them at the end of the text, and Emma supposed those were emojis. Claire must have overestimated the ability of Emma's new phone to receive modern hieroglyphics.

Reading the message again, Emma shook her head to clear her mind. A *sexy* time? That wasn't on the agenda at all. She hadn't even considered that there might be men in Ireland until this very moment. But of course there would be men there, just like men were everywhere, in every country of the globe. Huh. That was an interesting thought. It wasn't an *entirely* unwelcome thought, but it was a weird one, nonetheless.

Emma put the idea out of her head and settled back into her seat, diving into her book. It felt like her vacation was already beginning—she couldn't remember the last time she'd held a paper book in her hands, rather than just scrolling through an e-book on her phone or tablet. The feel of the book under her fingers, the turning of the pages...it was a real treat.

"If this is analog life," she said to herself under her breath, "Then maybe it's not so bad after all. *Maybe.*"

When the captain came on the loudspeaker to announce their impending descent into Galway, Emma jolted awake. She pulled the mask off her eyes, sat up from her reclined

position, and took a solid thirty seconds to regain her bear-
ings. She was in the air, over the ocean, rapidly approaching Ireland. According to what the captain had just said,
her airplane would touch down in this unfamiliar country
in less than half an hour. Now would be a great time to
take a video out the window and post it on SLICE, but of
course she couldn't do that...

A swarm of butterflies circled through Emma's stomach. This was happening. The flight had been one kind of
adventure, sure, but the landing on the ground, stepping
off the plane, finding her way through the airport and to
her hotel and around the city...

"Are you alright, ma'am?" Kind eyes blinked at Emma as
the flight attendant squatted down to her level.

"I..." Emma began to respond to her, realizing quickly
what had attracted the flight attendant's attention in the
first place. Her heart was racing, her breathing was getting
shallow and fast, and there was a good chance she was
sweating, too. "I...I'm fine," she managed to say, forcing a
smile as she stared back at the woman in front of her.

"Are you a nervous flier, then?" The flight attendant
asked, making Emma aware of her lilting Irish accent for
the first time. "We're incredibly safe, I assure you, and
the captain is an excellent pilot. Just take deep breaths
and think calming thoughts. If you need to breathe into
a paper bag, there's one in that pocket over there."

"Thank...you," said Emma.

How could she tell this woman it wasn't the flying that
was making her nervous, but everything that was going to
happen after the flying was over? The closer they came to
their destination, the more she wondered what the hell she

was doing with her life. Two weeks was a long time when you were in a new country where you didn't know anyone and weren't even entirely sure which side of the road they drove on.

"What side of the road do you drive on?" Emma blurted the question, words running together until her sentence was nearly unintelligible.

The flight attendant—her name tag read "Aoife"—blinked back at her. "I'm sorry?"

Emma pulled herself together, focusing her energy on the very specific questions she had for Aoife, rather than on the two weeks of uncertainty ahead of her. "This is my first time traveling to Ireland, and I just realized I don't know what side of the road people drive on there. I feel like a silly American tourist wondering that, and I know I could just wait and see...but you're here, and I'm pretty sure you know the answer."

Aoife smiled brightly. "I most certainly do know the answer. We drive on the left side of the road, and the driver sits on the right side of the car. So if some Irish lad or lass is taking you out on a date, make sure you remember that. We always have a good laugh when one of you Yanks struts over to the driver's seat like you're going to drive our own car." She chuckled once, like a tinkling bell. "It's a gas."

"I'm sure it is," Emma agreed. "And thanks...Aoi-fee. Sorry, that can't be right. How do you pronounce your name?"

"It sounds like *ee-fa*. Fair warning, there's lots of tricky Irish pronunciation to get used to. But if you can see the humor when people laugh at you, you'll be grand."

"Thank you, I'll remember that," said Emma. Having her anxiety met with kindness—and the reassurance of a few facts she would need to know—had eased her nerves.

As Aoife stood up and resumed walking through the cabin, Emma used the television screen built into her chair to track the flight path. The tiny airplane on the screen was nearly at the end of its arced line, and as the image zoomed in, she saw they were only ten minutes away from the Galway airport. She resigned herself to the uncertainty that was coming, making herself as comfortable as she could in her seat and reopening her book to the page it had been on when she'd drifted off to sleep. She couldn't stop the plane from landing in Ireland, she couldn't snap her fingers and be back in New York, and, actually, she was experiencing exactly what she had signed up to experience. There wasn't much point in resisting her arrival or getting too bent out of shape about it. Best to just take Aoife's advice and try to see the humor in whatever came her way.

Until Emma left the airport, everything went smoothly. The captain landed the plane with the absolute minimum of bumps, exiting from first class was way less stressful than waiting in the slow moving line of coach, and both baggage claim and passport control went off without a hitch. It was only when Emma exited the airport, standing outside and breathing the Irish air for the first time, that she considered she had no idea where her hotel was or how to get there.

That hadn't been a problem when she'd left her apartment for the airport. The reservation information was stored in her email on her phone, and she had planned to access it from there. Of course she hadn't taken the time to write it down—who did that, anymore? She had also intended to use one of the rideshare apps on her phone—she'd already checked and ensured they operated in Ireland—but of course that was no longer an option anymore either. She should call Claire, never mind the fact that it was the wee early hours that could only be considered morning on a technicality. It was Claire's fault she didn't have her phone, and Claire could make this problem go away just by opening up the phone and taking a scroll through her email.

Emma was just pulling out her phone to call Claire and give her a taste of her own medicine when divine inspiration struck. Or, not exactly divine inspiration...but her short-term memory performed a minor miracle and spat out the name of the hotel she had booked in Galway. It was called Eyre Square Hotel, and how she had come up with that just now, she did not know. Now all she had to do was figure out how to get there.

Spotting a taxi stand down at the end of the airport, Emma dragged her two suitcases there as quickly as she could. For the first time, she regretted packing as much as she had. Having enough clothes that she wouldn't have to think about how to do laundry in a foreign country had seemed like a great idea when she was in her apartment. Now that those clothes were nipping at her heels in two oversize suitcases, she was less sure about that decision.

When she made her way to the taxi stand, a smiling gray-haired man wearing a hat that reminded Emma of her grandpa greeted her. "Hello there, miss. Looking for a cab, is it? Where to?"

Emma followed him to his vehicle, learning along the way that "Eyre" was pronounced like "ire" and not like "air" as she'd tried to tell him. Once they knew they were talking about the same place, Emma climbed into the backseat of the car, feeling surprised despite Aoife's warnings to see the driver sitting on the right in front of her. That was going to take some getting used to.

As the cab left the airport and pulled out onto the main road, Emma discovered that the location of the driver's seat was the least of the things she was going to have to adjust to. Driving—or riding, thankfully, because she couldn't even begin to imagine driving a car—on the left side of the road was unnerving at best and terrifying at worst. It was even more terrifying when they exited the highway and turned onto the small city streets of Galway. Some of these streets were so narrow they had Emma questioning whether they were one-way streets. She found herself leaning to the left side, as if her movements could keep the car from scraping into oncoming traffic. Naturally, they could not—though there was no need. Tony, as the driver had introduced himself, was much more accustomed to these roads than Emma was and had no trouble at all navigating them. He did seem to be getting amused at her expense when he glanced back in the rearview mirror and saw her jolting away from all the surrounding cars, but at least he didn't laugh in her face.

When Emma was able to take her attention off the other cars on the road, she noticed the cute buildings surrounding them on every side. There were charming bed and breakfasts, shops she hoped to wander into, and restaurants and pubs that got her mouth watering just wondering what she might find inside. The anxiety she had been feeling about being in a new city ebbed as she felt the small-town feel of Galway. This wasn't New York City, daunting with its skyscrapers and angry drivers. This felt...doable, somehow. Like she wasn't going to get lost. Like she was going to learn her way around these streets relatively quickly. Like she could even feel comfortable here, and not out of place.

Tony left her in front of the Eyre Square Hotel, where the friendly front desk staff checked her in and showed her to her room. A bellhop helped her carry her suitcases up the stairs—there was no elevator, and she was grateful for the help hauling her behemoth luggage around.

When she was alone in her room, SLICE-related stress came back with a vengeance. Her fingers itched to scroll through a newsfeed, to Google her own name. Her old faithful companion, the headache that rarely left her alone, reminded her of its presence with a subtle but persistent thrum.

But there wasn't much that Emma could do about any of it now. Sure, she could stay in her hotel room and order room service—if they had that here—and spend the rest of the day obsessing about worst-case scenarios. But after the drive-by tour of Galway she had gotten, she was itching to be back in the city. She wanted to wander up and down the cobblestone streets, pop into a pub for a pint of Guinness, sit near the shore and watch the waves. And right now, she needed to be distracted.

Without another thought, she picked up her purse, closed the door behind her, and set off for an adventure.

# Five

T he first full day that Emma spent in Galway came close to being a perfect day. After she had spent the previous afternoon walking far more than 10,000 steps by her best estimate (though she'd never know without her phone), eating, drinking, and listening to live music (which would have made *great* SLICE content), she had slept more deeply than she had in years. She had slept like she was a woman with no sources of chronic stress in her life, in fact, and she couldn't remember the last time that had been an apt description of herself. But the bedding had been comfortable, the darkness had been absolute thanks in part to how short the days were this time of year, and her body had been exhausted and confused from the abrupt change of time zone.

On that nearly perfect day then, Emma woke up early, feeling rested, refreshed, and without any sense of doom hanging over her head. She had been too tired to even have stress dreams, it seemed. For a glorious moment upon waking, SLICE was the furthest thing from her mind, though it didn't take long for her concerns and anxieties to return. She had to get moving—and soon—before they took over her day.

Once she was dressed and ready to go, she asked the front desk staff for a recommendation of where to go for breakfast. They directed her to an adorable restaurant nearby and instructed her to order the "full Irish." Having no idea what that meant but embracing her sense of adventure, she did just that.

When her breakfast arrived, Emma sucked in a breath. It was massive—there were eggs, sausages, toast, tomatoes, beans, and some sort of patties, one dark and one light. They also brought her a small pot of tea and a pitcher of cream. It was an intimidating spread, but only because she wanted to taste it all.

And so that's what she did. Taking her time, savoring every bite, and finding herself continually surprised by the flavors, Emma worked her way through the plate. What had appeared far too big for her to eat by herself eventually vanished. She was equal parts proud of herself for getting to enjoy all of those savory nibbles and ready to take a nap.

When the waiter came to clear her plate, Emma asked him about what it was she had just eaten. "I recognized most of it, but those patties were just delicious. What were they? I thought maybe they were sausage patties, but the taste and texture weren't quite like that."

"Ah, the black and white pudding, you mean? I'm pleased to hear you liked it. It's one of my favorites, too," said the waiter, walking away with her empty plate.

"Well huh," Emma said to herself. "I'm going to look up black and white pudding later. Though considering how savory it was, I'm a little nervous about what I might learn when I find the ingredient list. That wasn't like any pudding I've ever tasted before."

After Emma had finished her pot of tea and paid for her breakfast, she had spent the morning walking through the shops in the downtown area of Galway. She had discovered that charity shops were the Irish equivalent of a second-hand store, with each one benefitting a different charity, and she had enjoyed making her way through every one that she found. She had snagged a few gifts to take home with her, and she'd even found a gorgeous Irish-made sweater that would have cost a small fortune if she'd bought it at full price.

When she was ready for a break from all the walking, eating, and shopping, she made her way to the Spanish Arch. At the hotel, they had told her it was a great place to sit and enjoy some people watching and sea gazing, but the front desk worker had also mentioned that it was a lot more popular in the summer. As Emma sat there shivering, she understood why and simultaneously realized she hadn't put on quite enough layers today. Regardless, the combination of the ancient arch, the deep gray of the sea, and the hum of people walking by with their shopping bags, no doubt full of Christmas presents, warmed her from within. For the first time in years, she felt herself getting into the holiday spirit.

By that time, her jet lag was catching up to her, and she made her way back to the hotel. An afternoon nap was just what she needed. On her way there, however, she stumbled across a small gathering of people. They seemed to be handing out brochures, standing in front of placards, and her curiosity was piqued. She approached with some hesitation, only realizing as her feet carried her in that direction that she might be about to get roped into signing a petition or getting a lecture about a new cause.

But that wasn't the case at all. The folks with brochures were selling spots on their tours, and the placards they were standing in front of were covered in pictures of their destinations. There were tour buses heading to the Cliffs of Moher for a few hours or Connemara for a day, and even some more ambitious salespeople advertising a three-day tour of the Ring of Kerry. Emma planned to see the Cliffs of Moher at some point during her trip, but she wasn't interested in getting on a bus anytime soon—especially not after how stressful it had been riding in the taxi. A wide bus navigating these narrow and windy roads would be worse, if not only for her road-based anxiety, but definitely for her car sickness.

And then she saw another poster that caught her eye. It read "See the Cliffs of Moher from the water," and as she got closer, she realized it was a boat tour, both to the Aran Islands and along the coast of the Cliffs of Moher.

"That's perfect," Emma said to herself. "I don't have to get on a bus, and I can kill two birds with one stone." She approached the young man standing in front of the poster. "Excuse me," she said to him. "What time does the tour go tomorrow?"

The young man looked surprised, like he hadn't expected to make a sale all day. "We leave at half nine, as long as the weather is good for sailing."

*Oh right, sailing*, Emma thought. *I hadn't even considered that.* She looked out at the sea nearby and the waves that were marring its calm surface. "Is it usually pretty smooth sailing, or...?"

The young man smiled. "It's a bit choppy at times, but you'll find your sea legs. If it's really bad, we don't sail, and we'll refund you or exchange your ticket for another day."

Emma threw whatever caution she had about getting sick at sea to the wind and purchased a ticket. After confirming and double checking that "half nine" meant nine thirty, Emma headed back to the hotel with a new bounce in her step. Galway was already an adventure, but her trip had just gotten even more exciting. She could hardly wait to see what the next day would bring.

Emma had opted to spend the rest of the day relaxing and getting ready for her big outing the next day. Back in her hotel room, she had attempted to take a nap before it became obvious that her reptilian brain and its ability to identify threats and sources of stress were going to make that impossible. After lying on her back with her eyes closed for half an hour, she decided she was as rested as she was going to get, and then she treated herself to a nice hot bath in the small tub in her bathroom.

Once she had soaked herself to the consistency of a cooked noodle and scrubbed herself within an inch of her life, Emma emerged from the tub, put on the fluffy robe she had brought with her, and flopped onto her bed. She switched on the television, flipping channels from soap operas to news programs and everything in between, searching for something to distract her from the intrusive thoughts that were sure to come back as soon as she was alone with herself again.

The temptation to check in with her team back home, to ask Beth or Dean how things were going with SLICE, came up once or twice. She even came dangerously close to reaching for her phone and firing off a text message. But then she stopped herself, settled back into the pillows, and sighed. She was doing what she had been instructed to do, what was essential for her mental health and probably for her business, too.

When the temptation to feel another bout of guilt or work-related stress threatened to bubble up again, Emma jumped up from the bed. She couldn't stay here and risk her lounging turning into wallowing, no matter how comfortable her bed was. She dressed, blow dried the last bits of moisture from her hair, and headed out in search of dinner and a pint.

The pint found her first. Emma walked down the same roads she had traveled earlier that day, stopping in front of a pub that had caught her eye that morning. Only now, it was an appropriate time for a Guinness, and there was lively Irish music flooding out of the door. She went inside, drawn as if by magnetic force towards the leaping melodies that seemed to call to her very soul. There was a feeling the music was stirring up that she couldn't quite explain. Despite it being what sounded like a cheerful tune—a jig, if she remembered correctly—there was a melancholy inside her, almost as if her soul had been craving it, like it was a returning home.

She ordered a pint of Guinness, then waited at the bar for a long time to receive it. The music made the time pass more enjoyably, but she was still aware that it had been far longer than she would wait for a drink back home.

Glancing back behind the bar, she saw a nearly full pint of Guinness sitting unattended under the spout. As she was watching, the bartender approached the pint, topped off the last bit of the glass, and then carried it over to her, depositing it on the bar in front of her.

"Why do you do that?" Emma blurted before she could stop herself.

"Do what?" the bartender asked.

"The pint was sitting there for a long time. I was just wondering why you do it like that."

The bartender looked amused. "Ahh, the classic question of an American in an Irish pub. Well, my dear, the Guinness needs to sit there until it has settled, until it's finished cascading. You see the line here, between the stout and the head?" He gestured to the side of her glass, where the creamy head was distinctly separated from the dark—almost black—beer in the glass. "That line is only obvious when we let your precious Guinness sit for a bit. Otherwise, it's just a foamy mess, and no one wants that."

"Huh. You learn something new every day," said Emma. She thanked the bartender for his help, tipped him well, then made her way closer to where the live musicians were sitting.

Observing the music from this close was like nothing Emma had ever experienced before. The musicians were sitting in a circle, and as far as she could tell, there was no conductor, no sheet music...just a connection that was almost otherworldly. When one tune would end, there would be a brief silence before one fiddler would start playing another tune and then everyone would join in. They played tune after tune, and it was almost entrancing. She wished she could film it to listen to it again later—or to post it on SLICE once she was back online, but since that wasn't an option, she had no other choice but to get lost in the music. Emma listened and sipped her pint, unaware of the passing time.

It wasn't until her drink was long gone and the musicians were taking a break of their own that she even bothered to check her watch. It was late, later than she had intended to stay up if she was going to be alert and feeling good tomorrow for her boat trip. She also didn't want to stay up too much longer in case she got a second wind and then ended up awake all night—jet lag was a real pain in the butt, and she hadn't figured out yet how to master it.

She opted to skip dinner and make her way back to the hotel. She could get a snack on the way, but she didn't want to spend all the time it would take to find a restaurant and then wait for a meal to be prepared. As she rounded the next corner, though, she saw something that made her stop in her tracks.

It was a small building, unremarkable from the outside. But through the glass windows she could see a stainless steel counter and two men behind it wearing kitchen uniforms. The smell coming from it was greasy, salty, and everything that made her mouth water, especially after drinking that last beer. Above the shop, the sign said "Fresh Chips," and that was more than enough to convince her to venture inside.

Inside, the smells were even more enticing. The men behind the counter greeted Emma, then continued helping the customers in front of her while she examined the menu above the counter. Every option sounded delicious, but she settled on "Cheesy Bacon Chips" just before it was her turn to order.

She left the shop with a large paper cup in her hand, steam emanating from the top of it. The cup was full of chips—more like steak-cut French fries, if Emma was going to explain it in American English—as well as chunks of bacon and a large helping of shredded white cheddar cheese. Emma held the cup in one hand and a fork in the other, and she continued on to her hotel with a smile on her face, delicious salty snacks in her mouth, and a newfound lightness in her heart.

The next morning, Emma woke early again, much earlier than she needed to be up for her boat tour. After devouring her snack the night before, she had settled into another comfortable night in her cozy bed, getting a solid eight hours of sleep like it was no big deal at all. Prior to arriving here in Galway, she wasn't sure when the last time she had slept for eight hours straight was—possibly in college.

Emma had a couple of hours to kill before she needed to be at the tour pickup spot, so she left the hotel in search of caffeine and breakfast. As much as she'd enjoyed her full Irish breakfast, her body was craving something that wouldn't make her feel like she needed to go back to bed to sleep it off. She stopped at a cafe she had noticed the day before, opting for a latte and a scone and taking a seat outside to enjoy them both. It was a chilly morning, but the sun was shining, warming Emma from the inside out and filling her with hope for what the day ahead would bring.

She popped back into the hotel one last time before making her way to the departure point. Since she was going to be gone for the whole day, she needed to be prepared. She traded in her purse for her small backpack, then stuffed a granola bar, a bottle of water, and the disposable camera from Claire inside. For good measure—because she was in Ireland, after all—she forced her raincoat in there too, making it nearly impossible to zip the backpack shut. She wrapped her scarf around her neck, pulled on her knit cap and a pair of mittens, and then set off.

The tour group met in Eyre Square and then took a shuttle to the boat. Emma was disappointed to find herself once again on a bus, but she didn't let it get her down. Soon enough, she'd be out at sea, on a boat, making her way towards Inishmore. That was the plan for the day, according to the pamphlet she'd read again during breakfast this morning. There were three Aran Islands, but this tour only docked on Inishmore, the largest of the three. There would be some time to explore before returning to the boat and taking a cruise along the Cliffs of Moher on the way back.

When they pulled up to the dock, Emma did a double take. *That* was the boat they were going to be taking? It was smaller than she had expected, and even though the sky had been clear and sunny during her breakfast this morning, it was looking gray and full of rain now. Most of the boat was uncovered, though there was a small indoor cabin to take shelter from the rain. She felt a familiar knot of anxiety return to her stomach, and she wondered for the first time if she was making a terrible mistake getting on a boat, especially here, in this weather.

But she wasn't a quitter, and she wasn't going to turn around now. She turned to the tour guide, a different man from the one she had bought the ticket from yesterday. "This is safe, right?" she asked him, trying to keep her tone light.

"Of course, lass," he assured her. "We run this tour every day, with no more serious problems than the typical sea sickness."

"That's common, then?"

"Absolutely. But we've got plenty of bags on board if you need to hurl into one. None of that being sick over the side of the boat, that's the surest way to fall into the sea."

"Ahh, that's good to know," said Emma, bile rising into her throat at the mere thought of being sick on a boat...or being surrounded by others who were sick on a boat. She looked out at the waves, which were looking larger and rougher here than they had back in Galway proper. "Do you ever cancel these tours?"

The man nodded. "If it's too rough, we don't sail." Judging by the fact that he didn't add "like now" to his statement about it being too rough, Emma deduced that the waves out there were child's play as far as he was concerned. She had no interest in seeing what he considered "too rough," and she was struggling to stop herself from overthinking about all the things that could make her stressed or terrified right now. It would be better to get moving than to sit here second guessing her decision to take this trip today.

After an overview of the plan for the day and the safety rules of the boat, the tour guide led them aboard. Emma strapped on a life jacket along with everyone else, then took her place inside the cabin, away from the potential rain that was going to start falling any minute from the look of things. As the engine roared to life, she reminded herself that this was an adventure and, if nothing else, it would make for an excellent story later.

# Six

To put it mildly, the journey to Inishmore was rough. The waves were choppy, and despite its speed, the boat didn't exactly skip over them. Instead, with every rise and fall of the sea, the boat soared high and then crashed back down, the horizon moving up and down faster and more abruptly than Emma knew it could do.

She had realized quickly that being in the cabin was a bad idea. Not only was she trapped inside where seemingly everyone around her was getting sick and using the bags the tour guide had told her about, but apparently the front of a boat was actually rougher than the back. Or at least, that's what one of the deck hands had told her. That's how she found herself sitting as far back as she could get, chilly rain lashing her face as the little boat made its way to the mass of land she could just barely make out on the horizon. Her eyes stung from the cold wind, and she could taste a hint of salt on her lips from the sea air.

Emma tried not to think about the fact that she was going to have to repeat this journey in the opposite direction again today, but it was hard to put that idea out of her mind. What had she been thinking, signing up for this tour in the first place? By some minor miracle or act of divine mercy, she wasn't sick, but she wasn't feeling great either. Her stomach was twisting and turning, but through sheer force of will, she had managed not to lose her breakfast. Now that she had left the warmth of the cabin, at least the sound of the rushing wind and the crashing waves was drowning out the orchestra of her travel companions emptying their stomachs.

When the boat docked on Inishmore, Emma was tempted to cheer like people did at the end of a great movie or a long flight. Judging by the way her fellow passengers were shuffling off the boat like a zombie army, she figured she would have been the only one clapping and kept her hands in her pockets.

Her first impression of Inishmore was that it must have been a hard place to live. That impression had been made on her before they even docked, while they were traveling over the stretch of sea separating the island from the mainland. To live there, you had to be hearty, probably made of tougher stuff than Emma or anyone else joining her on this tour was.

She looked around at the island, and she saw a harsh beauty. There was a lot of green, like Ireland was known for thanks to all the rain it received, but the gray sky and the sideways rain made this island unlike any of its tropically located cousins. Where they docked, there were a few buildings, including a pub that their tour guide pointed out. "You'll have some time to explore on your own," he said, "And we'll meet at the pub to depart. They do a grand hot lunch there, if I may recommend it." The scattered groans told Emma that a number of her new friends would not be able to bear the thought of eating anything for at least the rest of the day.

As their group dispersed, it became clear to Emma that the tour company's "tour" portion was limited to the boat. The tour guide and the boat crew headed to the pub, while the tourists on board were turned loose on the island. Emma saw some of them wandering towards the beach, others walking along the main road to check out the "downtown," of Inishmore, if you could even call it a downtown.

She set off by herself, wandering up and down the stone-lined roads and losing herself in taking photos. She snapped pictures of sheep, close ups of the rock walls, and some artistic shots of old tractors and thatched roof cottages. For the first time in a long time, she was so absorbed in the beauty around her that she lost track of time. As she continued to walk, she came across an old cemetery and ventured inside.

Cemeteries had never really scared Emma, at least not in the light of day. They were interesting places, where you could get a glimpse of the names that were popular at different times in history or the fonts that were used on gravestones, or even the lifespans of people at different times and in different locations.

That was how Emma lost herself in the Inishmore cemetery, wandering up and down the rows of headstones. She noticed the wind- and rain-beaten stones, some barely legible after years of exposure to the elements. She saw the last names, with lots of O'Donnells and Lowrys dominating the area. She was just starting to do some fast math to see if her suspicions—that life on this island was harder than back on the mainland—about the lifespan out here was correct when it happened.

She was walking closer to one particular gravesite, jogging from under one tree to the next one to stay out of the rain, when her foot hit a stone that was slippery with moss. Her heel slipped out from underneath her, and before she could stop herself, she fell and landed with a crash on her tailbone. "Ouch!" she exclaimed, reaching back to push herself up to standing. As she pushed herself up to a crab-like position, her hand slipped on the same mossy rock, bringing her back down again, right on her tender tailbone.

By the time she was able to get herself to a stable standing position, she was more than a little gun-shy about slipping again. Her tailbone was tender to the touch, and she didn't want to risk falling on it again or twisting her ankle. Either of those things was a surefire way to ruin the rest of her vacation. And so she began to make her way out of the cemetery, eyes planted on the ground to ensure that wherever she was about to step would not prove to be the equivalent of another slippery banana peel.

Emma was hobbling back in the direction the dock, trying to regain the ground she had covered on her way out at a much slower pace than she had gone the other direction. As she came to a fork in the road, she felt a moment of cold panic. *What time had they said the boat was going to leave?* She remembered they were supposed to have four hours to explore, so that meant they were due to be boarding again around 3:30 pm. She checked her watch and felt her stomach drop as she saw it was only five minutes away.

She was *pretty* sure she recognized this particular fork in the road and that she needed to go to the left to get back to the dock. The only problem was that she knew she was well over five minutes away. But what choice did she have beyond continuing to make her way back, step by step by step, hoping all the while that the boat wouldn't leave without her? Surely they'd do a headcount before they departed...right?

Despite the cold, Emma felt herself sweating. Not that she was booking it; she was still hobbling along, nursing the parts of her body that were getting more and more tender by the minute. No, the sweat had come when she remembered the tour guide saying that the boat would depart at 3:30 on the dot. He'd even encouraged all the participants to be back by three o'clock, spending the last half hour in the pub right near the dock just to play it safe.

*What would happen to someone who was left behind?* Emma wondered. *Would there be another boat today? Would they* really *leave without one passenger? Surely, that strict warning to be on board right on time was just that—a strict warning. It was intended to keep the passengers on their toes, but it didn't mean they'd actually leave one behind. That had a lawsuit written all over it, if they did that.* Another voice in Emma's head reminded her that she didn't know how the legal system worked in Ireland, and it was entirely possible that it was completely different from that of the US.

She reassured herself that there was no way the boat was leaving without her and continued to make forward progress towards the meeting point. She prepared herself for the punishment awaiting her—a boat full of impatient passengers and an ornery boat crew, no doubt—and she practiced her contrite apology. "I'm really sorry, everyone. I slipped and fell down in the cemetery, and I think I hurt myself. I couldn't walk back as fast as I needed to, and I'm really sorry that I made you all wait. Please don't be mad."

*Please don't be mad, please don't be mad, please don't be mad.* Emma repeated that phrase over to herself like a mantra with every step that she took. She hated the thought of letting anyone down, let alone an entire group of people like the one on the boat. But there was nothing that could be done about it now. If she could go back in time and avoid the cemetery altogether, she would definitely make that choice. Heck, if she could go back in time and skip all of her explorations today, opting to spend the entire Inishmore visit sitting in a dark and dingy corner of the pub, she'd take that, too.

It was after four o'clock by the time the dock came into view. As Emma crested the last hill, the view awaiting her made her heart drop. There, next to the pub, was the dock. And there, if she remembered correctly—not that it was a massive dock—was the spot where her ride had been tied up. It was empty. In fact, there wasn't a single boat at the public dock. Sure, there were boats, but they were all privately owned. Not a single ferry, tour boat, or even a water taxi.

Emma looked out to sea to confirm her suspicions, hoping against hope that the tour boat would be close enough that they could come back and get her. But if the boat was there at all, it was a distant blemish on the horizon. The captain had made good time—or else they hadn't waited even an extra minute for her. Or both.

Emma stopped where she stood, bending over to put her hands on her knees. She tried to catch her breath as the panic started to rise again. She was stranded on this remote and, frankly, inhospitable island. It was the terrain and the weather that were inhospitable; she hadn't met a single local in the hours she'd spent here and couldn't voice an opinion one way or the other about their hospitality.

The boat she'd taken here wouldn't be returning her to the mainland. There probably wouldn't be another boat today even, judging by how low the sun was sinking in the sky.

"Great. Just great," Emma said to herself. "Am I about to get my first—and hopefully only—experience of sleeping on the street? I can't imagine that's ever comfortable, but in this weather, I'm almost definitely going to catch pneumonia."

Emma was about to pull out her phone to see if there was a hotel anywhere on this island, or anything that remotely qualified as a place to stay—but then she remembered that the phone in her pocket was an ancient brick with no concept of what the internet even was.

But even if she couldn't look anything up online, she could call Claire and make her be her own personal Googler. That would serve her right for confiscating Emma's phone in the first place.

She looked down at the phone screen and was surprised to find she had almost two full bars of coverage. It wasn't great, by any stretch of the imagination, but it wasn't as terrible as she had anticipated.

The real challenge, though, was making a call without having her voice drowned out by the wind. It was whipping Emma's hair in every direction at once, and no matter which way she turned, somehow it blew on both her face and the phone's microphone.

"Claire? Hello?" Emma called into the phone.

"—that you, Em—?" came Claire's voice.

"It's me! Sorry it's so windy. Claire, I got stuck on Inishmore. There's no boat back until, gosh, I hope until tomorrow. Can you imagine if the tours only run every other day or once a week? Oh crap oh crap oh crap, I didn't even think of that until just now..."

"—ere are you—?"

"Inishmore! It's one of the Aran Islands. Listen, Claire, I need your help. I need to see if there's a hotel or some place I can stay here. But I don't have my smartphone, so I need you to look it up for me. Can you do that?"

"Emma! Can—hear me?"

"Oh, for crying out loud," cried Emma. "This is never going to work. I'll call you later, Claire! Thanks a lot for taking my phone, by the way!"

"You're...welcome?" Those were Claire's last words before the line died.

"There's got to be another way to figure this out," said Emma to herself. "I'll just go ask someone in the pub. They'll know what to do."

•❤•❤•❤•❤•❤•

Emma walked into Ryan's Pub twenty minutes later, and she was shocked by the darkness and the silence. This was nothing like the lively place she'd enjoyed the evening before. Reminding herself not to judge, she recalled it was still the afternoon, and it was unlikely that *any* pub was particularly festive and musical before the sun had even gone down.

She made her way over to the bar, where two old men with weatherworn faces were sipping their respective pints. She nodded at them when they turned to look at her, then leaned across to get the bartender's attention.

The bartender was considerably younger than his two patrons, and Emma registered a brief twinge of surprise, wondering what life would be like for someone her age on this island. He was preoccupied with something—either a crossword puzzle or a sudoku, judging from the texture of the paper, which was all that she could see. Emma cleared her throat, and he looked up at her.

"Yes?" he asked, looking puzzled to see her. Whether that was because of her age, her appearance, or just the fact that she wasn't a local, she couldn't tell. "What can I do for you?"

"Yeah, I got left behind by my tour boat," said Emma.

The bartender grimaced, reaching up to stroke his neatly trimmed beard. "Ah. That does happen sometimes. I'm sorry to tell you they won't turn back for you. No matter *who* you are. You best make yourself comfortable here, and you can take the next boat back."

"About that..." said Emma. "When *is* the next boat? Please don't say it's next week."

The bartender chuckled. "It's tomorrow at the same time. I'm sure you can survive life on the island until then."

"Is there anywhere to stay here? I mean, for someone like me. I'm sure you all have houses of your own."

"That's a marvelous observation, miss. We *do* all, in fact, live in houses here. Not a lot of apartments on the island. Not many chateaus, either." He had set down his paper, his hands now busy wiping what appeared to be clean pint glasses.

Emma forced a smile. This guy was trying her patience. "And what lovely houses they are, from what I've seen today. I don't suppose one of them is a bed and breakfast? Or that there's a hotel on the island?"

He laughed again. "If there were a giant commercial hotel, don't you think you would have noticed it? And don't you think it might be just a bit hard to keep it in business, considering the number of tourists willing to stay overnight here?"

Emma conceded. "That's probably true. There weren't that many people on my boat in the first place, but I'm sure none of them were heartbroken that they couldn't stick around until tomorrow. And you're right. I didn't see a single skyscraper on the island as we came over, but I could have missed it. I'm not the most observant person, you know."

"No, I should think not. Did you fail to observe what time it was, or how exactly was it that you got left behind by your boat, anyway?"

"I didn't lose track of time," Emma sighed. "I slipped and fell in the cemetery and bruised my tailbone. I'd wandered pretty far away from the dock, and I couldn't move nearly as quickly on my way back."

The bartender seemed to be holding back a smile. "I'm very sorry to hear about your tailbone, and I wish you a speedy recovery. If you need anyone to take a look at it, this gentleman here is our resident doctor." He gestured to one of the white-haired men at the end of the bar, who looked up in response to the attention directed his way.

"What did you say, Connor?" he asked the bartender.

Connor the bartender waved him away. "Nothing to worry about, Sean. This tourist here..." He raised his eyebrows at Emma, asking her to fill in the gap in the information he was about to share.

"Emma," she supplied.

"Right. Emma hurt herself exploring the old cemetery today, and I was just telling her that if she needed any medical care, you're the man to ask."

"That's me, alright." Sean turned to Emma. "Where was it you hurt yourself?" His eyes were wandering over her frame, as if looking for any gaping wounds or dislocations.

Emma glared at Connor and spat out her words through gritted teeth. "I'm sure I'll be fine." She turned to face Sean. "I just landed pretty hard on my tailbone when I fell down. I'm sure it's just bruised."

Sean put up his hands. "I certainly won't insist on checking it out, especially not in the bar. If it's still bothering you in a few days, you can come to my office."

"Thank you," said Emma, smiling at Sean. "I'll be leaving tomorrow, but I appreciate the offer very much."

Sean shrugged and turned his attention back to his companion, while Emma turned hers back to Connor.

"So *Connor*," she said, willing all the frustration she was feeling to come out in her tone, "Thank you *very* much for your help. If you're done embarrassing me by talking about my butt with grandfatherly types, then I think I'd best be going. I've still got to find a place to stay for the night, since you were no help at all with that."

The look on Connor's face made Emma understand the phrase "Irish eyes were smiling," and she cringed inwardly at the recollection of that old chestnut. "I'm just taking the piss out of you, Emma. I'll help you figure out some shelter for the night."

"You're *what*?" Emma asked, her eyes widening.

Connor laughed. "I always love getting that reaction out of the tourists. You all think it means I'm trying to make you pee your pants or something like that. It just means that I'm teasing you, making fun of you. Like a friend would."

"Ah," said Emma. "Friends, huh? I've got to tell you, this hasn't felt like the friendliest interaction I've had since arriving in Ireland."

"Has it not?" Connor asked. "Well, we'll have to do something about that, won't we?"

"Be my guest," said Emma. "If you think it's possible to redeem yourself from this terrible first impression, I'd love to see what you can come up with."

Connor looked thoughtful. "Well, I do know a place you could stay tonight. I'm pretty sure all the bed and breakfasts are closed for the season, but I just need to check a few things. In the meantime, why don't you take a seat over by the fire and warm up? What would you like to drink?"

Emma stared at him, surprised by the sudden turn the conversation had taken. "Um...a Guinness, I guess? And I will, thanks...it was chilly out there, and the wind does *not* play around."

"It certainly doesn't. I'll get you that Guinness."

"Thanks, Connor. I really appreciate the help. I honestly don't have a clue where I'd go if I left this pub."

"That's what I'm here for, doll. Helping stranded tourists and rescuing damsels in distress." He winked before he turned his back to fill her glass, and Emma went and found the table closest to the fireplace. She still didn't know what to expect tonight—Connor hadn't told her *where* she'd be staying, after all—but at least she wasn't going to be left out in the elements until her boat came back.

# Seven

A few pints later—she couldn't be sure of the exact number, since Connor kept clearing away the empty glasses—Emma had nearly forgotten her troubles. The pub had filled up with regulars, and the mood had taken a 180-degree turn for the better since she had arrived there stranded and facing a long night in the great outdoors. There was music playing—not live music, but it was peppy and upbeat, and everyone seemed to be in great spirits.

In fact, the pub wasn't like any bar Emma had ever been to. There weren't just single people looking to meet a special someone and thirsty people looking to drown their sorrows in some alcohol. There were families with children and people of all ages. It all just felt so warm, and that wasn't just the proximity to the fireplace talking.

When Connor came to Emma's table with a pint glass full of water, she accepted it readily before raising her eyebrows at a family with two young children seated near her.

"What's with the kids?" she asked in a whisper that came out far louder than she had intended.

"We're the only restaurant on this side of the island," Connor explained, "And we've got a great cook, if I do say so myself. It's a family-friendly place, though we don't serve the young ones beer no matter how nicely they ask."

Emma's stomach rumbled, making her aware for the first time that it had been quite a few hours since she enjoyed her scone in Galway. While the seasickness had made it impossible to think about food for a long time after that, she was firmly on land now and the Guinness she had been drinking had only whetted her appetite.

"Do you have a menu?" she asked. "Or a recommendation?"

"No menu necessary," said Connor. "It's fish and chips night. I can whip up a plate for you, if you'd like."

"Are...are you the cook? I mean, on top of being the bartender, you do all the cooking, too?"

Connor shook his head. "I don't do it all alone. I've got my little brother helping me out in the back. He washes all the dishes, and he does the basic stuff. The kind of thing he can't mess up too much, peeling potatoes and the like. But don't feel too bad for me. Business isn't exactly booming here when there aren't tourists around, present company excluded. During peak tourist season, my family comes in for the lunch rush to help out."

"Ahh, that's nice," said Emma. Her stomach had dropped in disappointment—much to her surprise—when he'd said the word "family," and she pasted on a smile now to cover up what she was feeling. "How old are your kids? Do they like helping out here?"

Connor laughed. "Jaysus, love, if you'd wanted to know if I was married, you could have just asked. No, it's not my kids that are helping out here anyway, it's my ma and da and my sister. In addition to the brother who's always here."

Emma's cheeks had blushed dark red, she was sure, but she could explain it away with the heat from the nearby fire. "That's nice that you're so close to your family."

"And that I'm not married," said Connor with a wink. "Not even in a relationship, in case you were going to wonder that next. Now, if you'll excuse me, I've got a plate of fish and chips to prepare and a bar full of locals to serve. I'll leave you to ponder my eligibility and what it means to you, then." He turned on his heel and walked back to the bar, his steps a little bouncier than Emma remembered them being on his way over.

The plate Connor placed in front of her a brief wait later was still steaming with heat. There were two massive pieces of battered cod, along with a heap of chips—Irish chips, of course, not American chips. Despite having eaten a significant amount of potatoes for dinner just the night before, the sight of another mound of steak fries just made Emma's mouth water. She silently thanked her ancestors, especially the two great grandparents who had emigrated to the US from Ireland generations before. They had surely given her a predisposition towards loving potatoes, and she was confident they were smiling down on her and this tower of taters now.

As Connor walked back to the bar, Emma dug into the plate in front of her without waiting even a second longer for it to cool. Missing lunch—or rather, spending most of the lunchtime period feeling supremely nauseated—had caught up with her, and even if she burned her mouth in the process, she was going to *eat*, damn it.

The fish was flaky and delicious, the potatoes crispy on the ends and steamy in the middle. She paused to wipe a sheen of oil from her lips and fingertips, considering for a second that she might want to eat a vegetable that grew *above* the ground at some point during her trip, before diving back in. She had never been one to feel guilty about what she enjoyed eating, and there was no sense in starting now.

When Emma had a full stomach and a clearer head, thanks to all the glasses of water Connor had been dropping off, she nearly got so comfortable and cozy in her chair by the fire that she just fell asleep right there. The music was still playing, all the children had left the pub, and it had been dark outside for so long she couldn't remember what this place even looked like with light streaming in through the windows.

Behind the bar, Connor wiped his hands on a rag and cleared his throat. "All right, everyone, it's last call. If you need your pint topped up or one for the road—only if you're walking, of course—now's the time to order it."

A series of groans echoed through the room from the people who loved the pub more than they loved braving the cold and dark to return to their homes.

"Not tonight," said Connor. "You won't convince me to stay open 'just a wee bit longer,' so don't even try it.

Meet me at the bar to order your last round and save the grumbling for someone else."

While Connor filled glasses and poured shots, Emma looked around her to gather her things. She put on her gloves, coat, and hat, making sure everything else she'd brought with her to Inishmore was still in her backpack before slinging it over her shoulder. As she got to her feet, she stopped and sat right back down.

She had no idea where she was going. She had gotten so swept up in the ambience and the tasty fish that she hadn't asked Conner the most basic and important follow-up question to his announcement that he knew a place she could stay. Um...*where? And with whom? And was that person aware she would be staying there, or were they already asleep?* What a mess.

As the crowd around Connor thinned out, Emma approached the bar. He smiled when he saw it was her at the end of the line, then he winked and went back to the glasses he was wiping. Clearly, he had not anticipated what she was here to say. He probably expected her just to thank him for the dinner—she'd tried several times to pay him, but he hadn't allowed it—and be on her way.

This was *so* awkward. He had definitely forgotten about the promise of finding her a place to stay. But he'd been so nice after that, the last thing she wanted to do was ask one more favor from him. Emma Kells didn't mind accepting help, but she had her pride too, damn it. Rather than asking this nice man—this snarky, troublemaking, yet impossibly nice man—for one more favor, she'd just have to find a spot outside that was protected from the wind and sleep there. It had been dark for hours; surely it would be morning soon.

"Thanks for everything, Connor," she said, raising her hand to wave goodbye at him. "Have a good night."

Connor put down the glass he was wiping and raised an eyebrow at her. "Forgetting something, are you?"

She raised her eyebrow back at him. "What do you mean?"

Now he was rolling his eyes. "Where are you staying tonight, Emma? Or did you find a place while I wasn't paying attention?" A horrified expression crossed his face. "You're staying with Sean, aren't you? I *thought* I saw some sparks flying between the two of you when he offered to examine your bruised tailbone..."

Despite herself, Emma laughed. "Yeah, that's exactly what's happening." She looked down at the bar, refusing to make eye contact with him. "Actually, I thought you may have forgotten the suggestion you made, and...well, it's dumb, but I felt like you'd already done enough. I didn't want to ask another favor, so..."

"So you were going to sleep on the dock? Emma, darling, I may enjoy teasing you and giving you a hard time—"

"Taking the piss out of me, I believe you mean."

"Right, that. It's certainly been fun, but that doesn't mean I think you should sleep out under the stars. I'm sure it would be lovely in the summer, if it weren't raining, and I'd be happy to join you if you want to come back then for a romantic evening in the back bed of my truck..."

Emma cleared her throat. "I think you're getting a little carried away there, buddy..."

Connor smiled impishly. "Right. We'll talk about that another time. Anyway, it's absolutely ridiculous that you'd rather go sit under a tree all night than remind me of a favor you think I'd forgotten."

"It may be ridiculous, I agree," she said. "But I'm in a pretty uncomfortable position here. The only people I know on this entire island are you and Sean, and I find myself at the mercy of your kindness. That's...kind of terrifying. I'm fairly confident you're not a serial killer..."

"There aren't enough people on this island for *anyone* to be a serial killer," Connor interjected.

"That's a *super* comforting thing for you to say," Emma answered, rolling her eyes sky high.

"I meant it to be reassuring, but I can see how you might have misunderstood. Anyway, I hadn't forgotten about you or your rather unfortunate situation."

"You hadn't?"

"Not at all," he said, the faintest hint of pink just starting to color his cheeks. "That's why I made last call a bit early and pissed off half my clientele."

"Oh." Emma's brain failed to find the right words, touched by his actions.

"I just assumed you knew what I was up to. Though I guess I can give you a pass this one time since we've only known each other for a few hours and spoken for a sum total of maybe...ten minutes?"

"Thanks," she responded. "For the free pass and also for not forgetting about me."

"You're welcome," he said. "Someone had to show you a bit of Inishmore hospitality, since the folks in the cemetery clearly didn't."

Emma laughed. "No, they sure didn't. Though I'd blame the moss and the rain more than any of the dearly departed souls."

"How diplomatic of you," Connor teased.

"Well, I suppose I should ask you the last question that's been hanging over my head."

"What's that?"

"Where, exactly, am I staying? You said you knew a place..."

Connor's cheeks flushed a deeper red. "Is that how I phrased it?" He laughed. "I swear I wasn't being willfully deceptive."

"Wha-?" Emma quirked an eyebrow in his direction.

"I believe what I should have said was, 'I *have* a place you could sleep.'"

"What? No. No no no. No, that's not going to work." Emma was shaking her head and holding up her hands.

Connor sighed. "Not like that. I didn't mean it that way. Christ, I definitely shouldn't have flirted with you tonight. That's making all of this so much worse, isn't it?"

Emma nodded. "It is. Though I appreciate you admitting you were flirting, because that wasn't one hundred percent clear."

"Was it not? I'll have to try harder next time."

"What? No! That's not the point." Emma was getting exasperated. "I don't understand. You said you had to check with someone. I thought that meant you had to check with someone to see if they had space. Like, someone with a spare bedroom or someone who runs a bed and breakfast during the peak tourist time."

"Ahh, I can see how you'd think that," said Connor. "But no, I don't know anyone like that."

"Then *who* were you checking with?"

"Well, I didn't actually check with her. She doesn't know how to use a phone. I just asked myself if she and I could make it work and I figured out that we could. So that was that."

Emma sighed audibly. "I know you're not married. I know you're not even in a relationship. I *do* think you're being cute right now, trying to make me wonder who this 'she' is."

"Guilty. It's too much fun messing with you, Emma. I don't know what to tell you."

"Tell me who 'she' is, and then tell me what your plan is for the evening so I can know how fast I need to run in the other direction."

"First of all, it's an island, remember? If you run too fast in any direction, you're liable to run right into the sea. Unless you can walk on water, that's a terrible idea." Off her groan, he continued. "Right. The 'she' I'm referring to is my dog, Lady. She usually sleeps with me in my bed, but I was going to change the sheets, give you my bedroom, and sleep on the couch. I was just wondering how Lady would feel about sleeping on the couch. Probably just grand, since I'd bet you fifty quid that's where she's sleeping right now."

Emma was silent. That wasn't how she'd expected his explanation to go.

"I probably should have told you all of this sooner. I didn't want you to think I was trying to get you back into my bed or anything like that. I mean, I *am* trying to get you into my bed, but I'm under no illusions of being in that bed with you. At the same time. You know?"

She nodded. "I think I get it. I just don't know if I feel comfortable, no matter what. I don't exactly make a practice out of going home with men I don't know, let alone sleeping over within a few hours of meeting them. Especially not when I've been out drinking. There are just too many horror stories that start that way."

"I know, and I understand. I mean, I understand that as best I can as a man." He paused, off something on her face. "What? You don't need to look surprised. My sister gave me my feminist education years ago, and I was embarrassed I didn't already know all those things. How unsafe she felt at night—not here, not on the island, but pretty much anywhere else."

"Your sister sounds like a smart woman. It's not easy to enlighten our male family members about experiences they'll never have, and if she managed to do it with *you*, of all people..."

Connor put up his hands. "Hey now." His eyes brightened with a new idea. "Do you want me to call my sister? She can meet us at my house, help you settle in, show you how to lock the door if it makes you feel safer."

"You'd do that? I mean...would she even want to do that? What time is it?"

He looked at his watch and winced. "I would definitely do that, but I would feel bad about it. Nora has probably been in bed for about two hours by now. She helps out one of the farmers who's gotten a little too old for the early morning milkings, so she's an 'early to bed, early to rise' kind of gal."

Emma cringed. "Waking her up from a dead sleep just to reassure me that her brother is a good guy sounds like a good way to make a terrible first impression. I've got to say, the fact that you suggested calling her in the first place, and that you mentioned a lock on the door for my comfort...both of those are points in favor of me taking you up on your generous offer. It's just the fact that I've been drinking that still makes me a little nervous."

Connor nodded. "That's fair. Though I will remind you, with no agenda of my own other than getting the facts straight, that it's been approximately two hours since you last had a drop of alcohol. It's been just water, fish, and potatoes since then. Which frankly sounds a bit disgusting when I say it like that, but you get the point."

"Huh," said Emma. "I hadn't realized that much time had passed. Does that mean you were looking out for me?"

"Something like that," said Connor. "I didn't think you'd want to spend your first night on Inishmore falling down drunk, and I saw how green you were when you got off the boat. Figured it had been a while since you'd been able to keep down any solid food, and as the only bartender on the island, it's kind of in my job description to make sure people don't get too sloppy drunk."

"I didn't realize that was part of the job. The last time I was at a bar in the States, it seemed like the bartender was more interested in good tips than in keeping everyone relatively sober."

Connor shrugged. "I imagine it's a bit harder to be the veritable guardian angel when you're in a packed bar with more souls than you can count." He gestured to the room around him. "Here, I've known every single one of these people since either I was born or they were. It's hard not to care when you're in that position."

"That's nice," Emma admitted. A yawn snuck out before she could stop it. "I guess I can't hide the fact that I'm getting a *little* tired, but I'm still not sure what the responsible thing to do is in my position. I'm not getting bad vibes from you, I'm more sober than I realized, and I think sleeping on your couch is better than sleeping on one of the tables here in the pub." Connor nodded in agreement. "But if I don't tell *someone* where I am and what I'm doing, then I'm a major hypocrite. Every time one of my friends meets someone in an online dating app, I'm that friend who insists they share their location with me. If I wander off to your home and they don't hear about it until I'm back home, I can only imagine how much crap I'll get. Hang on a sec."

Emma wandered over to a booth in the corner that was somewhat isolated from the music and reverie that hadn't died down even a bit since Connor's last call announcement. She slipped her phone out of her pocket and called Claire's number. It was late here, so that meant it was a reasonable time to be calling just about anyone back in the States...but she still chose Claire. Claire was the most likely to understand Emma's situation and offer good advice, with the added benefit that she was already the only person who knew about Emma's whole "stranded on a remote island" situation.

"Emma!" Claire answered on the first ring. "I'm so glad you finally called back."

Emma smirked. "Are you? You know, you could have called me at any time in the last few hours."

"Has it been *hours* already since we talked?" Emma could hear the surprise in Claire's voice. "I swear I just lost track of time. I was writing this scene, and the words were just flowing and didn't stop. It's like the opposite of writer's block. Which is great, but I mean…I also haven't gotten off the couch in an obscenely long time. Or remembered to call you back. Or, apparently, eaten or gone to the bathroom in far longer than a human should wait. I'm starving! And I really have to pee. Here, I'm taking you with me. Don't listen."

"By all means, don't let me stop you," said Emma. "Though that's not *exactly* why I called."

"Right. Duh. What's going on with you?"

"Well, I'm still stuck on the island…"

Emma heard a sound that was most likely Claire smacking herself on the forehead. "Oh my gosh, that's right! Wow! I really *have* been on another planet. I mean, I kind of couldn't hear what you were saying on the phone anyway, so maybe I didn't actually know that until now. What are you going to do? It's got to be super late there, right?"

"It is," said Emma. "There's no boat until tomorrow, and I've been at the pub for the last few hours." She cleared her throat. "There isn't actually any place open tonight that I can pay to stay at…"

"What? That's terrible! Are you just going to stay at the pub all night? It wouldn't be the first time, but, I mean, I'm not sure about you, but I haven't pulled an all-nighter since college."

"Luckily, I won't have to do that. The bartender, Connor…he's been nice and helpful. He offered to let me crash at his place." She bit her lip, anticipating with a cringe the reaction Claire was going to give.

And there it was. "Ooooh! The plot thickens! This is like something straight out of a novel. Let me guess, there's only one bed?"

"I haven't gone with him yet, because I wanted to call you first. So you know where I am. He's been a perfect gentleman, and this is not, like, a hookup technique..."

"But if it were, would you be up for it?" Claire asked.

It wasn't that Emma hadn't thought about it, but admitting it out loud was a whole different animal. "It's not like that, Claire. It's just a place to crash. I'd share my location with you, but..."

"I know, I know. An evil witch stole your phone. Anyway, you have my blessing. Go have a sleepover, and feel free to make it a romantic one. You're on vacation!"

Before Emma could protest, the call had ended. She rolled her eyes and looked up to find Connor's eyes already on her, watching her from the bar.

# Eight

Emma wasn't in the habit of going home with men the same day she met them, and the thought alone made her chuckle. After her call with Claire had ended and she'd confirmed her plans with Connor, he had cleared the pub out quickly. A few patrons had tried to convince him to just stay open a bit longer, but he had caught her yawning and told them to scram. Not before filling a glass or two for a few folks who were walking home, reminding them to bring the glasses back—and the ones they already had in their kitchens at home, too.

After the last customer had left, Connor beckoned Emma to come back behind the bar. He locked the front door, switched off the lights, and flipped over the open sign. Then returning to Emma's side, he grabbed her hand and led her in the dark back into the small kitchen and out the back door. He dropped her hand to lock the door, and Emma was grateful for the darkness to hide her rosy cheeks—why a platonic and practical hand holding had made her blush was something she didn't care to examine or explain right now.

It was cold outside, and Connor turned up his collar. Emma pulled her hat down further over her ears and crossed her arms over her chest, bracing herself against the wind.

"Where are we going?" she asked. "Are we driving? Do you live near here?"

"I'm just up the lane," said Connor, gesturing to the narrow road leading away from the dock. "It's a short walk. Follow me."

Emma jogged to keep up with him. His legs were longer than hers, and he was familiar with the route. It seemed he had better night vision than she did, too, because the dark sky didn't slow him down one bit.

"Slow down," she panted as she caught up with him. "I can't see a thing, and I'm just trying not to lose you."

"Ah, right," said Connor, looking up. "I forget sometimes that folks expect things like street lights. Here, give me your hand." She felt a thrill low in her belly as he tucked her right hand in the crook of his left arm and continued on his way, more slowly than before.

When the sprinkling rain started to get heavier and more sideways, Connor turned his head and looked down into her eyes. "You've got two choices," he said. "We can keep crawling along as slow as tortoises and get soaked to the bone..."

"Yeah, what's the other option?" Emma asked, blinking against the rain in her eyes.

"You can trust me, hold on tight, and we'll make a run for it."

Emma laughed. "I already fell on my butt once today, sir. I'm really not interested in that happening again."

"I'd say it's a lot more likely to happen once this street is slick with rain," he pointed out. "I walk this street in the dark every night of the week, Emma. Do you trust me?"

Surprising herself, she nodded. "I guess I do. But if I fall and re-bruise my tailbone, I'm rescinding all my trust forever and ever amen. And it will be one hundred percent your fault."

Connor nodded back soberly. "That's only fair. Hold on tight then." He linked their arms even tighter then, gripping her hand between his arm and the side of his torso. Then he took off at a jog, pulling Emma with him.

Despite all the reasons she shouldn't—it was dark, she had hurt herself once already today, and she hadn't known the man next to her for more than a handful of hours—Emma was having fun. The jog, the rain, and even the cold were exhilarating. And there was something about not being able to see the path ahead, about just grabbing tightly onto the (very solid) arm she'd been offered, closing her eyes, and moving her feet. She felt like she was flying, like a little girl dancing with her father, her feet off the ground.

She was surprised how willing she had been to trust Connor. First, she'd taken him up on his offer of staying at his house, and now she was letting him lead her through the dark and through the rain to get to that house. This story had all the makings of a horror story, but...

...it also had the makings of a completely different kind of story. One of adventure, joy, and maybe even a little bit of romance.

She felt her stomach flutter at the mere thought, tingles activating all her nerve endings even in the cold. Her life had been consumed by SLICE for so long that romance had been the furthest thing from her mind for years now. In this moment, with Connor, she didn't know what to expect—and she literally couldn't see the next step in front of her—but she had a feeling it was going to be something wonderful.

Too soon, they arrived at Connor's house. It was too soon, because as soon as they got there, under the light of his porch lamp, he stepped away and broke the physical contact between them. The side where he had been standing, anchored to her like they were in a three legged race, felt colder than any other part of her body with his absence.

They were both panting from the exertion, and Emma looked up to see Connor's face flecked with raindrops and a broad grin smiling down at her. There was a bareness to him, to the way he was looking at her. It was like the layers of joking and teasing had been washed away in the rain and wind, revealing something rawer and more real underneath.

"Well, I'd say that was half successful," he said. "We got here faster, but you're still all wet." He looked her up and down, heat traveling along with his eyes.

"Excuse me?" Emma said, a blush coloring her cheeks.

Connor laughed. "Get your mind out of the gutter, you. We both got soaked. It turns out we couldn't actually outrun the rain. Who knew?"

"Right, yes." She looked down at herself, seeing the raindrops dripping off of her jeans for the first time. "The raincoat was a great idea, but it looks like I needed to bring some rain paints, too."

Connor was unlocking the door, and with the sound of his key jiggling in the lock, a few faint "woofs" began emanating from inside. "I'll find something dry for you to wear."

"Thank you, but that's not—" Emma's words were cut off by a streak of fur bursting through the open door and leaping onto her. Paws touched her midriff, and a long pointy nose was craning towards her face. There was whining and a pink tongue that couldn't quite reach her face, no matter how hard it tried.

Emma laughed, holding the dog's front legs in each of her hands. "It's nice to meet you, too, er..."

"Lady," said Connor, reaching over to grab Lady's collar and gently set her back on all four feet. "And we've been working on jumping, we really have. If you'll notice, she didn't jump on me. She's really got that down perfectly. It's just that she jumps on everyone else... I'm sorry about that." He was rubbing Lady's head, looking down into her eyes. "She'll get it one of these days, won't you, Lady?"

Emma dusted off the front of her coat, where Lady's paws had been. "It's really okay. I love dogs, even when they misbehave a little. I've really missed having a dog, so I might just have to steal some puppy cuddles while I'm here." She reached over to Lady, who lurched forward to lick her fingers, her tail wagging rapidly and hitting Connor's legs at each end of its swing.

"I'm glad to hear it, because it's entirely possible she's not going to understand the whole 'you're sleeping on the couch tonight, Lady' thing. If you want puppy cuddles, you can have them all night long." He winked at her with his final words, then turned back to the open door, walking inside his house and whistling for Lady to follow him.

Before Emma walked through the door, she took a minute to look at Connor's house. It was a cottage, just the right size for a man who lived alone with his dog, but she was surprised by how cute it was. With its thatched roof, white walls, red door and matching flower boxes under the windows, it felt more like something out of a fairy tale—or maybe *Beauty and the Beast*—than a bachelor pad. It was certainly different from any bachelor pad she'd ever seen before.

Emma entered the cottage, closing the door behind her. Following Connor's lead, she slid off her wet shoes in the entryway and hung her dripping raincoat from the empty hook of the coat rack. She followed a short hallway to the living room, where Connor was lighting a fire in the fireplace, Lady at his side.

He looked up at her, no doubt noticing right away that she was dripping on his wood floor and shivering with the cold. "Let me get you some warm clothes. Can you finish getting this fire going?" He held out a few small pieces of kindling and a box of long matches, pressing them into her hands and walking away before she could respond.

Lady stayed behind in her owner's absence, and Emma turned to the dog, staring into her deep soulful brown eyes. "Can you give me a hand here, Lady? I don't exactly have a lot of opportunity to start fires in New York City... But how hard can it be?"

Lady's eyes conveyed a complete lack of faith in Emma's ability to create heat for all of them, and she exhaled audibly as she curled up on the rug in front of the fire, placing her head on her outstretched paws.

Emma turned to the fireplace, where Connor had already placed a few larger pieces of wood. She looked at the smaller pieces in her hand, then added them to the pile. She lit a match, tossed it on top of the kindling, and waited for the fire to roar to life.

Which didn't happen. A few short seconds later, the match had burned out, and she was back where she had started.

"Let's try that again," she said to herself. Luckily, the box in her hand was full of matches, far more than she would need...

She hoped, anyway.

She was determined to get the fire lit before Connor got back, for a reason she wasn't entirely sure about. Either he assumed she couldn't light a fire because she was a city girl, in which case she wanted to prove him wrong. Or else he assumed she *could* light a fire—and easily at that—because he'd never even met someone who lacked such a basic life skill. In which case, she definitely *didn't* want to be the first person to do so.

She lit another match, and this time, one of the pieces of kindling actually managed to catch aflame. Emma celebrated under her breath—she was that much closer to succeeding at her task.

Until it, too, burned out just a handful of seconds later.

Connor came back in the midst of her struggle, a small bundle of clothes in his arms, which he set on an armchair. Emma noticed he was still in his dripping wet jeans and plaid shirt, and she was touched and surprised by it. He'd gone in search of warm, dry clothes for her, but he hadn't bothered to put them on himself yet.

But when Connor looked at the fireplace and started grinning like a fool, her warm, fuzzy feelings for him extinguished themselves like another of those faulty matches he'd given her.

"What?" she asked. "I'm trying! I think there's something wrong with these matches."

He took the matches back from her, swiping one hand down his face to cover his smile. "That must be it. My apologies for the broken matches. I'll take them back to the store tomorrow and see if I can get a refund. In the meantime, I'll try to get this started some other way, maybe with a magnifying glass and the sun. It should be coming up anytime now."

"Har har," said Emma, rolling her eyes. "I can't remember the last time I started a fire, actually. It was probably a bonfire in my parents' backyard, and we probably doused all the wood in gasoline and just threw a match at it. Not the safest plan, and definitely not applicable experience in this situation."

Connor raised his eyebrows. "Indeed. In that case, I'm quite grateful you didn't siphon gas out of my car, throw matches at the fireplace, and burn the whole thing down. That was a great call." He kneeled down in front of the fireplace, reaching in to rearrange the small pieces of kindling. He nodded his head towards the armchair. "Those clothes are for you, bathroom's down the hall. Go ahead and get changed. If you need anything else, I'll see what I can do. But I'll warn you now, the fashion choices really don't get any better than that, so don't be trying to exchange anything."

"I'm sure it'll be just fine," she said, picking up the clothes. "Anything would be better than this." She gestured towards her flimsy sweater and the soaked jeans that were sticking to her skin. "Thanks, Connor. I really appreciate it."

"I'm not doing it for you, love," he said, not looking up from his work. "If you're going to be sleeping in my bed, I can't have you getting my sheets all wet, making them smell like wet dog."

"I do *not* smell like wet dog!" cried Emma, affronted.

"No, you don't," Connor gestured towards Lady with his head. "But this one will, and if she's curled up next to you, then so will you."

"Ah." Emma nodded. "Got it."

She headed off down the hallway and found the bathroom immediately. There were only three doors off the hallway, a bathroom, what looked to be a laundry room, and a closed door at the end of the hallway that she guessed was the bedroom.

Emma entered the bathroom, closing the door behind her. There was an unopened toothbrush on the counter, an unused towel folded and placed on the back of the toilet. Inspired by the sight of the towel, she reopened the door and called out for Connor.

"Yeah?" he responded, voice raised to travel down the hall.

"Do you mind if I take a quick shower? Just to warm up a bit?"

"Of course not," he called back. "Can you figure out how it works, or do you need me to give you a lesson?"

Emma laughed. "We've got showers too in the US. I'm sure I can figure it out."

"Suit yourself!"

Emma's pride wouldn't let her admit to Connor that she needed help figuring out the shower. Never ever.

But it had been ten minutes since she'd last called down the hall to him, and she was still fully clothed, sticking her hand into the running water and pulling it back quickly because the water was freezing. It hadn't warmed up one bit, no matter how much she adjusted the tap. She'd tried everything, every possible combination. She'd even reasoned that, if they drove on the opposite side of the road in Ireland, maybe "hot" and "cold" were on opposite sides of the faucet.

That hadn't worked. Nothing had. And she was about to give up and call it a day when there was a knock on the door.

"Everything okay in there?" asked Connor through the thick wooden door.

"Why wouldn't it be?" Emma called back.

"So you figured out the immersion, then?"

"The what?"

She heard Connor chuckling on the other side of the door. "Let me in, and I'll show you. I'm sure you're still fully clothed, just sticking your hand into the shower and marveling at how cold it is."

Emma recoiled, jerking her hand back and slamming the tap down at the same time. If Connor was going to come in here and show her how to make the cold water warm, the last thing she was going to do was give him the satisfaction of conforming precisely to his expectation.

She stalked over to the door and opened it to find Connor leaning against the frame, an impish grin on his face. "Your knight in shining armor has arrived, m'lady," he said, sliding through the door next to her and brushing against her in the narrow space. Her breath caught in her throat at the nearness of him, and she coughed and shoved her hands in her pockets just to give herself something to do.

Connor switched on the shower, stuck his hand in the flow of water, and nodded before shutting it back off. "Just as I suspected. Ice cold." He walked back out the door, turning back to look at Emma. "Come with me if you want to learn the single most important tip for surviving in an Irish home."

He walked to the other door, the small room she had assumed was a laundry room. Sure enough, there was a washing machine inside, but there was something else, too. It was a massive tank on the wall, covered in lights, switches, and dials.

"This," said Connor, gesturing to the room as a whole, "is the hot press." He pointed to the tank, turning one of the dials. "And this is the immersion. It heats the water. It's off to save energy when I'm at work. We'll just let it wait for fifteen minutes or so, and then you'll be all set to take your shower."

"Ah," said Emma, looking around her. "There was definitely no way I was going to figure that one out on my own."

Connor shook his head. "I knew that, of course. I'd have been very surprised if you started opening doors looking for the hot press. That might not be that strange for an Irish houseguest, but I imagine it would seem quite rude for an American one."

Emma nodded. "That's true. I was weighing my options that wouldn't require me to ask you for help. I was definitely leaning towards just telling you I was suddenly too tired to shower and needed to go right to sleep."

"What was the other option?"

"Taking a cold shower like a horny teenager."

Connor's eyebrows lept up his forehead. "I see," he said, looking down at her with a question in his eyes. "And would that be...necessary for some reason?"

"Absolutely!" cried Emma. "I mean, have you smelled me lately? Cold water or not, a shower is definitely necessary."

He rolled his eyes at her. "Sure, that's exactly what I meant, smartarse. Come sit in front of the fire while you wait for the water to heat up. The time will go faster if you're warm, at least."

Emma followed Connor back to the living room, where the fire was burning nicely in the fireplace. She noticed most of the kindling had been placed underneath the metal log holder, and she made a mental note for the next time someone asked her to start a fire. She was going to *rock* fire starting the next time the opportunity presented. Heck, if there were such a thing as adult Girl Scouts, that would be the first badge she would earn.

Emma settled in one of the armchairs near the fire, and Lady came over to sit near her feet. Emma petted the dog's head, scratching behind one of her ears, while Connor opened and closed drawers and cabinets in the kitchen. It was all one big room, the kitchen, dining room, and living room, but her back was to him in the chair and she didn't turn around to see what he was doing.

When he joined her, sitting down on the stone in front of the fire and setting a small tray on the coffee table between them. The tray held two steaming mugs, a sugar bowl, a small jug of milk, and a cylinder of something wrapped in plastic. Connor scooped a tea bag out of each mug, depositing them on a small saucer.

"How do you take your tea?" he asked, pointing to the milk and sugar in turn.

"A little sugar, a lot of milk," Emma responded, accepting the cup gratefully from Connor when he placed it in front of her.

He opened the cylinder—of cookies, it seemed, when the mystery was revealed—and held it out to her. "Digestive?" he asked.

Emma wasn't entirely enticed by the idea of eating something called a *digestive*, but she was pleasantly surprised when she took a bite. The cookie—*biscuit*, she reminded herself—was similar to a graham cracker, but somehow way better. With a cup of tea in one hand and a digestive in the other, she found herself, for the first time since she'd entered Connor's house, feeling totally at ease. Like all was right in the world. She no longer felt like an awkward weirdo who couldn't figure out how to take a shower or who said accidentally flirtatious things to her attractive host. Instead, she just felt comfortable sitting here in silence with him, sipping their tea, munching on biscuits, and getting warm in front of the fire. It was an oddly natural feeling, like they had known each other longer than for just a meal, a rainstorm, and a few laughs. If she closed her eyes and squinted, she could almost trick herself into thinking she was sitting in front of her boyfriend's fire, about to go use his shower and then fall asleep in his bed like it was the most natural thing in the world.

Only in that scenario, she probably wouldn't be sleeping in his bed alone. *Details, details.*

"Thank you, Connor," Emma blurted. "I'm really sorry for all the inconvenience. You're probably exhausted after a long day of work and I'm totally ruining your plans. But I really, really appreciate you taking me in. I don't know what I would have done without your kindness. And no jokes, please. I really mean it, and I hope you can take my gratitude seriously."

Connor smiled, a devastatingly genuine and handsome smile that made Emma's heart crack open. "You're absolutely right to admonish me. I was just about to dismiss you with a joke again. But you're welcome. Anytime. And you didn't ruin my plans at all. If anything, you made my evening eleven times more interesting and fun."

"That's an awfully specific number," said Emma.

"It's what the calculations came up with," Connor shrugged. "I don't argue with the math, I just report it."

He reached over and picked up Emma's hand from her knee, squeezing it. "You never have to be alone. Just ask for help, and trust that the right person will provide it."

"Are you the right person?" Emma asked, her pulse beating like a drum in her throat. She wasn't even entirely sure what she was asking, but it felt like the biggest, realest, and most important question.

"I don't know," said Connor, looking down. "But it doesn't feel like an accident that you're here. And I'll take that."

# Nine

Waiting for the water to get piping hot had been worth it, in every sense of the meaning. Not only was the shower Emma was currently taking gloriously toasty, but the time she had spent with Connor had been different. More real. It had given her butterflies in her stomach, tingles up and down her spine, and so much to think about in the shower that she was pretty sure she had just washed her hair twice rather than conditioning it.

The banter had been fun, more fun than Emma would have admitted if he'd asked. From their first meeting, Connor's playfulness and quick wit had kept her biting back laughs and rolling her eyes to cover up just how much she was enjoying it. But there had been glimpses of something else tonight, too.

That look when they landed on his doorstep. That authenticity in front of the fire.

Meeting him had been a reminder that no matter how much you think you understand someone through a first impression, you're only scratching the surface. There's so much more beneath the depths than any of us show at first glance.

Emma groaned out loud. "What a profound revelation for a social media app developer to have," she said to herself. "And here I am encouraging people to keep it all surface level. To really invest in building that outer identity until it's bombproof."

She got out of the shower, toweled off, and then wrapped her hair up on top of her head in the same towel. Twisting to peek in the mirror, she was surprised that she couldn't see a purple bruise on her butt, sore as her tailbone still was. Satisfied with what she saw, she finally looked at the clothes Connor had left for her and laughed out loud.

The sweatpants were nothing remarkable—a pair of dark blue men's sweatpants that fit fine around the waist even if they were a little tight in the hips and long in the legs. But the long-sleeved shirt he had selected made her crack up every time she looked at it.

"Regional *hurling* champs?" she asked Connor as she entered the living room, dressed in his clothes. "Is that, like, a vomiting championship? Because, where I come from, that is definitely what hurling means."

Connor looked up at her and an unreadable expression crossed his face before he chuckled. "Hurling is an ancient game, and I'll not have its good name besmirched in my very own home, of all places." He looked her up and down, his eyes landing on her own. "Did everything fit alright?"

Emma nodded. "It did, thank you. I wasn't sure what to do with these." She held up her wet clothes. "I remembered the washing machine in the hot press, but I noticed there's no dryer in there."

"Nor in most of the country. But have no fear, we'll hang these up in the hot press, and they'll—probably—be dry by morning. If not, you're welcome to take the hurling shirt home with you."

"Wow, thanks," said Emma, turning back to hang up her wet clothes. She called back over her shoulder. "I might just throw these old clothes away in that case. I can't miss my chance to own a hurling shirt!" The sound of Connor chuckling softly to himself brought a smile to her face she couldn't swallow back down. She was having too much fun with him, and she didn't have any intention of putting a stop to that any time soon.

Emma returned to the living room, plopping herself next to Connor, who had moved to the sofa. When he looked over at her, she was tempted to feel self conscious about her makeup free face and unbrushed hair, but his smile—along with the reminder that whatever makeup she had put on this morning had been washed off by the elements hours ago—quickly extinguished that concern. This wasn't the way Emma would have chosen to show up for a first date given the choice, but then again, this wasn't exactly a first date, was it?

Sure, the flirtation had been there. And the attraction too, at least on her part. Heck, Connor had even bought her a meal, and if that wasn't the most traditional first date activity, then what was? A movie?

Perhaps it was the fact that they had entered into the "staying overnight" phase of their knowing each other with no game playing or questioning the implications of what it meant that had her so confused. Because it didn't mean anything, of course. Connor was a nice person, helping her out in her time of trouble. Knowing him—or at least based on her first impressions of knowing him—he would do this for anyone who was stranded on the island. Or rather, for anyone who was stranded on the island who could put up with his teasing long enough to get to the other side, where the genuine offer of help and goodwill came.

"Are you tired?" Connor asked, interrupting her reverie.

"Not really," admitted Emma. "I don't think I've totally adjusted to the time zone difference, and even though it's dark outside and I know I should feel tired, I just don't."

Connor nodded, picking up the TV remote from the table next to his place on the couch. "I'm usually too wired after a shift to go to sleep right away. But—and I mean no offense by this—I'm also usually too burned out on talking to humans that I can't bear the thought of making conversation." He pointed the remote towards the TV and raised his eyebrows in question. "You up for a movie? I could make popcorn..."

Well, that settled it. Dinner and a movie, and even an overnight visit. Emma had officially convinced herself she was on a date, and she didn't care who tried to prove her wrong. She nodded at Connor. "That sounds great. I can look for something good while you make popcorn..." She laughed at the expression on his face. "...or, since you clearly don't trust my taste in movies, you can point me in the direction of your popcorn making equipment and I can leave you here to select a movie that we'll both enjoy that won't make me question your taste or you feel self-conscious about it."

"Hmm, you've got a point there," said Connor, fiddling with the remote. "What kind of movies do you like, anyway? How do you know you'll be so much better at this than I am?"

"Easy," said Emma. "Everybody likes to laugh. Can't go wrong with a good comedy. Action movies, romance...those can be excellent or terrible. Horror is just horrible. Always. I'm pretty sure that's where the word horrible comes from, actually. But comedy is a safe bet. Especially if we go with a classic."

"Define classic. Are we talking 90s Adam Sandler? 2000s Will Ferrell? Earlier?"

"You know your *Saturday Night Live* alum, I'll give you that. But I was thinking something a little older. Go make popcorn and I'll see what I can find."

He handed her the remote. "You know how this thing works?"

Emma laughed. "As long as this isn't another iteration of the hot press slash immersion fiasco, I can handle it."

Halfway through *What About Bob?*, Emma's exhaustion caught up with her. Confused about time zones or not, she had expended a lot of energy that day walking all over the island. In order to share the bowl of popcorn more effectively, Emma had scooched over next to Connor on the sofa, sitting on the center cushion and leaving the far left one vacant. Or it was vacant until Lady hopped up and claimed it.

Perhaps sensing Emma's tiredness, Connor moved the popcorn to his lap and pulled a lever on the side of his seat, popping out a footrest and reclining his section of the sofa. "Don't be jealous," he said, before she could say anything in protest. "I did it for you. Go on, scooch a little closer and put your feet up. You know you want to."

Emma did as he said, relishing the comfort of lying back and putting her feet next to Connor's on the footrest. The right side of her body was pressed along the left side of his from the shoulder through the leg. It should have been uncomfortable, but it wasn't. Apart from the shoulders, actually, which seemed to be fighting for space on the couch. Just as she was about to suggest rearranging themselves for maximum comfort, Connor spoke again.

"Let me try something," he said. "Lean forward for a sec. If this is weird or uncomfortable, we can change it." He sat a little higher on the seat, extending his left arm along the back of the sofa and gesturing to the empty seat next to him. "Come here to me. Put your head on my arm like a pillow."

Emma raised an eyebrow. That man's arm looked far too muscular to make a good pillow, and as she settled in, she was proven correct. With her head awkwardly angled forward, she laughed and Connor joined in.

"That was a better idea in my head," he said. "It's been a long time since I shared this couch with someone besides Lady and I may have forgotten how it works."

"Let's just go back the way we were," Emma suggested. "It was a little awkward, but at least it was better than this."

"Suit yourself," said Connor, replacing his arm at his side. Emma sidled next to him, twisting her torso slightly, so that she was leaning against his side rather than fighting for space.

When she opened her eyes again, the screen was dark and the fire had burned out. The lights were still on in the room, and she, Connor, and Lady were all still on the couch in approximately the same positions they had been.

They were only *approximately* in the same positions because Emma had woken to find herself cuddling embarrassingly with Connor's biceps. Her head was leaned against his shoulder, where by some small act of grace she *hadn't* drooled. Her body was turned towards his, her chest pushing against his arm and both of her hands cupping his forearm.

It would be far more embarrassing if he were awake, but judging from the way his head was lolling back on the headrest and his mouth was hanging open, Connor was just as asleep as she had been thirty seconds ago.

Emma knew she needed to go to bed, that she and Connor would both sleep a lot better if they weren't jammed onto this single seat of the sofa. But she also didn't want to wake him up...not just yet, at least.

It hadn't been terrible having someone to cuddle with, after all. In fact, as she remembered the last seconds of sleep before she had jolted awake, they had been deliciously cozy and comforting, without a trace of anxiety or restlessness in sight. And if she woke Connor up now, would that be awkward? Weird? Would he feel like a bad host for falling asleep? Or what if he was such a deep sleeper that he didn't even budge? Why was it always so awkward dealing with people in different levels of consciousness?

"Oh good, you're awake," said Connor, rubbing his eyes.

"Yep," she nodded, forcing a more casual smile than she felt after the way she had spooned with the man's arm. "Looks like we both dozed off there and missed the end of the movie."

Connor was shaking his head. "I saw the whole thing, actually. It was a great choice you made, if I do say so myself. But you...well, you fell asleep pretty much as soon as I reclined the seat. And the way you grabbed onto me like a spider monkey, well, I couldn't really go anywhere. I guess I fell asleep too, waiting for you to wake up."

Emma's face was crimson, burning a brighter red than she was sure it ever had before. He had *seen* her fall asleep? How bad had it been? She wiped her face again, reassuring herself that at least there hadn't been slobber. But had there been snoring? Sleep talking? Strange noises?

No doubt noticing her expression, Connor laughed and reached the arm closest to her down, patting her amiably on the knee. "Relax, Emma. You didn't do anything embarrassing. I just didn't want to wake you up because I knew you'd had a long day. And admittedly, there was something kind of cute about the way you were clinging to my arm like a koala climbing a tree."

*Cute.* That was something. And he hadn't pushed her away the second they were both conscious again, so that was probably a good sign, too. Right?

"I'm glad to hear that," she said. "Nothing kills the chemistry like sleep farts, am I right?"

Connor shook his head, a single quiet laugh escaping from his mouth. "They never stop, the tasteless jokes. But at least you admitted there's chemistry." He looked up at her then, a playful grin and wiggling eyebrows just for her.

"Like I'm the first one to make a joke every time the two of us talk. I believe the expression is 'It takes one to know one,' sir."

"Touche. So what do you say? Is that enough couch chemistry for one night? You should probably sleep in a bed, and I should probably kick you off this couch and keep it for myself."

A wild thrill of excitement awoke in the pit of Emma's stomach, and her next words slipped out of her before she could even think to stop them. "It's so late, it almost seems pointless to make up the couch. Why don't we just share the bed?"

Connor's eyes were wide as he stared at her, their faces so close she could practically count his eyelashes. "Miss...Emma, whose last name I now realize I don't know, are you...propositioning me? Is this the way you seduce a man?"

Emma blushed again, hurrying to explain and backpedal any momentum she had started in the wrong direction. "It wasn't a sexy invitation, so hold it right there. I'm just assuming the bed is big enough for two people to sleep in it, especially if those two people have already managed to sleep on a single sofa cushion together. No funny business, though. Lady can sleep in the middle and be our buffer just to ensure no one gets any wild ideas."

Connor laughed and leaned forward to look at Lady. "Oh, she would definitely love that. And what kind of human companion would I be to deny her getting to sleep next to not one, but *two* warm human bodies? Emma, my friend, you've got yourself a deal." He held out his hand to shake hers, then kicked in the footrest and stood up from the couch. Turning back to offer her a hand, he spoke again. "Let's give this dog a night she'll never forget."

Emma shook her head. "That sounds *so* wrong, and you know it." She reached down and scratched Lady's head. The dog had jumped down from the couch and was standing at their feet, wagging her tail. "This good girl deserves all the cuddles. Don't you, Lady?"

Lady licked Emma's hand in response, before trotting off down the hall to show them the way to the bedroom.

•♥ · ♥ · ♥ · ♥ · ♥•

In hindsight, Emma didn't know what she had been thinking when she suggested sharing the bed like siblings in a hotel room on a family vacation. Whether the buffer in the middle was a waggy tailed dog or a wall of pillows, it was never conducive to the best sleep. Emma made a mental note: *If you're going to share a bed with someone, it should either be 100 percent romantic or 100 percent platonic. Otherwise, no one is getting any sleep.*

As exhausted as she had clearly been on the couch, she was now wide awake, staring into the darkness. She felt the urge to toss and turn, sure she just needed to move one more time to get comfortable...and yet she also felt painfully aware of her every breath and movement. She couldn't hear a peep from Connor's side of the bed, which meant he was probably sound asleep, and if she so much as exhaled forcefully, she was in danger of waking him up.

That was all really unfortunate because, for some reason, both her breathing rate and her pulse seemed to be just a touch faster than normal. Something was putting her on edge, making her feel nervous...but what could it be?

She heard Lady's tail thwapping against the bed and looked down to see the dog's dark eyes staring back up at her, the only thing gleaming in the darkness.

"Can't sleep either?" Emma whispered, patting the mattress near her to invite the dog to creep up higher, where her head would be in reach for scratches.

Connor groaned, giving away the fact that he was clearly awake, too. "That makes three of us," he said, rolling over to face her and petting Lady's belly while Emma scratched her head.

"It's weird, right?" Emma blurted out. "Sharing a bed, I mean. I thought it wouldn't be a big deal, especially after we both fell asleep on the couch, but..."

"It's definitely weird," agreed Connor. "It's always a bit strange at the beginning of a new relationship, you know? You're not sure if the other person snores, or you don't want them to find out about the weird thing you do in your sleep, like kicking or grinding your teeth or whatever perfectly normal human thing it is. It's ages before everyone can get some rest, finally."

"Hmm," murmured Emma. "You're right, I think. It's been a while since I went through that phase with someone, so I'll have to take your word for it."

"Well, I'm just speaking from memory," said Connor. "Ancient memory, at that." He flipped onto his back and settled into the mattress deeper. "So what is it that's kept you from having someone special in your life?"

"We don't have to talk about that." Emma wrinkled her nose in the darkness. Talking about her workaholic tendencies wasn't exactly her first choice for a fun topic.

Connor exhaled audibly. "We may as well. Otherwise, we're both awake and staring at the ceiling, pretending we aren't. At least this way it's not awkward for anyone."

Emma thought about it for a moment. "That's fair. It's not like you and I see each other every day...or probably ever again, actually. I guess that makes it a little easier, to be honest."

"Sure. That's one way of looking at it."

Emma took one more breath, then it all poured out of her. "The truth is, I've just been way too busy with work. That's such a cliche, isn't it? I'm under no illusions that I'm the first person to sacrifice my personal life for a career." She laughed mirthlessly.

"You certainly aren't." Connor's voice pierced the darkness. "I've been there, too."

Emma turned to face Connor, staring at his profile in the deep dark of the room, trying to make out his expression. "I can't tell if you're teasing me right now. Are you teasing me right now?"

He turned his head to look at her and shook it. "No, I'm not. I'm not talking about the pub. The pub is my retreat from what I was doing before. The life I'm living right now, the version of me you met...it's not who I've always been. It's weird to think that there are people like you who will never know that version of me."

"That sounds ominous. Who were you? What did you do? A spy?" She gasped. "A serial killer?"

He shook his head again. "You first. You started this topic, anyway."

"Fine," she sighed. "I work in tech. App development. Have you heard of SLICE?" Connor shook his head, drawing a laugh from the depth of Emma's being. "This really is a different world, and I think I love it. But anyway. SLICE is, like, the next big deal in social media apps. I developed it. It's my baby. And it's launching to the world...soon. *So* soon."

"Then what are you doing here?"

"There's a bit of a public relations mess happening at the moment, with someone claiming I stole it from him. My team and I decided the best thing was for them to handle it and me to get a bit of a reprieve from...all of it." She was silent for a moment. "I'm guessing this all sounds so inane to you. So silly. It's an app on your phone, for crying out loud, and yet I've made such a big deal out of it. Sacrificed so much—especially so much human contact—for it."

"It's not silly or inane at all." Connor reached over Lady and put his hand on Emma's. "And...I understand more than you know. Really."

"Really?"

"Really. Before I moved back to Inishmore, I was in Dublin for years."

"Dublin? Does that mean you were working in tech, too?"

Connor nodded. "Search engine development, actually. Not quite the same thing, but I get it. The long hours, the sacrifices, the feeling that it's all worth it because you're somehow moving humanity forward. Only it's all a crock, isn't it? None of that matters."

"What happened?" Emma asked. "Why did you leave?"

"I couldn't stay there anymore. It...wasn't good for me."

Emma noticed how he hadn't exactly answered her question, but she didn't push.

"My parents said they could use some help at the pub, so I came back to be with my family. I thought it would just be for a while, but...I just couldn't go back. I couldn't convince myself that the work I had been doing was important anymore. So I sent my letter of resignation by email, and I stayed here."

"You never went back?"

Connor shook his head. "It was a bit shocking how easy it was to leave the life I'd built for years. A few friends called me, sure, but that was it. Nothing real. Not like here."

Emma squeezed his hand. "I'm glad you figured out the right decision for you. I bet it was hard when you were still discovering what that was. I kind of feel like that's where I am now. If I'm honest—and I haven't admitted this to anyone yet—I have my moments where I doubt what I'm doing at SLICE." She shuddered. "I can't believe how scary it is to say that out loud."

"Hmm," murmured Connor. "Awareness...that's the first step to changing anything, isn't it? And if you're scared to tell it to yourself, that's one thing. But there's no need to be scared to tell it to me and Lady, now is there? We won't tell a soul."

Emma smiled into the darkness, their hands still clasped together. "Well, thank you both for that." She fell silent then, turning over the words she had said in her mind until she slipped off to sleep.

# Ten

Emma woke the next morning unsure where she was, which made sense considering she had arrived in the dark, was wearing clothes that didn't belong to her, and was still adjusting to being in Ireland in the first place—never mind on a remote island where she had never intended to stay the night.

She stretched and rubbed her eyes, opening to find the source of the *thump thump thump* sound that was coming from the near distance. Deep brown eyes looked up at her from the foot of the bed, where Lady was wagging her tail.

"Good morning," Emma greeted the dog, her morning voice rising an octave with the cuteness of the animal. Lady army crawled towards the head of the bed, propelled the entire way by the intensity of her wags.

"She's already been fed, so don't let her tell you otherwise," said Connor as he entered the room. He was still wearing the sweats he had slept in last night, but he had a mug in each hand.

Emma felt a wave of embarrassment wash over her. Last night, she had told things to Connor that she hadn't told anyone else, not even Claire. It hadn't felt that strange, emboldened as she had been by the darkness and the knowledge that she would never see Connor again. But here it was, just nine hours later and...she was seeing him again. And while that shouldn't have felt like a surprise, for some reason it did.

Connor looked sheepish, too, with a tinge of pink to his cheeks that she hadn't seen before. "I wasn't sure if you'd want coffee or tea in the morning, so I made you one of each." He set the two mugs on the nightstand next to Emma, then turned to leave the room. "I'll give you some privacy. Wasn't trying to intrude on you and Lady's special time together."

Emma smiled as the door shut behind him. "Your dad's alright, you know that?" she said to Lady, scratching her ear. She picked up the mug closest to her and took a sip. "Ugh!" she groaned, setting it back down. "That answers my question about coffee and tea being interchangeable in the morning. Turns out it really does matter how you get your caffeine." She picked up the other mug, took a sip, and sighed with pleasure. "That was a sweet gesture, though. You don't drink tea, do you, Lady?"

The idea of leaving the bedroom and joining Connor in the living room or kitchen, wherever he was, hung over Emma's head. She wanted to be a good guest, and she wanted to spend more time with him, but she also had the nagging feeling that she had overshared last night. Or that both of them had overshared, not that she had minded listening to what he'd had to say. It just felt like *a lot*, especially for something that wasn't even a first date.

It wasn't like there was an alternative, though. There was no back door to sneak out of, and even if there were, she'd still be on the same tiny island as Connor. And he'd still be the only person she knew here. (Sean the doctor didn't count; she didn't even know where he lived.) She also didn't have the option of hiding out in this bedroom all day, either. Connor would need to come back in to get his clothes out of the closet, at the very least, and Lady was bound to need a walk, a potty break, or a meal before long.

But even more than all of those reasons, Emma knew she needed to be brave for once. She was brave when it came to taking professional risks, to putting herself out there in the ways that most people only put off for "someday." But with humans—especially with men—she wasn't exactly a pillar of courage. No matter how much it scared her today, something real had happened with Connor last night. She had told him things she hadn't said out loud before, and she was guessing he had done the same. Even the way he had reached for her hand, the way she had squeezed his...she was pretty sure they had still been holding hands last night when she fell asleep. She could pretend it hadn't happened, that everything was still the same between them and just make a dumb joke, setting the tone for the day ahead. Or she could join him in the kitchen right now, without overthinking it, smile, say something nice—something real—to him, and walk the path less traveled. Less traveled by Emma Kells, at least.

Before she could chicken out, Emma called Lady off the bed, picked up the second mug, and headed towards the living room. She hadn't bothered to stop in the bathroom or to look in a mirror yet, but that was all part of this vulnerability experiment she was undertaking right now. There wasn't much she would have been able to do to alter her appearance, anyway; it wasn't like Connor had a cosmetic bag full of all her favorite products lying around. (She had checked. After she'd found conditioner in his shower, all bets were off. Alas, the conditioner was the full extent of his going above and beyond the normal bounds of masculine hygiene.)

"Good morning," she said to Connor, who was sitting near the fireplace, reading a book. He had a pair of black-framed glasses perched on his nose, and Emma felt an unexpected ripple of sensation travel through her at the sight of him. He had so much else going for him appearance-wise, she was woman enough to admit, but there was something about adding the glasses that pushed it over the edge. The smile, the accent, the arms, and now...the geek chic? If she wasn't careful, she was going to be full-on crushing on Connor before she ever got on the boat back to Galway.

"Morning," he smiled as he looked up at her. "Did you sleep alright?"

She smiled back. "I did, actually." And then, before she could breeze past it and into a new day, she plowed forward, into the unknown land of open-hearted sharing in the light of day. "Thank you for talking with me last night. It really helped."

"I should thank you, too," he said. "I hadn't thought about that time of my life in a while, but it's always good to get a wee perspective check." He nodded to the mugs in her hands. "Did you decide on a beverage, or are you double fisting it?"

"I'm a coffee gal, through and through, I'm afraid." She lifted the tea mug to draw his attention. "Should I pour out this tea, or—?"

Connor was already waving his hands, beckoning the mug towards himself. "Give it here. A good Irishman never lets a cup of tea go to waste."

"I took a sip—"

"Like that's going to stop me." He took the mug from her and took a large gulp. "Just the way I like it. How did I know this mug was going to end up right in my hands before I even delivered it to you? Did I make that happen with my powerful brain?"

But Emma wasn't paying attention to what he was saying. Ever since he'd put the mug up to his mouth, his lips pressing right where hers had been only a few minutes before, she'd been distracted. The intimacy of sharing a cup, of being separated from a kiss by nothing more than time and a bit of ceramic, was filling her mind with images and desires that had no business there. Especially not before anyone had brushed their teeth. But after Connor's next sip, he had licked the rim of the cup, and her mind had gone completely blank. Presumably, he'd just been using his tongue to catch a drop of tea that was threatening to roll down the side, but it felt an awful lot like he was torturing her with temptation.

Only he wasn't even aware of where her mind had gone. "Emma?" he asked, waiting for her to respond to whatever it was he had said while she had been blacking out.

She sat down, sipping her coffee again. "Sorry, what did you say? I'm still only half awake."

"I just asked if there was anything in particular you wanted to do today. I know you did a bit of exploring on your own yesterday, but we have better to offer on Inishmore than just the old cemetery, you know."

Emma stared at Connor, not fully processing what she was hearing. "Sorry, I think I missed something," she said finally. "Are you asking what *I* intend to do today? Or are you asking for suggestions of what we should do together? Because it kind of sounded like the second one, until I started talking out loud and realized I may have horribly misread the situation."

Connor was smiling wider the longer she spoke. Finally, he put her out of her misery. "Oh, I was definitely talking about going with you. If I know anything about you for certain, it's that left to your own devices, you're liable to injure or maim yourself. Speaking of which, how *is* your bum today?"

Emma shifted in her seat, leaning back until she yelped in pain. "I thought it was better, but apparently I just wasn't sitting on it. Whatever we do, it probably shouldn't be a tailbone-intensive activity."

Connor raised an eyebrow. "Well, I'm not entirely sure what that is...but I assure you, we won't be sledding or riding horses...not even a mechanical bull. So what is it that you *do* actually want to do?"

"Honestly?" She shrugged. "I'm leaving that up to you. You live here...you know what's special way more than any travel blog I can read or boat tour guide I can ask. And I'm just here to enjoy...to experience life the way you all do on the island. I'm not trying to fit every single experience into my time in Ireland."

"So if I told you that what people do here is take their dogs for walks and make lunch and visit their parents...you'd be okay with that?" There was a glint in his eye that told her he was kidding, but she didn't think it was a good joke.

"Um...yeah! My life has been seriously lacking normal experiences. And rest. So even if you're making a joke, I'm up for doing everything you just said."

"You want to meet my parents already? Jaysus, woman, I know we held hands, but I don't even know your last name yet."

Emma felt her cheeks color at the reminder of the emotional intimacy they'd shared. "It's Kells. So now you do."

Before breakfast was going to happen for Emma and Connor, Lady had some urgent needs to attend to. Finding that her clothes were still a bit damp from the night before, Emma pulled her raincoat and boots on over the sweats that Connor had loaned her. He offered to stay in his own lounge wear out of solidarity, and Emma took him up on it gladly after he'd reassured her that no one they saw was going to care.

"This is a small community, though. Won't people gossip about you?"

Connor shrugged. "It's also quite a close community. It has to be, considering how rough the weather can be here. Whether I go out in sweats or a suit, no one's going to be looking at me funny. They will, of course, *all* know that you slept over and probably want some details about that." He looked unfazed at the thought that an entire community was going to be prying into his love life. "If I have to choose between being comfortable or not, comfort wins every time. It's not like these folks haven't seen me in sweats. A good number of them even changed my diapers, I don't mind telling you."

"Perhaps you *should* mind telling me that," Emma laughed. "I'm hoping you aren't talking about something that happened recently..."

Connor rolled his eyes. "What a clever joke, Ms. Kells! Now if you don't mind, we've got a dog who needs a walk, so whenever you're done with your profane humor, we best get on that."

"I'm ready!" Emma insisted. "I was waiting for you to make up your mind about your fashion choices. Now, if *you're* finally ready, then let's get out of here."

Lady didn't need to walk on a leash, making this particular dog-walking experience unlike anything Emma had ever experienced back in the States. But the path they walked was one Lady had been on many times before, and the folks they encountered on the road all seemed as familiar with Lady as they were with Connor. Emma was the only wild card of the equation, though the friendly souls smiled and greeted her all the same.

After one older gentleman continued walking in the opposite direction, Emma turned to Connor with the question that had been bothering her since the first friendly pleasantries they'd exchanged. "I didn't understand a word the two of you said to each other. Is the accent that strong, or is there something wrong with my ears?"

"That depends," said Connor, his face deadpan. "How good is your Irish?"

"What do you mean?" asked Emma. "Irish what?"

Connor shook his head. "Your tour guide did a real bang-up job yesterday if he didn't bother to tell you that a lot of people still speak Irish here."

"You speak Irish?"

"Of course. We all learn it in school, but the Aran Islands are one of the few Gaeltacht regions of Ireland, where you still find people using it in their daily lives."

Emma nodded. "I learned a bit about the language before I came here, but I had no idea how what Wikipedia told me would play out in real life. Until recently, I still thought it was called Gaelic. I honestly thought all the Irish signs, like the city names on buses and things like that...I thought all of that was done for tourists. For novelty."

"Right." Connor paused in thought. "I can see how you'd think that. I'm sure a lot of people do. But it's all part of an attempt to save—or even revitalize a dying language. Languages like Irish or Welsh, they don't tend to get taken too seriously by the rest of the world. But they aren't a novelty to us; they're part of our culture, our history. Of course, we don't want to see them die out, even if Irish class *was* one of the most difficult lessons in all my school days."

"Isn't that always the way?" asked Emma. "The things we appreciate the most as adults, we resented when we were kids. Sometimes I think about the classes I practically slept through in middle school, high school, even college...but some of those subjects are just fascinating to me now. If someone wanted to pay me to go back to school and learn them all over again, I'd definitely be up for that."

"It's good to know what a supreme nerd you are, Emma," said Connor. He smiled affectionately. "It's endlessly amusing how full of surprises you are."

"How could I be anything *but* full of surprises?" She checked her watch. "We've known each other for about twenty hours, and we were asleep for eight of them. You can't seriously think you've already managed to figure me out."

Connor shook his head. "Not at all. In fact, I get the distinct feeling from you that, even if I knew you for a lifetime, you'd always be finding new ways to surprise me."

Emma's chest puffed out at the compliment, her spirit buoyed by the affectionate tone of his voice. The idea of knowing each other for a lifetime, for the implications of what that could mean, thrilled her all the way down to her toes, warming them in her flimsy boots.

Just as the wind was getting to be a bit too much on their faces, it was time to turn around and head back to the cottage. Lady trotted ahead of them, in a hurry to get home where her breakfast was waiting for her.

As Lady scarfed down her bowl full of kibble, Connor opened cabinets and drawers, pulling out a frying pan and a toaster.

"I was thinking of frying some eggs and making toast for breakfast. Does that sound good to you, or should I make some porridge instead?"

Emma's stomach rumbled with hunger at the mere mention of eggs. "Toast and eggs sound great. What can I do to help?"

"Why don't you fill the kettle again and boil some water for tea? Or if you're anti-tea at all times, you can make another coffee or a hot chocolate for yourself."

"I'm not anti-tea," said Emma. "I just don't want to drink anything other than coffee first thing in the morning. Not orange juice, not tea, not even a glass of water, which I realize is probably not the healthiest confession I've ever made. I wasn't always like this. I swear, I used to drink water...herbal tea...even the occasional kombucha."

Connor nodded knowingly. "Did all of that change when you started working in the tech field?"

"Yeah, actually. How did you...?" She looked up at him and nodded. "Right. The same thing happened to you?"

"Let's just say, I had some serious unlearning to do when I moved back here. Sleeping, hydrating, going outside during the daylight hours. Those were all things I was pretty rubbish at in Dublin."

"I think it goes with the territory. When everyone around you is more concerned with success and forward momentum than their health, then taking a break feels like admitting weakness."

He looked at her with a scrutinizing eye, searching her face for an answer before he even asked his next question.

"What's that look for?" she asked, her discomfort growing with every second.

"You just...you sound like someone who *used* to work in tech," he said. "Not someone who's only taking a break from it. Someone who's been out of the office for what...three days?"

Emma's heart sped up, guilt consuming her. Did she really sound like that? How dare she resent SLICE when it had been the cause of everything good in her life? She'd barely thought about work since arriving on Inishmore yesterday, and that didn't sound like something a founder would do. Not someone who *deserved* to be a founder, anyway.

Connor's soft throat clearing caught her attention. "Emma? Where did you go? Was it something I said?"

She forced a smile. No need to let him in on the full extent of what was going on in her brain right now. "No, it wasn't. Just...well, thinking about that might bring on my second existential crisis of the day, and I'm not quite sure I'm ready for that yet."

"What was the first one?"

Emma supposed she had to admit it, since she hadn't exactly intended to say that. "Waking up here. With you. It just felt vulnerable...more vulnerable than I'm used to. It kind of made me want to run out the door, rather than talk to you. That might make me a terrible person, but I didn't do it. And honestly, I'm kind of proud of myself for that."

"From the sound of it, you should be."

"You don't sound surprised."

"Well, I woke up a little earlier than you did, so I had a moment or two to freak out about those same things before you were up. That way I could pretend to have my act together while you were driving yourself mental."

Emma chuckled. "That's awfully big of you to admit it now, when you could have just kept up the charade."

Connor was flipping the eggs in the pan when the toaster beeped. Emma buttered the toast while the tea steeped, and within a moment or two, they were sitting at the kitchen table together preparing to dig in.

Between bites, Emma asked the question that had been brewing in the back of her mind since it had been mentioned that morning. "So...I'm going to meet your parents today?"

Connor swallowed his bite and took a sip of tea to wash it down. "Do you want to?" he asked, cocking an eyebrow.

"I think that depends on the expectation," said Emma. "I mean, I definitely do want to meet them. I *love* parents, and not to brag, but they love me, too. Friends' parents, classmates' parents...I've always been good with them all. I was just wondering what they would think. If that might be a problem for you."

"It's no problem for me," said Connor. "And I'm honestly clueless what they'll think. They've never actually met any special ladies in my life, so we'll find out together how they handle it. Maybe Da threatens you with a shotgun, maybe Ma gets out her old wedding dress to see if it'll fit you. Your guess is as good as mine."

"You've *never* brought someone home to meet your parents?"

"Don't look so shocked, Em. Weren't we just talking about my workaholic Dublin days? Is it any surprise then that I wasn't exactly taking weekend trips back home with special gals every chance I got? Considering how similar the two of us are, I'd be pretty surprised myself if you said your parents had met a whole bunch of your boyfriends."

Emma shook her head. "You got me there. And I vote we *do* meet your parents today. We can make sure they know we're just friends, so they don't get their hopes up for a spring wedding or anything like that."

The expression on Connor's face was one of utter bafflement. "You have something against spring?"

# Eleven

Emma was still dressed in Connor's clothes when it was time to go to his parents' house, but at least her bra had dried—and she had traded in the hurling shirt for a borrowed plain black sweater. She was still wearing his sweatpants, since the man didn't own another pair of pants that would fit on her body, but her hair was combed and her teeth were brushed. It was as good as things were going to get.

"You ready?" Connor asked as they slipped on their shoes in the entryway.

"Sure," said Emma, her voice betraying the nerves she was feeling. "Just realizing I'm a little less sure of myself than I let on. Your parents do speak English, right?"

Connor chuckled. "I'm so tempted to mess with you and teach you to memorize Irish phrases on the way over...but even *I* know that's mean. But the answer is yes. They definitely speak English. I imagine there are a handful of folks on the island who don't, but it's pretty hard to get by in the world when Irish is your only language."

"Thanks for not messing with me." Emma stuck her tongue out at Connor. "From what I know of you so far, you'd probably tell me you were teaching me something perfectly harmless and then it would end up being totally inappropriate." Off Connor's growing laughter, she probed further. "I'm right, aren't I? What were you going to teach me?"

"*Pog mo thoin*," said Connor. "It's a classic."

"*Pog mo thoin*," repeated Emma, cringing as she butchered the pronunciation. "And what does that mean?"

"Well, it's not a friendly greeting, as you may have already guessed from context."

"I did, believe it or not."

"Grand. It means 'kiss my arse.'"

Emma nodded. "Okay, yeah. I get it. I see how that would be a fun way to have fun at the expense of a tourist. To take the piss of them, if you will."

Connor's face was turning red from laughter. "Take the piss *out* of them," he clarified. "Don't forget any words, or it totally changes the meaning. Jaysus, woman. I can't have you embarrassing yourself in front of my parents. Whatever will they think?"

Emma swatted him on the arm. "Alright, that's enough. Are we getting out of here now, or what?"

The two of them left the house, and with a whistle from Connor, Lady was close behind them. He led Emma over to an old truck, nodding towards the passenger seat to remind her which side to sit on. Admittedly, she *had* forgotten, and when he'd nodded, her first thought had been, "What? He can't be serious. He wants *me* to drive?" This time, however, she managed to keep her thoughts to herself and even to keep her face from betraying them to the world, or at least to Connor.

As she settled into the front seat and buckled her seat belt, she turned to Connor. "Where are we going, actually? I thought everyone lived so close that we'd just walk there."

"They're not in the village; they're a little more remote. It's certainly possible to walk there, but I figured it'd be wise to have the truck in case it's raining when we want to come back."

"A wise decision." Emma nodded. "I suppose you learn things like that when you live here long enough. Can't be getting soaked to the bone and hanging your clothes in the hot press every single night, can you?"

"It's not advisable, no."

Emma paid attention to the scenery around her as they left the area where Connor's and his neighbors' houses were. They were driving away from the "downtown" area—if you could call it that—where the pub and the harbor were. The road followed the coast, and she stared out the window at the vast gray expanse of sea. Staring at it brought back unpleasant memories of yesterday's journey on the boat, and, before she could stop herself, she groaned out loud.

"What was that about?" Connor asked. She could practically hear his eyebrows climbing up his forehead without even looking at him.

"Just remembering my boat journey yesterday. I think I could enjoy looking at the sea a lot more if the thought of getting back on a boat didn't make me sick to my stomach."

"It was a bit rough then, yeah?"

Emma nodded. "*A bit*, yeah. I've never seen that many people throwing up at once, and I honestly don't care to see it again anytime soon."

"You're still planning on going back on the boat today?" He cleared his throat and nodded towards the sea out the window. "It looks to be quite a bit choppier today than yesterday, so I wouldn't blame you at all if you wanted to wait it out another day."

She turned and studied his face. Did he want her to stay longer? His expression, his tone...none of it gave away what he was thinking. "What do you mean? It's not like I've got another option...I appreciate your hospitality very much, but I don't think I can just decide that I'm going to be your new roommate, you know."

"I'm very much uninterested in having a new roommate, so that's a good call." He paused, pursing his lips before his next words rushed out. "However. I would not be opposed to having your company for another day, or even a couple more days, if you wanted."

"Really?" Emma swallowed a face-splitting grin, letting only a demure curve of the lips show. Why did his admission make her so happy?

He nodded, eyes on the road. "I'd like to continue that conversation we started last night. I like you, Kells. I like spending time with you, and I think you might feel the same way. So why wouldn't we spend more time together? Life's too short not to do what you like, and all that."

There was a rush of energy coursing through Emma's veins. She hadn't entertained, hadn't even *considered* the idea of staying in Inishmore longer than planned. This morning, she had been comforting herself for her over-sharing with the thought that she would never see Connor again.

But now, here he was, vulnerably offering to let her stay longer in his house. Telling her that he liked spending time with her. Implying—if she was reading the signals correctly—that there was a potential *something* between them.

The thought of that something thrilled her. And it terrified her. At the same time, in the same body, she was holding those two conflicting emotions, and she didn't have the first idea what to do about them.

Connor was looking at her with a question in his eyes, so she smiled at him. "Can I give you an answer a little later?"

Almost imperceptibly, his face shifted. Like he was having to mask disappointment when he'd been wanting to bust out the world's biggest grin.

Emma rushed to explain. "It's just that all my things are still in Galway, in the hotel. It's not like anyone will miss me there, but..."

"But you're going to get tired of wearing my clothes soon?"

*As if.* What was it about wearing a man's clothes, especially his comfiest, most well-loved items that was simultaneously like a hug and an aphrodisiac? She hadn't been the first teenage girl to "forget" to return a borrowed hoodie to a cute boy, and she certainly wouldn't be the last. Even Connor's offer of his hurling shirt—which *may* have been a joke, she was big enough to admit—was thrilling and enticing in oh so many ways.

"Just basic hygiene stuff, frankly. Deodorant. Socks. Undies. All the things that stop me from smelling like a swamp thing."

Connor was shaking his head and laughing. "You sure know just what to say to a man to get his mouth watering with excitement. 'Ooh baby, tell me more about that deodorant!'"

Emma snorted with an unexpected laugh. "You asked for the truth, so you got it." She shifted in her seat. "But seriously. Is it alright with you if I let you know in a few hours what I've decided about going back to Galway?"

"Of course. As long as you let me know before today's boat leaves, so we don't end up with a repeat of yesterday."

At the memory, Emma put her head in her hands. "I have no interest in repeating that day—or at least, that *part* of that day again, ever."

"Are there other parts you're interested in repeating?"

Emma nodded. "There definitely are."

The genuine smile spreading across Connor's face made Emma's heart melt. "Good," he said. "Me too."

In hindsight, there was nothing Emma should have been nervous about when it came to meeting Connor's parents. For one thing, it wasn't like she and Connor were dating, which meant there was no pressure for them to like her. But for another, far more significant thing, Iris and George

Ryan were probably the two sweetest people she had ever met.

From the moment they had arrived, Iris had swooped in like a mother hen, offering tea and local anecdotes, treating Emma like she was just one of the family. There had only been the briefest of flashes, when they had first arrived, that had given away to Emma that Connor had *not* warned his parents he was bringing a visitor. George had been intrigued to learn Emma lived in New York, and he had been full of questions. In fact, between all the things Iris wanted to tell Emma and all the things George wanted to hear from Emma, it was nearly impossible for her to take a sip of tea or a bite of biscuit. Or for Connor to get a word in edge-wise.

From the looks of it, though, Connor wasn't minding that at all. He sat off to the side, watching Emma and Iris on the sofa with an amused smile on his face. Amused, and something more, too. There was a certain wistfulness about his expression, like he was capturing a moment he knew would never come again. Not that any moments ever repeated themselves...but if there was one he'd like to replay, maybe it would be this one.

When they'd been visiting together for about an hour, the front door burst open, and a young woman came inside in a flurry of activity, bustling about to fling off her shoes and get a drink of water like she'd just finished running a marathon.

"Nora dear, we have company!" crowed Iris, patting the sofa seat next to her. She had scooted closer to Emma to make room for Nora, who Emma remembered as Connor's sister based on what he'd told her last night.

Nora's eyes went as wide as saucers at the sight of Emma. "Where in the world did you come from?" she asked.

Emma stood up to shake her hand. "I guess you don't get a lot of random visitors dropping over here, do you? I'm Emma. I got stranded here last night, and your brother was kind enough to put me up for the night."

"I bet he was," said Nora, walking over to her brother to clap him on the back. "What a hardship, eh? Having to put up with a beautiful woman, to rescue a wee damsel in distress. You'll get a gold star for this one, I'm sure."

Was...was Connor Ryan *blushing*? Emma had seen hints of it before, but she'd almost been able to convince herself that she'd imagined them. But here, in front of his family, at the mercy of the teasing of his kid sister, he was red faced and at a total loss for words.

And it was the most adorable thing Emma could even imagine. Even cuter than Lady's puppy dog eyes and wagging tail. No, it was *dangerously* cute, and she knew for certain right then that she would be staying in Inishmore longer.

It might be today. It might be tomorrow, too. It might be the rest of her time in Ireland. But what Emma knew with 100 percent confidence was that she wasn't going to forget about Connor Ryan anytime soon. And that she wanted to spend more time with him before she had to leave.

Following that thought like a shadow was a second thought. This one reminded her how frightening it was to feel this way and how inconvenient it was, too. After all, she had a business to run back in the real world.

But as the two thoughts warred in her mind, her heart declared itself the judge. *There's plenty of time to be afraid, and there's plenty of time to put work over everything else. Just for today, choose what gives you butterflies. And if that's this man, then even without the promise that it's going to last forever, choose him.*

With the peace that knowing that brought, Emma sat back and smiled, taking in the scene around her. Iris was trying to get Nora to sit down for a cup of tea, while Nora was insisting she needed to shower after "running all over the bleeding island to help Old Dec find his missing sheep." Connor had moved next to his father, and the two were huddled in a conversation that, from the occasional words that reached her ears, was about the pub. And there was Lady, sitting at Emma's feet, gazing up at her as she rested her chin on Emma's knee.

*This is a good choice*, thought Emma. *This is a happy, warm, comforting, and exciting choice. And I'm about overdue for one of those.*

Emma had intended to wait until she and Connor were alone again to let him know she'd made up her mind and was going to stick around a little longer. But as she was saying goodbye to Iris and noticed the older woman's eyes filling with tears, she couldn't resist spilling the beans. Iris was trying to fit in all the kind words and well wishes she'd give to someone she liked but knew she would never see again, and Emma just couldn't take it anymore.

She took both of Iris's hands in her own and squeezed them gently. "Don't give me all your Irish blessings at once, okay?" She glanced at Connor, pleased to see that he was listening intently. "I don't think you can all get rid of me that easily. I may stick around for a few more days."

Iris's eyes brightened, and she squeezed Emma's hands back. "That's just wonderful news, dear! Oh, we'll have to get together for a proper roast dinner. When shall we do it—tomorrow?"

Connor interjected then. "How about Emma and I talk a bit about her plans and we'll figure out a good day?" He winked at his mom. "I'll see how long I can convince her to stay. Maybe I'll use the promise of your roast dinner to extend her visit a wee bit longer."

Nora gave Emma a hug, pulling her in close to whisper something in her ear. "I'm glad my brother met you. He seems to really like you. He deserves to have something good happen to him, and I hope he doesn't mess this up."

Nora abruptly ended the hug, pulling back and smiling at Emma, who was floundering for the right words to say. "No...we're not..."

Nora just winked, gave her a nod, and stepped back so that George could give her a hug, too.

Once they were back in the truck, Connor turned to face Emma straight on. "So. It seems like you made up your mind about staying for another day." He was smiling. "It sounded like you were thinking of staying for *several* days, actually."

Emma ducked her head. "I was going to wait to talk about it with you when we were alone again. I didn't want to overstay my welcome or over-promise how long I would stick around. But, just...your mom seemed so genuine in her well wishes, and I didn't want her to say all these nice things, only to find out I'm not actually leaving."

"That makes a strange kind of sense," said Connor. "I've got to admit, I find it kind of adorable that you wanted to make my mom happy."

"Your whole family, they just seem like such great people. Thanks for bringing me to meet them."

"Well, don't speak too soon. You haven't met my brother yet."

"Oh, right! The one from the pub. Is he there now?" A beat passed. "Wait, do *you* have to go to the pub today? I totally forgot that you have a job, embarrassing as that is to admit."

"Nah, it's my day off today. Patrick runs the place by himself one day a week. The kitchen is closed on those days, since he's absolutely useless with a stove. But he knows how to fill a glass, and the locals understand I need a day off."

"You do." Connor had started the car and begun the drive back to the other side of the island, and Emma was staring out the window. "You're reminding me yet again of something that's been missing from my life back in New York."

"Do you mean you're missing a handsome Irishman?" His eyes were twinkling mischievously. "Or that you're missing days off in your life?"

"Oh, I've got a surplus of handsome Irishmen." Emma rolled her eyes. "Days off are not exactly encouraged, you know. It's like, if I take 24 hours off from work, everyone is afraid the competition will outpace me so badly that I'll never catch up."

"That sounds about right." Connor's eyes were on the road. "Somehow they're managing without you while you're here, though. How's that?"

"Well, it helps that they specifically told me to go away. To take time off. To leave this particular problem to them to solve."

"So it's like a onetime deal?"

Emma shrugged. "I guess so? This is uncharted territory. Something like this has never happened to me before, and I certainly hope it doesn't happen again. I mean, I hope the intellectual property theft part doesn't happen again. I think I really do hope that the vacation part happens again, afraid as I am to say that out loud."

"Have you been checking in back home on the situation? Any news?"

Emma shook her head. "My friend Claire—you'd like her, she's far too tricky and too much of a smartass for her own good—took away my smartphone and replaced it with a prehistoric piece of technology. I can make calls, but I can't go online, check any social media, or even send a text. I can't access my own app, for crying out loud."

"Are you having withdrawals?"

"From SLICE? I admit it feels really strange to be away from it. Like if I'm not on there, sharing slices of my life at regular intervals, I'm just becoming more irrelevant with every passing minute. It doesn't help that I know how the algorithm works—everyone does, it's one of our main selling points. But knowing how it works, I know for damn sure that every day I take off from posting there, I sink lower and lower with my reach. That's not a good look for the founder of a social media app, you know?"

Connor was quiet, thoughtful. "Is that really a necessity? To not only create the damn thing, but to be one of its most prominent users? Seems like two completely different jobs to me."

"You might have a point there. The concern is just that SLICE is so new. If I'm not using it religiously, then it's kind of like the chef who won't eat her own cooking. It makes you wonder what's *really* inside it."

"Ahh," Connor exhaled. "I hadn't thought of it like that."

"To be fair, I hadn't really thought of it from that perspective you just shared, either," said Emma. "Because there's a part of me—probably the part of me that's a total control freak, but I'd rather not think about that too much right now—that is *very* uncomfortable with handing over the 'influencer' part of my job. Like, if some other people are the ones making all the content on SLICE, then how can I know what direction the app is going to go? You know? What if it gets nasty? Or inappropriate? Or just plain dumb?"

"You've launched this app to the masses, right?" Connor asked. As Emma nodded, he continued. "Then I'm afraid 'just plain dumb' is inevitable. Let it go. Do the part you're good at and step away from the rest of it. Trust that no matter what you create, there are going to be people who use it to put meaningful, educational, inspiring content into the world. And a lot of those people are going to be struggling to build an audience while everyone else focuses on makeup tutorials and celebrity gossip."

"Hey now," said Emma. "Don't poo poo the makeup tutorials. That's an art form. But yeah, the gossip does seem to lack any kind of redeeming value."

They had stopped in front of Connor's house, but before they could exit the car, he put his hand on Emma's arm. "What is it you get from social media? From the posting, I mean? And are you dying here without it?"

"That's a valid question. This trip is the longest I've gone without being connected in longer than I care to admit. I thought it would be a lot harder than it was, but it's been surprisingly easy...mostly because there's no self control involved. My phone simply won't do the same things as the phone Claire confiscated. Otherwise, if I had my regular phone...I hate to admit it, but I'd be experiencing this whole trip through the lens of what would look good to other people. What pictures I should take, what videos I should share, what filters I should use... All the moments I've been experiencing would just be mined for content."

Connor leaned in towards her, his hand sliding down until it clasped her hand. "What about this moment? Or any of the real moments we've shared, when it's just the two of us and the jokes stop for a minute? Do those feel less than just because they haven't been curated for public consumption?"

Emma's breath had caught in her throat at the nearness of Connor. "Oh no, I'm happy to keep these moments for myself."

He smiled wickedly, then pulled back, giving her hand one last squeeze before dropping it. "Good," he said. "Me, too."

# Twelve

Back inside Connor's cottage, they both flopped onto the sofa. The meal Iris had prepared had left them both uncomfortably full, even after the journey home. Emma stifled a yawn before turning to Connor and catching him in the middle of an epic one of his own.

"Oh good," she said. "I thought it was just me. I'm exhausted!"

Connor yawned again, audibly this time. "It's definitely not just you. We've still got a couple hours of daylight, and I don't want you to waste your time here. We could get some caffeine in our systems and then head back out to do some exploring? Maybe go check out some of the old Celtic ruins?"

"I absolutely want to see some ruins. Yes, please!" said Emma. "...but maybe not today. If I'm going to be staying longer, we've got more time, more days than we need to cover every square inch of this island, I'm guessing. But I'm not the kind of traveler who can just go go go."

"What do you want to do instead, then?"

"Honestly? A nap sounds like heaven."

Connor's eyes widened in surprise. "Wow, that is *not* what I thought you were going to say."

"Disappointed?"

"On the contrary, I'm pleased as punch. I'll get you a blanket, put something inane on the telly, and we can both pass out reclined on the sofa."

"That sounds like a perfect plan," said Emma, cuddling into her seat. "Can I make one request for what we watch?"

"Your wish is my command, m'lady."

"Would it be possible to watch some hurling?"

Connor laughed. "Ahh, I thought you'd never ask. I would be honored to introduce you to the noble sport of hurling. Coming right up."

Hurling was not at all what Emma had expected. Mostly because she had remained convinced it was some kind of competitive vomiting tournament up until the moment the match started. As it turned out, hurling was a sport that had been around since ancient Irish times. And, like pretty much any other sport Emma had ever tried to watch on television, it made her fall asleep within ten minutes.

The couch was comfortable, the announcers' voices were like soothing white noise lulling her to sleep, and

Lady's head on her lap provided just the right amount of grounding calm.

For the second time in as many days, Emma woke up on Connor's couch in the dark.

"Dang it," she said to the dark room. "What time is it?"

She heard Connor's weight shifting at the other end of the couch, then a mumbled, "Huh?"

"Is it, like, the middle of the night again? Did we sleep the whole evening away?"

Connor's voice got muffled again as he turned on to his side. "Not possible," he said. "Anyway, the sun sets at, like, half four this time of year. I'm guessing it's five o'clock, at the latest."

Huh. How had Emma not noticed how early the sun had set yesterday? That's right, she'd been in a pub with very few windows for the entire evening. That explained it.

Convinced that Connor was going to be snoozing longer than she cared to stay on the couch, Emma shuffled to the kitchen and opened the fridge. Connor had done a stellar job of feeding her so far in the time that she'd been under his care, but it would be nice if she could return the favor.

As she was scoping out the produce bin, a thought stopped her in her tracks. Where did people on this island actually get their groceries from? If Connor was trekking to the mainland for his carrots and potatoes, he might be less appreciative of her kitchen experiments. Emma wasn't the *best* cook...because cooking wasn't exactly her favorite activity.

While she was standing in front of the open refrigerator door, she became aware of footsteps behind her and turned to greet Connor's sleepy face. "What are you doing?" he asked, rubbing his eyes.

"Well, I *was* thinking about cooking something for you...until I remembered we're on an island and I don't know how difficult it is for you to get groceries...and then I got too intimidated to do anything but stand here, stare into your fridge, and waste your electricity."

"Thanks for the thought." Connor leaned close behind Emma and reached forward to shut the door. "We do actually have a supermarket here—a small one—so you don't need to worry that I'm, I dunno, swimming to Galway and back with a bag of food trailing behind me."

"That's good to know." Emma was struggling to find words with Connor so close behind her. He hadn't moved back, even though there was no need for him to be standing so near. Why hadn't he stepped back? Did the man have no concept of personal space?

Emma started to speak again, to ask Connor what they should cook for dinner, when she felt his hand land on her lower back, the other hand on her upper arm. She turned around to face him in the darkness, wondering what expression she would see on his face if there was any light at all in the room.

"We need to turn on a light," she blurted, stepping back.

Connor chuckled. "I wouldn't have guessed you were afraid of the dark, Emma."

"It's not that. We already had one intense conversation in the dark; I'm not sure we should make it a habit. It makes it that much more awkward when we're back in the light of day and realize all the things we shared—or overshared—with each other."

"Ah." Connor stepped across the kitchen to flip on a light switch. "That's a bad habit, isn't it? Waiting until the cover of darkness to say the things we're really feeling. Or act on the impulses we've managed to suppress during the day."

Emma nodded. "Darkness and alcohol both have that effect. Last night we had both working together, making us share all our deep, dark secrets. So, whatever happens today, I don't want it to be under the same influence, you know? I don't want to wake up tomorrow morning wondering why I said what I said or did what I did."

Connor took a step back closer to her. "Hmm," he murmured. "And what did you think was going to happen today?"

"I don't think I imagined your hands finding me in the darkness."

He shook his head. "No, you didn't. Did you not want me to do that?"

"Not at all," Emma protested. "That's not what I'm saying. Just that, if something *were* to happen, I wouldn't want it to feel like we were sneaking around in the darkness. Like there was something embarrassing or shameful about it."

He took another step towards her. "I think I'm following what you're saying, but I don't want to get the signals wrong. Why don't you tell me what it is that you *do* want me to do?"

Emma's feet moved towards him on their own. "I don't think a kiss would be out of line at all."

"No?" he asked, reaching a hand up to cup her neck, his thumb stroking her cheek. "I don't think so, either."

"That's good," Emma said dumbly, feeling her body weight shift forward of its own volition. Her lips found Connor's just as her eyes closed, and it was like electricity was flowing from his mouth to hers and back again. One kiss turned into another and another, their hands traveling up and down each other's backs, into their hair, their faces...it was like they couldn't get close enough, feel each other deeply enough.

When Emma had gone long enough without air that she was starting to see stars—or was that just about the nearness of Connor?—she pulled back to breathe. Their arms were still around each other, but now, in the light of the kitchen, she was staring into Connor's eyes. His pupils were nearly the size of his irises, giving away just how much he was enjoying the moment.

As much as she was, if she was honest with herself. And why shouldn't she be honest about what she was feeling? This connection with Connor wasn't the kind of thing that happened every day. For one thing, it didn't usually happen that she found herself stranded on a remote island. And even if that had been a commonplace occurrence, what were the odds that the only person there to help her was a handsome, single Irishman who was interested in her? As if that weren't enough, he understood her, he wanted her to stay, and his family was a delight.

Honestly, Emma was about to start checking the room for hidden cameras. This was all a little too good to be true, and it felt like it had been orchestrated by someone with some seriously masterful planning skills.

Maybe that was what fate was, actually. Like a really skillful personal assistant was arranging the best surprise party you'd ever been to. She might have been too cynical (and too busy) to believe in such a thing a week ago, but the last day and a half had started to make her wonder.

"What's going on in that head of yours?" Connor asked, his hands trailing her cheeks.

"I'm not entirely sure." Emma shook her head to clear her thoughts. "I'm just...surprised, I guess. By all of this. I swear it wasn't my intention to hook up with an attractive Irishman while I was here."

Connor smiled at her. "I'm surprised, too. I don't normally bring home stranded tourists, you know. And I really did intend to sleep on the couch last night. And to send you on your way today, but..."

"Yeah, I've definitely missed the boat again by now. Oops," said Emma, her tone giving away that she felt exactly zero remorse about staying here with Connor longer.

Still locked in their embrace, it was hard for Emma to look up at Connor without craning her neck. "What should we do now?" she asked.

"Well, I was thinking." He had a twinkle in his eye that matched the words he was speaking. "We *could* figure out dinner now. Or..."

"I'm listening."

"We could keep making out. Maybe even in the bedroom instead of the kitchen, just, you know, for the sake of being someplace a little more comfortable."

"And having privacy from Lady, of course."

"Indeed. She's such a stalker sometimes."

Lady was sitting at their feet, looking up at the two of them as her tail swished back and forth across the tile floor.

Emma looked down at the dog, addressing her directly. "Lady, if you'll excuse us, we need to leave you alone for a bit. You're in charge while we're gone."

And with that, she took Connor's hand, led him back to the bedroom, and shut the door behind them.

When they reemerged, Emma and Connor had worked up an appetite. As Connor guided her back to the kitchen, her hand in his, he asked, "So what was it you were thinking of cooking before my mouth and I so rudely interrupted you?"

Emma ducked her head. "I have no clue, actually. I was just staring into the refrigerator, hoping divine inspiration would strike."

"And did it?"

She shook her head. "Not at all. I'm not exactly the world's best chef."

"Huh," he said, sarcasm pouring through his words. "I would have thought most tech giants had all sorts of time to play around in the kitchen and learn how to prepare cuisines from all over the world. You must be the rare exception who doesn't have a sense of proper work-life balance."

"I must be," Emma said, sticking out her tongue at him. "I'm sure when you were working in Dublin you prepared four course meals every night."

"Absolutely," said Connor. "Cooking at the pub has really cramped my style. It used to be all homemade pasta, salmon with truffle aioli, caviar on toast...can you tell I don't really know that much about fancy food?"

"I never would have guessed that. But you do make a mean fish and chips, and that's good enough for me."

Connor frowned. "You're not eating the same thing two days in a row, even if it *is* the best fish and chips in the county. The county includes Galway, by the way, so don't think I'm underselling my abilities."

Emma shook her head. "I wouldn't have expected you to do that, and I wouldn't have agreed with you if you had. Though you still haven't answered the question of what we're going to eat tonight."

"Hmm." Connor opened the fridge and a couple of cabinets, as if making a mental tally of the ingredients at hand. Finally, he made his decision and announced, "Spag bol."

"I'm sorry? What language is that?"

"English. Or technically Italian, I guess. Spaghetti bolognese. Surely you know what spaghetti is."

"Okay, smart*arse*. I *do* actually know what spaghetti is. Spaghetti *bolognese*, I'm not so sure about, though. Why don't you just tell me what to do and I'll do it? I'll be the sous chef, and you'll naturally be the head chef."

"That's fair." He handed her a cutting board, a big knife, and an onion. "Why don't you start by chopping this?"

Onions, carrots, tomatoes, minced meat, and noodles later, Emma was quite pleased with the end result of their first foray into cooking together. While chatting and chopping, she had realized that spaghetti bolognese—or

spag bol, as Connor insisted on calling it until she gave in
and referred to it by its nickname as well—was a staple of
the Irish kitchen. Possibly of the European kitchen at large,
but she wasn't going to make that broad of an assumption.
It was one of the first dishes that kids or teenagers learned
to cook, and it only seemed right that it'd be the first thing
she cooked in...far longer than she cared to mention.

"Do you want to hear an embarrassing confession about
the way I normally make spaghetti back home?" she asked
Connor.

"I'm dying to," he said with a smile. "Let's have it."

She gestured to the pot on the stove where they had
boiled the noodles. "That part is the same. But the sauce?
It comes out of a jar."

"Seriously? A basic tomato sauce? You all don't just
whip that up from the fresh ingredients? If I can do it, I'm
pretty sure just about anyone can."

Emma shook her head. "No. I mean, I'm sure there
are those of us who do that. But judging by how big the
section of pasta sauces is at the grocery store, I'm guessing
they sell a lot of them."

"Is it as big as the aisle full of different kinds of cereals?"

Emma laughed. "So you're familiar with American su-
permarkets?"

"Just what I've seen on the telly. I'm no expert on pasta
sauce brands though, so don't worry. I found your anecdote absolutely fascinating."

He kissed her then, on the tip of the nose, before picking
up the plates he'd prepared for both of them and carrying
them over to the table. Emma felt herself warm all the way
down to her toes, so comforting was that easy affection.

It had been like that throughout the cooking process, actually. When the onion she was chopping had made her cry, Connor had wiped her eyes with a tissue before planting a soft kiss on each one. While he was stirring the mixture in the pan, she had wrapped her arms around his waist from behind.

It had been nice. Really, really nice. Like, *pinch me, because I'm not sure this is even real life* nice.

So it was only inevitable that something would interrupt the moment. It had all been too good to be true, hadn't it?

The interruption came in the form of Emma's phone ringing. By some miracle—or curse, now that she thought about it—the battery had survived the whole time she'd been gone from Galway, only losing one bar. Either they didn't make cell phone batteries like they used to, or this old brick had a lot less on it to entice her to eat up battery life.

"Sorry about that," she said as the ringing started. "I'm surprised anyone would even call me here. Pretty sure they're all under instructions to not contact me until I'm back in the States." She stayed sitting at the table while her phone rang in her backpack on the other side of the room.

"If you want to check it, go ahead. It's either something important or someone who forgot how time zones work."

Emma shrugged. "Or a wrong number." A beat. "But yeah, I should check it. Just to see."

She hurried across the room, determined to silence the ring before that annoying ditty it was playing got stuck in her head for the rest of time. Glancing at the screen, she saw Dean's name. That was...unexpected. If anything, she would have guessed Beth would be the only one entrusted with keeping her in the loop. If the call was coming from Dean, it might be something important. What if...?

"Answer it, Em." Connor's voice traveled across the room to her ears. "You look like you've seen a ghost. It'll be better to answer it and see if you're right than to leave it alone and assume the worst."

She nodded, then lifted the phone to her ear. "Dean? What is it?"

"Emma!" Dean's voice was in her ear as clearly as if he were in the same room. What kind of cell phone sorcery *was* this? "I didn't think I'd get you on the phone. Do you have a minute?"

"Not really." She looked at Connor, who was sitting at the table waiting for her to join him. He seemed to be studiously avoiding listening to her phone call as he was arranging and rearranging the salt and pepper shakers in the middle of the table. "I'm in the middle of dinner. Can you make it quick? Is something wrong?"

"Right, sorry. I didn't think about what time it was there. It's not an emergency, per se...it's just..."

"I'm going to need you to spit it out. You're giving me some major anxiety over here."

"We're rethinking our strategy for handling this whole Chad Bradley thing. You've been following the news, right?"

Emma sighed, reigning herself in before she could snap at her biggest donor. "I haven't. Claire confiscated my phone, and I've been offline the whole time I've been here. I can't lie, it's been pretty great."

"Huh," said Dean. "I can't imagine it, but that sounds terrible to me. Way too much to catch up on when you get back online again. Anyway, here's the deal. Chad Bradley isn't going anywhere. With every passing day and every exclusive interview, he's practically a staple of the daily news. I don't think the public is taking him that seriously, but...he's everywhere."

Emma felt like she was floating, aware only of the sound of her heartbeat in her ears and an electric feeling coursing through her veins. She wanted to bolt for the door, to run away from this discomfort until the feeling faded or her legs gave out.

"Emma?" Dean had kept talking, finally realizing Emma wasn't exactly *there* with him mentally.

"I'm still here." She hated how small her voice sounded to her ears.

"Well, we need you. We need to counter his...ahem...*eccentric* personality with one that's as charming and wholesome as yours. To have you be the face of SLICE, really out there for everyone to see. America's sweetheart, if you will."

"Oh," said Emma. She looked at Connor again, thinking of the conversation they'd had about the difference between influencers and founders. She felt a wave of nausea.

"It'd be the perfect way to jump on the wave of media that Chad Bradley is causing. Get some attention for SLICE. Build your personal brand. All that good stuff. So what do you say?"

"I'm going to need to think about it, Dean. The idea of a 'personal brand' makes me a little queasy, to be honest. But more than that, I'm not exactly sure what you're asking. Does the company expect me to come back early? Or to...what...get a new phone and start posting online 24/7? Neither of those are options."

As her tone had risen and her breathing had accelerated, Connor had looked up from the table, his eyes finding hers to offer the strength and reassurance she was so desperately craving. The wordless question, asking her if she was alright, was met with the slightest of nods. She needed to do this on her own.

"Actually, you know what, Dean?" Emma interrupted whatever Dean had been saying that she hadn't heard. "You all are going to need to do this next phase without me. I have every faith in Beth, in you, in the team. And I'm on a remote island without internet access. There's nothing I can do for you from here."

Dean scoffed. "Ireland's not exactly a remote island, Emma."

She rolled her eyes sky high. "I'm on Inishmore, Dean. I've been here for two days, and I'm not sure yet when I'm leaving. I appreciate the update, but I'm going to have to sit this one out."

"Well, okay then," Dean sputtered, surprised by her reaction. "I'll keep you updated, then."

"Thank you. Have a nice day. Goodbye." Emma hung up the phone with shaking hands, switched it all the way off, and dropped it back in her bag. When she stood up to return to the dining table, Connor was right in front of her.

He pulled her into his arms, pressing a kiss to the top of her head. He said nothing, just held her.

Finally, when her breathing had returned to normal and her heart rate had steadied, she spoke. "I don't know why that was so hard."

"You don't?" Connor asked, pulling back so that he could look into her eyes. "Are you sure about that?"

Emma shook her head. "It was just...I've never done something like that, not when it comes to SLICE. Said 'no.' Let down the people who are depending on me. I don't know if it was the right thing to do, but...but it just happened, I guess. They sent me here. They gave me a taste of life with proper sleep and without the headache that's been plaguing me for the last three years and...I'm not ready to undo all of that yet."

"There's nothing wrong with taking care of yourself, Emma." Connor was quiet for a moment, thoughtful. "I lost sight of that myself when I was in Dublin. If I'd been brave enough to do what you did, maybe things wouldn't have fallen apart like they did."

"What happened to you there?" Emma's curiosity was piqued, her attention taken off of her own anxieties for an unexpected moment.

"Too much work and no play, I guess." His lips briefly curled into a facsimile of a smile, then his expression dropped. "I worked too much, didn't take care of myself, barely spoke to my family...and would you believe it? But of course I got depressed. So down and blue I could barely get out of bed. My da and Patrick showed up one day and practically forcibly dragged me back here to the island."

Emma pulled him in for a hug, her arms wrapping around his waist. "I'm glad they did. I'm glad you're okay now." She looked up at him. "You *are* okay now, right?"

He nodded. "I am, but it took some work. Some rearranging of my priorities, for sure. Re-learning the joy of a slow Sunday meal with the family, cuddling up with a good dog on the couch, pulling a pint of Guinness at the pub rather than sitting at a desk until the sun's long gone."

While Emma could certainly relate to some of that, she couldn't imagine ever trading in her tech work and feeling satisfied. But maybe that was a fundamental difference between them.

"I don't know what I'm going to do after this vacation," she admitted. "If there's any way my life won't be consumed by work again. I've never been that good at work-life balance."

Connor was silent again. Emma noted the way he didn't rush to fill her silences with solutions and advice, and it made her squeeze him even tighter. He was a good man, and he was a good listener.

"I don't think I'm going to figure out the right path forward just now," Emma finally admitted. "I think we should eat. Enjoy our meal, relax for the evening, spend some more time cuddling and kissing...just...no more work. No more talking about it, and, if I can help it, no more thinking about it, either."

"That's a perfect plan, Emma dear." Connor picked up her knuckles to his mouth and kissed them lightly. "Whatever I can do to help, whatever support you need, you just let me know. Okay?"

She smiled back at him, the last traces of anxiety melting out of her. "Okay," she said, squeezing his hand.

# Thirteen

The comfort and ease with which Emma, Connor, and Lady spent their time together was disorienting, how natural and right it felt after such a short time. As far as Emma could remember, new flirtations or relationships—she still wasn't even sure what to call this—usually started with a lot more game playing and posturing. They should be getting dressed up to the nines, going out to the hottest spots to impress each other, or try to make each other jealous by stealing the attention of everyone around. Instead, they were, more often than not, curled up on the couch in sweats. Heck, Emma hadn't even had the option of wearing makeup in the time since she'd met Connor, to say nothing of dressing up in fancy clothes or shoes that weren't rain boots.

The next day, they had explored the ruins of ancient sites on the island. Emma had found herself humbled to the point of speechlessness by the reminders of the men and women who had occupied this space so long before them. Even Connor, who had no doubt seen the rocks and burial markers so many times before that they truly blended into the scenery, was quiet, almost reverent.

"How long has your family lived here?" she asked him, while they stood in the midst of Dún Aonghasa, awed by its prehistoric age and the stark, sheer cliffs dropping into the sea. "How many generations, I mean?"

"We're not actually born and bred islanders," he admitted. "Though that would be a much cooler story. My ma and da moved here in the seventies."

Emma had to pick her jaw up off the ground. "Really? That's so much cooler than I thought. Why did they move here?"

Connor shrugged. "They were newlyweds at that point. The way they talk about it, it's like they just got fed up with the hustle and bustle of big city life and all its demands. Which is kind of hilarious when you think about what 'hustle and bustle' meant in those days compared to what it is today. I imagine they'd be pretty shocked by the work you do. They haven't even bothered to get mobile phones, those two. They might be the only people I know who still have an old landline."

"Wow. You weren't kidding. And what about you? Did you like growing up here?"

"I liked it when I was a wee one. But when I got a bit older, Ma and Da and I butted heads a lot. I wanted to get into all the kinds of trouble the teens on the telly were getting into, but there wasn't a lot of opportunity for that here. I think that was the idea, right? They didn't want their kids to get mixed up in any of the petty crime or casual drug use that happens in the bigger cities. But my siblings and I, we just wanted to go to the cinema or kiss a boy or girl we hadn't known since we were in nappies. Our parents finally relented when we were in high school, and they let us take the boat over for the day by ourselves on Saturdays if we'd gotten all our homework done."

"And was that just the taste of freedom that you'd been craving?"

Connor nodded. "Definitely. I missed the last boat home once or twice, not entirely by accident. I just needed that experience, you know? I honestly went a little mad with it for a while and started to get mixed up with a bad crowd, some things I probably shouldn't have. But when my da sat me down and made it very clear to me that the only path off of the island was going to university and the only way to go to one of those was to do well on my exams, well..."

"You got your act together."

"I got my act together. Yes. Studied in Dublin, got hired fresh out of university, and stayed there until it all blew up and I ended up back here."

"Do you think you'll stay here, then?"

"I'm not sure. It gets a little quiet and lonely here sometimes, but for the most part, that's been good. It's usually just when I think about the fact that I'd like to have a family of my own someday that the island feels a little too small. Like the odds of me even getting a date my own age aren't great here." He smiled at her shyly. "Doesn't always feel like that, though."

Emma stepped closer and wrapped her arms around him. "Because sometimes beautiful Americans drop from the sky right into your pub and into your life?"

"Something like that. And even if you can't keep them forever, you should always appreciate a gift from above when it falls right into your lap."

"Oh, indeed." Emma was nodding forcefully. "There's no better place for attractive blessings than your lap, is there? You've got to thank the universe on behalf of your lap and make sure you don't stop the flow of good things coming its way."

Connor chuckled and pinched her playfully on the rear. "I'll keep that in mind for when I'm looking for lap blessings in the future. Right now, I'm all set."

"That's good. Because I am too." She smiled up at him before dropping a soft kiss on his lips.

That evening, Connor had to work in the pub. He'd offered to call in a favor with his brother to get the night off, but Emma wouldn't hear of it. The pub had been so much fun on her first evening, and she still hadn't gotten to spend any time with Patrick.

That decided it. Connor would man the bar, Patrick would be in the kitchen, and Emma would be the runner between them. After meeting Patrick and discovering he had the same snarky, witty sense of humor that Connor did, she was thrilled. This was going to be more fun than any of the work she'd been paid to do in a long time.

The time flew by, busy as the pub was that evening, and Emma relished the feeling of flow that came with being busy and having a job to do. It wasn't until hours later that she found herself, for the first time, taking a break from it all.

Emma was in the kitchen, helping Patrick get the last of the dishes washed and put away, when he stopped what he was doing and turned to her.

"It's been bothering me for days; I have to ask," he said. His tone was serious, but she thought she saw a hint of a smile playing at the corner of his lips.

Emma gestured for him to continue. "I reserve the right to not answer, but go ahead and ask."

"What in the world has kept you here this long? And are things, like, *serious* with you and my brother?"

Emma smiled. "I don't mind admitting that it's 100 percent your brother that has kept me here this long..."

"Jaysus, I knew it. Blink twice if he's holding you prisoner."

Emma rolled her eyes. "Not like that, goofball. I like him. We have fun together. And I can leave anytime I want to."

Patrick wiggled his eyebrows at her. "I can't help but notice that you haven't left yet. Any plans to do that or...are you planning on joining the family?"

"It sounds like you can't wait to get rid of me, Patrick. Don't you appreciate the kitchen help?"

"I do." Patrick was quiet for a minute, seemingly focused on the plate he was scrubbing, but Emma suspected there was more brewing under the surface, judging by the way his forehead was crinkling. "Look, I'll be honest," he said finally. "Connor's not usually one to play it cool. To have a casual fling or anything like that. I'm guessing he hasn't asked you what's actually developing between the two of you, but we're all wondering."

"You're *all* wondering?"

Patrick nodded. "Nora and I were talking about it this morning. Ma overheard us, and she and Da joined in, too. They're pretty much all wondering if we're going to get to keep you forever or if you're about to break Connor's heart and go back to America and forget we all exist."

Emma's eyes widened. "I...I'm not sure what to say. I appreciate the heads up, though. I really do. I think this is a conversation I need to have with Connor, though, don't you think?"

Patrick was quick to nod. "Oh God, yes. I've had all the heart to hearts I care to have for at least the next year. Please talk about this exclusively with my brother from here on out. Can you promise me that? That you won't try to talk to me about your feelings again, *ever*?"

"You're ridiculous." Emma was laughing. "You started this conversation, remember?"

"I'll never admit to that." A beat. "Just please don't hurt my brother, if you can help it. Let him down easy, if letting down is what you need to do."

"I promise I will."

*Would it come to that?* Emma hadn't exactly been making plans for her future with Connor, but she also hadn't been making plans to head back to Galway yet, either. It was one thing to just "wait and see" where a relationship would go when the two of you lived in the same city. But when you lived on opposite sides of the world—and one of you was on a remote island only accessible by the Motion Sickness Express...to say that made things *a lot* more complicated was a major understatement.

As if waking from a deep slumber, the realization dawned that Emma had only been speaking to Connor and members of his family for the last two days. She'd texted her parents to let them know she was alive, sure, but she hadn't even talked to Claire in days. How was she supposed to have a clear head about Connor when she'd literally been living in a dream world?

"You've got this under control here, right?" Emma asked Patrick. "I need to make a phone call."

"I've done it without you every other night I've worked here, but gee, I'm not sure I can handle it tonight. Hurry back, okay?"

Emma shook her head as she walked out the kitchen door. How had the Ryan children developed their trademark snarky humor when, as far as she could tell, both of their parents were as innocent as doves? It couldn't be genetic, then; there had to be some other explanation. Or maybe Iris and George just hid it really well.

Stepping outside, Emma slipped the phone out of her pocket, impressed again at the longevity of the battery. Between the battery life and how much better she felt not having the temptation to open up a time-sucking app every time she opened her phone, she was almost considering switching to this phone full-time when she was back in the US.

*Back in the US*. Something about that phrase filled her with a sense of dread...sadness...an ache for what she would be leaving behind here. She was epically failing at taking a vacation that would refresh her for the work she had waiting for her back home. Instead, she didn't want her vacation to end and could already predict that when it did, she'd be sinking into a pit of sadness as she mourned its loss.

Why couldn't she have gone on vacation in New Jersey? It certainly would have been more convenient. But she wouldn't have met Connor, and as inconvenient as it was to be developing intense feelings for someone so painfully far away, it was better to have found him than not to.

Why couldn't Connor be from New Jersey?

Emma chuckled to herself, shaking her head. What was with the sudden New Jersey fixation? And when had anything good ever come out of New Jersey?

"Alright, that's enough New Jersey disparaging," she said to herself as she called Claire's number. "That's not what we came out here for. Speaking of good things from New Jersey..."

"Were you talking to yourself about me?" Claire's voice resounded in her ear. "You know that's super weird, right?"

"Maybe I was, and maybe I wasn't," answered Emma. "For all you know, I'm on stage right now, talking about your home state, and I just called you up to be a part of a live demonstration."

"Uh huh. I'm sure there's a huge demand for keynote speakers talking about New Jersey at Irish conferences. I hear it's a really hot topic, especially during the holiday season." The sarcasm was pouring through the phone. "Anyway, what's up? How are things with your hot Irishman?"

"How do you know something's going on with us? I told you I was staying longer on Inishmore, but I'm pretty sure I never mentioned..."

"I'm your best friend, duh. When you mysteriously decide to stay on a teeny tiny island—I looked it up online, so I know exactly what you're working with there—for *days* longer than originally planned and then you stop checking in with me, it doesn't take an advanced degree to draw the conclusion that there's...ahem...*someone*...keeping you busy."

"You're good at this, Claire," said Emma. "You should be a detective."

"I'm a writer, love. It's practically the same thing. You spend enough time working with stories, figuring out how the pieces fit together, and then nothing surprises you anymore. So, tell me about the dude. I'm guessing that's why you called?"

"You're right again. Things are really great, actually. It's been kind of magical being here, like time stopped or something. There's no mad world rushing about just outside the door, it's just a much more laid back life. Connor and I have just been so comfortable, so relaxed together. It's easy to be with him, and it's kind of confusing me. Like...right now, I don't even want to think about leaving. His brother just took me aside to talk about where our relationship is going and letting Connor down easy if I'm going to hurt him."

"Oof. Intense."

"Yeah, it was. But also not really. I don't *want* to hurt him. But I've also pretty much only been talking to him and to his family, so I need you. I need some perspective in my life before I do something rash like decide to stay here forever."

"Whoa. Okay. Yeah." Claire's words were stilted, every syllable defying her wordsmith nature. "Are we talking, like, Stockholm Syndrome here?"

Emma sighed. Leave it to her best friend to look out for her best interests like a cynic rather than just getting swept up in the romance of it all. "I can see how you'd think I'm living in some sort of *Beauty and the Beast* warped reality. It's not like he's not letting me leave, dude. The first day, I missed the boat. The second day, the weather was bad enough that I couldn't sail at all. By the third day, that was yesterday...well, I just wanted to spend some more time here. The place is charming, and Connor is...well, he's special. I really like being with him."

"Okay...but when you say things like 'stay here forever,' even in a joking kind of way, you can see how that would freak me out, right?"

"I mean, yeah. Of course. I don't really mean it. I just meant that it's been great being here. And I'd like to be here longer. And when I think about leaving, about all of this being over...it just makes me feel a little sad."

"Is that just about Connor? Or is that about avoiding what's waiting for you back here, too?"

"You mean SLICE?"

"Yeah. It seems like you're really enjoying taking a break from it, so it seems like that could definitely mess with you when you think about coming back. It's like the Sunday Scaries times a billion."

"You're not wrong. I haven't been online at all." Claire coughed. "Thanks to *you*. I was going to say that. But whatever instinct led you to confiscate my phone...you were on to something. I needed to disconnect. To unplug. Now that I've done that, it's hard to want to plug back in again."

"Well, throwing your entire business away just because you like spending less time on your phone seems a little extreme, my dear."

"I know." Emma exhaled fully. "I'm not really thinking that. It's too drastic. But I think something's going to need to change. If nothing else, being with Connor is reminding me of how much more there is to life than just work."

"That's great, hon. I think you really needed that reminder."

"I'd pretend to be offended by that, but we both know it's true."

There was a moment of silence as they both sat with the weight of Emma's words.

Claire was the first to break it. "Emma?"

"Yeah?"

"Just promise me one thing, okay?"

"Of course."

"Promise you won't forget that no matter how magical everything feels right now with Connor...if it's real, it will survive time. And distance. You don't need to move in with him tomorrow to keep it from falling apart. And if it doesn't survive some time apart or some figuring out, then...well, then just appreciate it for what it is, I guess."

"Oof. Yeah. I know." Emma felt herself deflating with every word.

"I know you don't want to hear it, love. But it's just that I care about you. I wouldn't tell you something that would bum you out that much if I didn't care about you."

"I know. I appreciate it, even if it kind of hurts."

Claire sighed. "It's just...look. I write love stories, right? And there's nothing more thrilling than an instant love connection that makes everyone upend all their plans and change their whole lives. It's great on the page, but in real life? In real life, that's a really scary thing to see, especially when it happens to someone you love. If you and Connor are meant to be and this thing is going to be a forever kind of thing—"

"I mean, let's not get ahead of ourselves..."

"Let me finish. I'm just saying. If this is your person and the two of you are going to partner up for the rest of your days on earth, that doesn't mean that starting from the moment you met, you can never spend a night apart. Or that continuing to work on a company you built means that you don't love him enough. I know you know all of this stuff, but sometimes love makes us do and think and believe crazy things. Or...not love, exactly. Lust. Infatuation. All that excitement."

"Claire?"

"Yeah?"

"You said the 'love' word a lot just then."

"I did. What did you think about that?"

"...I...I'm not sure. It kind of resonated, actually. But it's too soon. I know it's too soon."

"Look, friend. I'm going to have to hop off the phone for a meeting with my agent soon, but I need to leave you with some parting wisdom. I wish I could help you figure all of this stuff out over the phone right now, but that's just not how matters of the heart work, especially when there are two people involved."

"True..."

"So let me just remind you of this. Lean in to your feelings. Trust your heart. Learn to listen to it again because, let's be honest, you've kind of been ignoring it for a while."

"Guilty as charged."

"Just don't be so anti-logic and reason that you forget that you have a brain, too. It doesn't have to be all or nothing, only one or the other. Life isn't all binary decisions, you know? Up and down, left and right, on and off."

"I *do* know what binary means. Try to remember all the years of computer science courses I took."

"...right. Anyway, it applies here, too. You've been all head-focused, and now you're moving in to your heart. That doesn't mean you have to cut off your head or turn off your brain. You can take turns listening to both of them."

"I'll try that, Claire. I really will. Thanks for talking to me...for the tough love and for the encouragement, too."

"Anytime, my dear. Well, not *any*time. There is a five hour time difference, so I'd prefer you didn't call me when it's ten o'clock in the morning there."

"Duly noted."

After hanging up with Claire, Emma walked around to the front of the pub and entered through that door instead of slipping back into the kitchen. She wanted to see Connor, especially after hearing Claire's words.

When her eyes met his across the room, the warmth that spread across her body dissolved the remains of the cold from the weather outside and from her sobering conversation. Whatever this was, whatever was developing between her and Connor, it was worth handling with care and taking the time to figure it out properly. Rushing into a committed relationship in a blaze of glory and then crashing and burning wasn't her speed at all. But spending some more time with this good, good man and having some necessary conversations about what the future held for them...that was just what her soul needed.

# Fourteen

On Emma's seventh day on Inishmore, she woke with an unpleasant realization. She couldn't keep putting off her return to Galway, and she couldn't keep putting off talking to Connor about it, either.

She lay in his bed, staring up at the ceiling and thinking over what would happen next. Was this going to be the end of a fling? Or the beginning of something longer lasting? She couldn't know the answers until she talked to him; this was not a one-sided problem to solve.

"Hey," said Connor, rubbing his eyes. "How long have you been awake?"

"Not really sure. I've just been lying here thinking."

Connor put his arm over her body and pulled her close, his head resting in the crook of her neck. "What are you thinking about?"

"I'm going to have to go, you know. Soon, probably."

"You're really not staying forever, then?"

"I know you're joking, but believe me, it's tempting. I hate the thought of leaving Lady. But I've got a flight back to the US in two days, and I need to do some Christmas shopping in Galway before then."

"Oh right. Christmas." Connor groaned.

Emma chuckled. "From the sound of it, I'm guessing you've had all your gifts bought and wrapped for months now."

He shook his head. "Not even close. And I'm going to look like such an arse if I don't remedy the situation. Ma always makes something homemade, a sweater or a scarf or something equally wonderful. And Nora is secretly one of Santa's elves, I swear. She always picks the perfect gifts."

"What are you going to do about it, then?"

Connor pushed himself up on his elbows and looked at her. "Well, I think I'll start by inviting myself along to Galway with you. If you don't mind, of course. I've got some errands to run myself, and I'm overdue for a trip to shore."

Emma was practically glowing from within. Her smile was so wide it almost hurt, but she didn't even try to contain it. "I guess I could be convinced..."

He pulled her in close again, planting kisses down her neck to her collarbone. "Let me see what I can do to help you make up your mind."

The day just kept getting better. Not only was Connor joining her back to Galway, but he'd arranged a special ride back for them.

"You mean we don't have to wait for the boat full of vomiting tourists?" she'd asked him when he told her the news.

"We can if you really want to." He winced at the thought. "But Patrick is making an errand run for some of the older folks on the island and he offered to bring us along."

"I love the sound of that," said Emma, smiling.

"It will take a bit longer. We'll make stops at the other two islands before we head back to the mainland."

"Really? I was hoping I'd get to see them, but that didn't seem super likely."

"Yep. It's one of Patrick's many side jobs, shuttling things around from one island to the other and Galway to boot. He'll be happy for the company, I think."

A thought crossed Emma's mind that made her heart beat faster. "Wait. You're not coming back with him, are you?"

"You think I can get my Christmas shopping done that quickly? Jaysus, woman, you've got more faith in my shopping abilities than I do. No, I thought I'd stay with you. Maybe even until you fly out, if that's alright with you."

"It absolutely is," she said. "It's perfect."

"Plus," Connor continued. "I already convinced Patrick to man the pub for the next two nights. I'm pretty sure he's already sent out invites for karaoke night." He shuddered at the thought. "I don't want to be back for that, and I'm sure he doesn't want me to be, either. No need to deprive the young one of all his fun, now is there?"

Emma laughed. "What a good big brother you are. Now you just have to find the perfect Christmas gift for him, and you'll be winning all sorts of Best Sibling Ever awards."

"That's not really a thing." Connor was shaking his head. "You only children never really get how the sibling dynamic works, do you?"

"How could we? None of it makes sense. You're always taking the piss out of each other, punching each other on the arms, rubbing your knuckles on each other's scalps..." She noticed the way Connor was looking at her, and her expression turned quizzical. "What? What is it? What did I say?"

Connor put his hand over his heart and let his eyes well up with insincere emotion. "You got the expression right. 'Taking the piss out of each other.' I just...I never thought I'd see the day. Well done, truly."

Emma shook her head, turning back to Connor's bedroom to check one last time that she had everything packed. It wasn't like she'd had a suitcase full of belongings, after all. She was, however, leaving the island one hurling sweatshirt richer, and as she tucked it into her backpack, she smiled at the thought.

The boat ride back was smoother than the original one Emma had taken, either because the weather was better or because Patrick was a more talented skipper. She was convinced it had everything to do with the wind and the waves, but Connor and Patrick both insisted it was all due to Ryan men's boat captaining skills. Whatever the cause, she was thrilled to be keeping her breakfast down with no convincing or firm self talk.

Their first stop was Inishmaan, the second largest island, before stopping at Inisheer, the smallest. They didn't get off the boat at either stop, just observed—with pride, on Connor's part—as Patrick navigated them to the dock and collected a crate full of crafts from someone waiting on shore. Connor had told her that Patrick was the local drug runner, but she'd figured out from context clues—and from peeking in one of the crates, because both of the Ryan brothers didn't know when to let a joke die—that the goods inside were handmade sweaters and other crafts.

The views had been beautiful, and Emma enjoyed seeing the way life on the three islands differed. Much of it looked the same, from the landscape to the houses, but the smaller the islands got, the more remote and isolated they felt. She was glad she hadn't gotten stranded on Inisheer where she might not have found a bed at all...but who was she kidding? She was glad she had gotten stranded on Inishmore, where both Connor and his bed were. No other place could compare to that.

The remainder of the journey had left Emma so awestruck that she didn't have any words to describe it. Though it was a bit out of the way, they had sailed within sight of the Cliffs of Moher on their way back to Galway. Judging from the way Connor was watching her watch them, she was pretty sure it had been his idea. The stark drop-off of the cliffs into the deep gray-blue water, the lush green grass above them, all set against a sky that was miraculously blue and empty of clouds left Emma feeling humbled at the power of nature. At the sheer beauty that could exist, without a human working for a lifetime to create it—it had simply happened on its own. As they approached by the sea, she imagined what it had been like for the first sailors to set their eyes on this sight all those years ago. What it must have made them feel, how it must have shaped their beliefs. Even the Ryan brothers were quiet, proving that when it comes to truly inspiring beauty, no amount of familiarity could breed contempt. You could never get sick of a sight like this.

Just after noon, Patrick had parted ways with them in Galway. He wished them a happy couple of days together, giving Emma a little extra squeeze during their goodbye hug that she was pretty sure was intended to remind her of their previous conversation.

Connor and Emma walked hand in hand, making their way first to her hotel room to drop off their things and so that she could change into her own clothes again. She'd been alternating between the outfit she'd worn to Inishmore and the clothes she'd borrowed from Connor, washing her undies in the sink and hanging them dry in the hot press. It had been like camping—far from her normal standards of cleanliness, but fine for the circumstances.

Still, a pair of fresh jeans, a clean t-shirt, and a cardigan she hadn't worn yet on the trip had her feeling like a new woman. She was tempted to slap on a bit of mascara and lip gloss to really bring out the big guns—give herself the full makeover experience—but she stopped short. If she still wanted to get fancy when it was time to head out for dinner, she could do it then. In the meantime, comfort and cleanliness were her top priorities.

While she changed, Connor had taken a seat at the small table in the room, where he'd borrowed a pen and a slip of paper. From the looks of it, he was jotting down a list of people to shop for, and without being too obvious in her peeking, Emma was pretty sure she saw her name near the top of the list.

"I'm ready if you are," she announced, after she'd slipped her feet into her brown leather booties.

Connor looked up from his piece of paper, and as his eyes landed on her, she saw his pupils dilate. "You look beautiful." His voice sounded thick.

"Amazing what a fresh set of clothes will do, huh?"

"Nah. You looked even more beautiful in my hurling shirt. I think maybe it's just the confidence that comes from knowing you look good. I'd love to stay in the room for another few hours and give you a thorough explanation, but..."

"But we're losing daylight." Emma grabbed Connor's hand, and he let her pull him to his feet. "Come on, sir. That list there looks long, and if we don't get started soon, we'll never be done with it."

"Alright, alright." He followed her to the door, and the two of them set off on the streets of Galway in search of Christmas gifts, souvenirs, and everything in between.

Four hours, two pints of Guinness, and three big shopping bags later, and the two of them were ready to be done for the day. They went back to the hotel to drop off the bags, get off their feet for a moment, and figure out a plan for dinner.

"Where would you like to go?" Connor asked. "Any particular places you've heard about? Or dishes you want to try?"

Emma thought about it for a moment. "You came here a lot as a teenager, right?"

Connor nodded.

"Then I want you to take me someplace significant in the history of Connor Ryan."

Connor groaned and shook his head. "You really don't want that, love. I was a teenager. I didn't exactly have discriminating taste in food."

"I don't care," said Emma. "It's more about taking a tour of your past than about going to a restaurant with Michelin stars."

"I hear what you're saying, but I'm warning you," Connor replied. "The only thing coming to mind right now is a pizza chain, and that's probably the last thing an American wants to eat in Ireland."

"As long as you've got some good stories to go along with it, I'm game. You do, right?"

Connor scoffed. "As if I'd tell you if I didn't. No, I'd make something up that was so good you'd never know the difference." He held out his arm so that she could rest her hand in the crook of his elbow. "Come on, m'lady. Let's get some pizza in you."

It turned out that Connor wasn't kidding when he said the restaurant was a chain. It was, in fact, an American chain—Domino's Pizza, to be precise. Still, Emma didn't complain. She learned, actually, that Irish Domino's chains had toppings you wouldn't normally find at a pizza restaurant in the States. Including, she was sorry to learn, corn. She'd never seen that back home, for sure. Emma tried to be an open-minded pizza lover, but she drew the line at corn. What was next, potatoes?

Nope, there they were. There was a pizza with potato wedges on it, and she had officially seen everything.

At least, to go along with the rather unusual meal, the company was delightful. Connor's stories about his high school friends and all their antics had kept Emma laughing, and his promise to find photos of his high school haircut—"a bit of a mullet," he had called it—had her excited both for the future laughs and for the hope that things between them weren't about to be finished forever.

They needed to talk about that. She knew it, and he did, too. But it never got less awkward to imagine initiating that conversation.

Maybe another pint and some craic would help. Emma had asked Connor the meaning of the word when she'd seen it on a chalkboard outside a pub earlier, and he'd nearly died laughing as she pronounced the word as "crayk."

"It's 'crack,' Emma."

"You're joking. Taking the piss out of me. You want me to go into a pub and ask someone about the crack and watch them just laugh and laugh and laugh at me? Well, it's not happening, mister. No way. I refuse to fall for another one of your jokes."

Connor's smile was so wide it made the skin next to his eyes wrinkle. "I swear to you, I'm not taking the piss out of you. I adore the way you have mastered that expression, that's true. But if you go around asking people, 'What's the *crayk*?' or telling them something was 'good *crayk*,' I'm afraid I'm going to have to excuse myself back to Inishmore a bit early. I'd lose all my credibility as an Irishman, and that really won't do."

Emma eyed him warily. "So you're telling me, with a straight face, that word really is pronounced like *crack*. Ugh, for the first time in days, I'm honestly really wishing I had my regular cell phone and I could fact check you right now."

"You don't trust me?"

"I actually do." She thought for a moment. "So I guess, on that note, I just need to let this go. If you're having fun at my expense, you'll get a laugh out of it. But if you're telling the truth, then there's no point for me to resist. I win either way. Either I've learned something new from you, or I trust you and get burned for it, and that makes you feel like a jerk."

"Indeed." He stood and offered her his hand. "For what it's worth, I really have no interest in feeling like a jerk because you trust me. So that's just another argument in favor of me telling you the truth right now."

The argument was settled once and for all when, at the first pub they entered, an old acquaintance of Connor's clapped him on the back and loudly asked, "What's the craic, man?" and the *crack* pronunciation was undeniable. If not for the moments they'd spent discussing that word, Emma would have found the question very disconcerting. As it was, she was merely pleased to learn that her boyfriend hadn't been having fun at her expense.

*Boyfriend?* Yes, she'd called him that, if only in her mind, to herself. That was yet another reminder of the conversation they were rapidly approaching. In fact, as soon as Connor was finished shooting the breeze with this old friend of his...

"That gobshite," Connor muttered under his breath. "Some things—some *people*—never change." The two of them were making their way through a crowd to an empty bar table in the back corner of the pub.

"Who was that?" Emma asked. "You two seemed friendly enough, but..."

"Nah." Connor shook his head. "He used to run tours to the islands and stop in at the pub, so I'm just used to playing nice with him. But the guy's an absolute arse. Always making promises to his tourists that he couldn't keep and I'd end up being the one paying for it. He'd tell them we had a gluten-free menu, or something like that, and then when it wasn't true we'd be the ones getting terrible reviews online. I've got no use for him."

"He's not running tours anymore?"

Connor shook his head. "Not to Inishmore, anyway. I'm sure he's still up to the same nonsense, but I made things unpleasant enough for him that he made up an excuse and gracefully bowed out of visiting my island. I'm not disappointed about it, either."

They stood in silence a beat longer, Emma working up the courage to ask Connor a question while he silently fumed about his former tour guide acquaintance.

"Connor, listen. I...I think we need to talk."

He looked up from the table into her eyes, the depth of the connection traveling far deeper than she had been prepared for.

He picked up his pint and took a long sip. "About what?"

"I really like you," she blurted. The words flowed out before she could stop them, before her nerves about what he might say could stop her. "These days we've spent together have been really, really special to me."

"I like you, too," he said, a sad smile coming to his eyes. "So why do I feel like there's a 'but' coming?"

"No no," she hurried to explain. "Gosh, I'm sorry. I didn't mean it like that. This isn't a breakup talk or anything. I mean...I don't even know what we are, so how could I possibly break up with you? Maybe you don't even think we're dating. Or maybe you have flings like this all the time. Or..."

He reached his hand across the table, placing it over hers. "I didn't mean to freak you out. I understand you aren't breaking up with me, but it sounds like we need to figure out what the hell we're doing together. Is that about right?"

She nodded back. "Yes. That's exactly it. I'm...so confused. I really like you, and I don't know what it means. Like...am I about to have my heart broken? Or am I about to go back home at the end of a casual holiday fling"—she said the words with all the contempt she could muster—"and pretend that I haven't had my heart broken?" She groaned and put her head in her hands. "I'm so terrible at this. I'm giving away all my feelings just like that and not even playing it cool at all."

Connor walked around to her side of the table and took her in his arms. "Hey," he said, waiting for her to look up at him. "I wouldn't want you to play it cool even if you knew how. I don't either...I just hide it well by making smartarse jokes when things get too real." He rubbed one hand up and down her back. "If it makes you feel any better, I'm feeling all the same things you're feeling."

"Really?" She looked up into his eyes, surprised and warmed by all the tenderness she saw there.

"Of course. How could I not? These days have been everything. Like I'm living a life I borrowed from someone else who's much, much luckier than I am."

She smiled. "I like that. It sounds about right."

"What if there's another option that doesn't involve breaking your heart or mine?"

"Like what?" Emma asked. "We can't just keep postponing our goodbye, delaying the inevitable."

"Maybe there's a 'both and' option."

Emma cocked her head at him. "You're going to have to elaborate, sir. I'm not following."

"I just mean...well, maybe we can delay the goodbye a bit longer. But also maybe it doesn't have to be a goodbye. Are you up for keeping this thing going even when you're back in the States?"

"You mean long distance?" When Connor nodded, she kept talking. "I've honestly never tried that before. I'd be worried I wouldn't be any good at it. Especially considering, you know, the crazy way I've let my work take over my life."

"Ah. You're right. Forgot about that." His posture deflated with his words.

Emma smiled. "I wasn't finished, though. I think, even if it's hard and messy and I'm not good at it...it's still better than saying goodbye and walking away from something good."

Connor frowned. "Are you sure? When you said that thing about work...what if we try this and it's too messy and we break up over the phone?"

Emma shook her head. "Okay, honestly, I said I might not be good at it, but that won't be true for long. I've never met a challenge I didn't rise to excel at, and a long-distance relationship would be the same way. I'm not cut out for failure, you know."

Connor chuckled. "Leave it to you to treat an emotional relationship like it's something you can win at. But okay. I'm game, too. I think we've got a plan."

"We've got a vision," Emma corrected him. "We don't have a plan yet, but when we get back to the hotel and I have something to write on, we can start working on one."

Connor pulled her to himself again, nuzzling into her neck with his stubbly cheeks. "You have no idea how sexy it is when you talk like that, do you?"

"Not at all," she said, rolling her eyes. "It seems like you're not into it in the least, so I must be doing something wrong."

He growled into her ear. "Okay, that's enough of this. You ready to get out of here?" She nodded, and they slipped out the door, hand in hand, with smiles plastered across both of their faces. The conversation they'd shared had lightened Emma's spirits, and she was ready to celebrate that.

# Fifteen

They woke the next morning to the sun streaming through the window into their eyes.

Emma groaned and turned to face the other way, pressing her back into Connor's chest. "I knew we forgot something last night. Why didn't I think about the blinds?"

Connor kissed her shoulder, and she could feel his smile pressing into her skin. "I believe that's my fault for distracting you. And I won't apologize for it."

Emma put on an affronted tone. "What a scoundrel! Why on earth not?"

He kissed her again. And again, his lips traveling up her neck to her nape. "For one thing, we can't stay in bed all day. We've got more shopping to do, I believe. Plus, we've got to eat. I'm starving."

"Ugh, fine," Emma groaned. "But only if there's good food and lots of coffee. I'm not getting out of bed for tea and oatmeal."

Connor tsked behind her. "Barely even awake, and she's already insulting my favorite breakfast. I see how it is."

"My one regret from my stay at your house is that I never tried your oatmeal. I'm guessing it's just as boring and tasteless as all the other oatmeal I've ever eaten, but...well now, I'll never know."

"Not with that attitude, you won't. But where's your faith in me? In our future? Do you really believe I'd let you go a whole lifetime without tasting the best porridge you'll ever have?"

"Not for a minute," she admitted. "I'm just giving you a hard time, but I have all the faith in the world that I'll be eating bland, boring oatmeal with you before we even know it."

"That's the spirit," he said, giving her one final shoulder kiss before flipping the duvet off them dramatically. "Now let's get this show on the road."

It wasn't until after her second cup of coffee that something Connor had said the night before tripped across Emma's memory.

"Hey," she said, looking up from her empty breakfast plate. "Last night you said something about 'both and.'"

"Yes..." He paused. "Is this the part where you ask me about my improv career?"

"No...I was just wondering. Were you talking about these days that we're spending here in Galway? ...or did you have something else in mind?"

"I was thinking..." Connor began. "Ahh, never mind. It's ridiculous."

"Oh, no no no. You can't say something like that and then expect me to leave it alone. What, pray tell, were you thinking?"

Connor paused, his cheeks flushing red. "Look, I know it's mad, and it's way too soon to ask you something like this. I just thought it might be fun if you stayed for Christmas."

Emma's heart buoyed with warmth at the same time her stomach sank with disappointment. "Oh, Connor," she said. "I love that you asked that. I really do. And trust me, it's definitely tempting. To be honest, I want to stay, I really do..."

"...but there's definitely a but coming, right?"

Emma grimaced. "It's just...Claire...and Christmas Eve Eve. It's our tradition, and it's the one thing I promised before I left. That I'd be back to spend it with her, just like we do every year."

"Ah, right." Connor's fallen lips were making Emma's stomach flip flop with sadness, but the way he was trying to rally, to force them back up into a smile, was making her feel even worse. "That's alright," he said. "Just a thought, not a big deal."

She reached across the table and took his hands in her own. "You know I'd stay. In a heartbeat. Right? If I didn't have this work mess hanging over my head or a best friend who's already suspicious of my newfound emotional side, I'd leave it all behind and sail right back to Inishmore with you."

Now his smile was genuine. "Would you now?"

She nodded.

"And you'd never leave again?"

"I mean, I'd want to visit my family and friends from time to time. And probably travel, like, once a year. But yeah. Other than that. And other than work, of course. I realize those aren't super romantic things to say, but I'm just being honest."

"I appreciate that." Connor's fake sincerity was forcing her to hold back her laughter. "I was afraid you were going to take my offer a little too seriously and become a squatter in my own house. Like, I'd have to stay there around the clock, too, just to be sure you didn't change my locks when I left and declare the whole thing your own."

"Hmm." Emma pretended to think about it. "It *is* a nice cottage, with everything a person needs for a good, simple life. Plus, it's got Lady. Yeah, I think I'd be all set there." She paused a beat before continuing, finally ending whatever agony she had caused Connor. "Okay, fine, I'll admit it," she said. "You're my favorite part of the island. If you weren't there, I'd have been happy to leave that first day and never come back. I'd be glad to have seen it, but it wouldn't feel like home at all."

Connor cocked an eyebrow in question.

Emma sighed. "And I didn't mean to insult your home just then. It was supposed to be a compliment, believe it or not. There are plenty of places I've visited and loved and don't really feel the need to see again. But the places where the people I love are? Those are the places I want to go all the time. Like, whenever I have a chance to go somewhere, that's where I want to be."

"Very interesting." Connor stroked his chin. "I couldn't help but notice your use of the word 'love' in that sentence. Would you care to elaborate on that?"

Emma was sure her cheeks were flushing fire engine red by now, but she didn't care. "Yeah, okay, maybe I didn't really mean to say that. But I did. I guess my mind grouped you in with all the people who are really important to me—my family and Claire, mostly—and since I love all of them, it applied the word to all of you. I'm sorry if that freaked you out. I wasn't trying to spring anything on you too soon or anything like that."

"Hey," he said, stopping her from continuing to explain herself and dig herself even deeper into the word hole she'd already created. "I wasn't accusing you of taking things to the next level. I was just checking my ears to see if I'd heard it correctly. Because honestly? I kind of liked it."

Emma exhaled. "Oh good. It's too much work pretending I don't like you as much as I do. I never was good at playing those kinds of games, and I'm not going to start now."

"Wait, wait, wait." Connor's eyes were blinking rapidly, like he was clearing the screen so that he could hear her more accurately. "Did you just downgrade me from *love* to *like*?"

Emma laughed, punching him lightly on the arm. "It's one thing to include you in the group of 'people that I love.' It's something else entirely to tell you to your face, 'I love you.' Surely you see the difference."

"I do. For what it's worth, though, I wouldn't have complained in the least if you'd said, 'I love you' to my face. I think I actually would have quite liked it."

"Hmm," said Emma. "That's good to know. When the time comes...maybe when you say it to me first, I'll keep that in mind."

"Grand," he smiled. "I'm glad we got that sorted out."

♥ · ♥ · ♥ · ♥ · ♥

It was the end of another wonderful day spent together, all the mundanities of day-to-day life transformed into something a lot more interesting and fun since they'd been doing them together. As evening rapidly approached and they were making plans for their last shared meal, Emma found herself getting quiet, the reality of her impending departure settling over her heavily.

She should be excited for Christmas Eve Eve with Claire, for the holidays with her parents, and even for getting back to work...but with every minute nearer that her flight crept, the more she dreaded it. She was getting scared of what awaited her in her "real" life. Of the work that would swallow her whole. Of being confronted with the truth that she didn't have the time or energy to be in a relationship with anyone. Of demand after demand after demand on her time and the peace and comfort that she'd experienced since she arrived in Ireland vanishing like a popped bubble.

Emma was sitting on the bed in the hotel room waiting for Connor, who'd wanted to put on a thicker pair of socks. He was talking to her over his shoulder while bending down to fix the new pair, but when he sat up and saw her expression, he stopped.

"Hey," he said, crouching to eye level in front of her and stroking her cheek. "What's going on? Where are you?"

She blinked away the thoughts that were spiraling out of control. "Sorry." She shook her head to clear her mind. "I just got a little stressed thinking about tomorrow. I'll try to shake it off; I don't want it to ruin our last night here."

Connor sat down next to her, putting his arm around her shoulder and pulling her close. "It's okay, you know. To feel whatever you're feeling, I mean. If you want to talk about it, we can talk about it. But you don't have to pretend you're not feeling it on my account."

"Thanks," she said, as she looked up into his eyes. "I just don't want to miss whatever happens tonight because I'm too busy thinking about what's going to happen tomorrow and the next day and the day after that. That's no way to live a life."

"It isn't," he agreed. "Why don't we try looking at it this way, instead—what's one thing you can do right now that will make tomorrow easier? And don't say 'pack my suitcase' because damn it, woman, we already agreed that would happen later and everything will be worse if we're both hangry."

"Oh trust me, that would be the last thing I'd suggest. Food is top priority right now." She pulled out her phone, chuckling at the ancient brick of outdated technology in her hand and the fact that she still expected it to be her old, reliable smartphone. "I thought of one thing I can do, if you'll let me borrow your phone."

Connor placed his phone in her hand, raising an eyebrow. "You're not going to make a crank call, are you?"

Emma laughed. "I promise I'm not, though that does sound like fun." She opened a browser on his phone and started typing. "I was just going to check in for my flight, for once. I never do it in advance, and when I'm at the airport waiting in that long line, I always wonder why I didn't. This time, I'll check in early and then not be stuck waiting forever and an age."

"Ahh." Connor pulled her closer, resting his chin on her shoulder to look at the screen with her. "So maybe we can even have a little more time together and not have to get you to the airport quite so bleeding early."

"Hey!" She elbowed him in the ribs. "I maintain my stance that three hours before departure time is an appropriate time to show up at the airport for an international flight. You can't convince me that's not true."

Connor sighed. "I think you'll find that's a uniquely American idea. I get it—it makes sense in your country, somehow. But here, well...pretty much any flight you take is international, so I guess it's just never quite as big a deal."

"Uh huh..." Emma was only half listening to Connor's jabs because something on the screen had caught her attention. She scrolled a little further to make sure she was reading it right, feeling her face blanch and her pulse accelerate at the same time.

"Em?" Connor pushed back the hair that had fallen in her face, tucking it behind her ear. "What's up? Is something wrong?"

"My flight..." she said, finally looking up at him. "They canceled it."

Connor's eyes brightened before her very eyes as a grin ripened across his face. "You're joking! Emma, that's fabulous news!"

"Is it?" she asked. "I mean…it's not like I *wanted* to leave, but…"

"But what?"

"But I think I feel guilty about staying. There's work to get back to…and oh my gosh. Claire. What about Claire?"

Connor took her face in his hands, dropping a kiss on the bridge of her nose. "I'm sure she'll be disappointed but understand. What was it that canceled your flight, anyway?"

Emma looked back at the phone in her hands. "They don't come right out and say it, but it sounds like it's about the weather."

"What's to feel guilty about, then, love? Unless you have some ability to control the weather that you've been hiding from me…" He winked at her. "Though that would make sense, too, honestly. It would explain why you couldn't leave Inishmore after that first night at the cottage. You couldn't come right out and say that you wanted to stay, so you just kicked up a storm to do your dirty work for you."

"That's it, exactly." Emma rolled her eyes. "You caught me." She looked helplessly at the phone in her hands, the news about her flight still displayed in bold letters across the screen. "I don't know what to do here. It's up to me to rebook my flight, I think. I'm just not sure…"

Connor put his hand over hers, lowering the phone from her eyeline. "What if you don't worry about that right now? What if you just stay? For Christmas, at least. Tell everyone back home that your flight was canceled because of the weather, and if any of them give you a hard time, then you can tell them to take it up with God. Or Mother Nature. The only other alternative I can see is you taking a boat across the ocean, and that will be much slower and much more likely to result in vomit."

"You're right," said Emma. "I think the guilt is just a symptom of saying yes to everyone else too much and not looking out for myself. I feel the same way whenever I take a sick day."

Connor laughed, but there was no joy in it. "Let me guess, you don't take a sick day unless you're on death's door."

"Right again. And even then, even if I'm too sick to stand up straight, I still spend most of the day justifying to myself that I do, in fact, need to be at home."

"That settles it then." Connor picked up the phone and held it in front of her face. "You've got ten minutes to let all the important people know. Your parents. Claire. Someone from work. Wish them a happy holiday and tell them you'll let them know when you have your plans figured out. And then we'll go out and celebrate."

"What are we celebrating?" Emma asked.

Connor dropped the phone in her outstretched hand, placed one hand on either side of her head, and kissed her squarely on the lips before getting to his feet. "We're celebrating the stars aligning in a way you can't possibly feel guilty about. We're celebrating more time together, and we're celebrating the fact that you'll be on the island for Christmas, too."

"The island?" Emma asked. "Inishmore? What about the weather? Will it be safe? And your family! I can't crash your family Christmas."

Connor was already shaking his head. "We won't go into the sea unless it's absolutely safe, so don't you worry about that. Most likely your flight was canceled because of icy conditions at the airport, and that won't affect us at sea." He bent down to look her in the eyes. "And what about my family? Can you imagine them being anything other than thrilled to have you spend Christmas with us?"

"I just don't want to make it awkward. It's already a big deal for your mom, preparing a meal like that for all of you. But then having an extra mouth to feed…and what if she feels pressure to make me feel comfortable?" She felt frantic now as the thought dawned on her. "Connor, I don't want them to be scrambling to get gifts for me or anything like that. I'd feel terrible adding all that stress. Why don't I just stay here? I could extend my hotel reservation, I'm sure—"

Connor cut her off with a gentle finger on her lips. "For one thing, Emma, it's awfully presumptuous of you to assume my ma is doing all of this herself. Don't you think she married a handy husband and raised all of her children, regardless of gender, to help out around the house? Heck, it's her sons who work in kitchens, for crying out loud."

"Right." Emma chuckled. "Somehow I forgot that. I'm glad she doesn't do it alone."

"Not at all. The preparation is the most fun part, and none of us miss out on it." He smiled at her warmly. "And as far as the gifts, don't you worry about a thing. I'll make sure no one thinks you expect them to roll out the red carpet. If Ma happens to have an extra scarf around, I'm sure she won't stop herself from giving it to you. But I won't let any of them pay for overnight Amazon delivery or anything of that nature."

"Are you really sure it's okay?" Emma was looking up at Connor, her eyes searching his face to read his expression more than the words he was saying.

He smiled and nodded. "It's more than okay, Emma. It's exactly what I would have wished for, had I known it was an option. I'm thrilled, honestly. Can't imagine a better Christmas gift."

# Sixteen

On Christmas Eve morning, Emma woke up in Connor's bed on Inishmore again, smiling to herself as her eyes opened. It felt like she was right where she belonged, and there was no better—or more Christmas-y—feeling than that.

They had stayed in Galway for an extra day, spending Christmas Eve Eve doing just what Emma and Claire would have done. Claire had been understanding of Emma's situation, as had everyone else. It turned out you really couldn't argue with the weather, after all. So, after everyone knew she wouldn't be home for the holidays, Emma had relaxed for the first time in a long time. She couldn't do anything to get home faster than she already was, and, in fact, it seemed as if that knowledge alone had freed her. She still hadn't booked her flight back, resting in the knowledge that if she was already missing Christmas, what was one more day?

Christmas Eve Eve had been a day of Christmas movie marathons and hot chocolate, just what would have made Claire proud—and surely what she was doing on the other side of the ocean, with just a few time zones' difference. The only distinction between the two friends' celebrations was that Emma had an attractive—and often shirtless—man snuggled up in the covers with her for *her* movie marathon. And she wasn't complaining about having to share the duvet at all.

The Ryan family tradition was to share lunch together on Christmas Day. Connor typically spent Christmas Eve at the bar with close friends and patrons, but he'd told Emma he'd be more than happy to pass that responsibility off to Patrick this year.

That's how Christmas Eve had ended up being a slow, leisurely day with the two of them and Lady, who'd been thrilled to see them when they arrived back on Inishmore the day before and retrieved her from Iris and George's care.

After Lady's walk and a pot of coffee in front of the fireplace, the preparations for Christmas Day lunch began. Iris and George were in charge of the main dish, a roast duck that Emma was very curious about. Nora was preparing the potatoes and another vegetable dish, and Patrick was on desserts.

"What does that leave you with?" Emma asked Connor.

He was tying on an apron, and handed her one to match. "I'm the baker of the family, actually." He rummaged in his cupboards, pulling out a bag of flour and a few measuring cups.

"Oh really? What are we making, Christmas cookies?"

He smiled warmly. "We're making soda bread, but judging by your expression right now, there's no way I'm getting away with not making cookies. I think it would break my heart to let you down like that."

Emma smiled, clapping her hands with glee. "This is perfect. I'm excited! I've never made soda bread before either, can you believe it?"

"I actually can. I don't think it's that common where you come from, is it?"

"Not at all. Now the really important question. What kind of cookies are we going to make?"

Connor opened a drawer and gestured inside. "Well, this is my baking drawer—"

"Wait wait wait," Emma interrupted. "You have a whole baking drawer?"

"Of course. I told you I'm the baker of the family...what did you expect?"

Emma stood up on her toes and pressed a kiss to his lips. "Just when I think you can't get more perfect..."

Connor smiled. "Yeah, that's nice. But as I was saying, before I was so rudely interrupted...have a look inside the drawer and see what you can make with what's inside. I don't have *everything*, but I have the basics. Butter's in the fridge. If you need something super specific, odds are we can't get it at the grocery store, so..."

"I got it. We'll make do with what we have."

Emma poked around in the baking drawer, the pantry, and the fridge, and pulled out everything they'd need to make butter cookies and a basic frosting. She had pulled up a recipe on Connor's laptop because, unlike him, she was *not* the baker of her family, and she didn't have things like that memorized.

Emma and Connor worked side by side, her mixing the ingredients for cookies and shaping them into perfect golf ball-sized balls, while Connor got his soda bread recipe just right. He had turned on a Galway based radio station that was playing non-stop Christmas music, and the two of them were humming along in companionable silence.

When the bread was in the oven and they had some time to wait, Emma perched on the countertop while Connor cleaned up and boiled the kettle for tea. "Are you sure about tonight?" she asked.

"What do you mean, about not going to the pub?"

She nodded. "I don't want you to change all of your plans because of me."

"Not at all." Connor shook his head. "I want to spend as much time with you as I can, of course. I see those folks at the pub every year, and who knows when I'll get to spend my next holiday with you."

Emma picked up the mug he'd handed her, using it to warm her hands. "You *can* have both, you know. I can come to the pub with you, help out, maybe even meet some of your friends."

He looked up at her with a start. "Would...would you want that? I thought a low-key evening would be more your speed..."

"That's true," she admitted. "But we've had a lot of low-key evenings lately. Even for a professional introvert like me, sometimes the option of going out and about sounds...good. Interesting. Exciting, even. Don't get me wrong, it doesn't mean I'll want to go out again the next day or anything crazy like that. And I'll definitely be spending New Year's at home on my couch. But one evening with your friends could be really fun."

"If you're sure..."

Emma looked up from her mug at the hesitation in his voice. "Do you not want me to come? Oh gosh, I'm sorry...I didn't even think. Here I am, offering to spend all this time together, when maybe that's just going to make things worse and harder for you when I leave. If it's easier to keep the two worlds apart, me over here and your friends separate, I totally get that. We can stay home."

"Emma." Connor was standing between her knees now, his hands on either side of her face. "Love, you are working yourself up into a lather. I wasn't trying to convince you not to come because I'm hiding some deep dark secret or don't want you to meet my friends. I...I just want to give you what you want."

She nodded. "Admittedly, considering how long we've known each other, it's not actually that easy to predict each other's wants and needs. It might feel like we're super in sync, but it turns out I can't read your mind and you can't read mine, either."

Connor shook his head. "I think I'd like to be able to do that...but I can't quite yet."

"There's no need for it. We're better off learning how to communicate properly than building up false confidence in our mind reading abilities. That way lies all sorts of trouble and miscommunication."

"I hadn't thought of it that way, but you're probably right." He nodded once. "So then. What do you want to do tonight, honestly? I'll believe whatever you say, I promise. No trying to convince you or double check or any of those shenanigans."

Emma threw her head back and let a laugh escape. "Then believe that I want to go to the pub. Really really. I want to meet your friends and celebrate with whoever's there. Then come back here when the night is finished."

"That settles it then." Connor held out his hand to shake hers. "It's a deal, Kells."

She smiled at him. "It's a deal, Ryan."

Ryan's Pub on Christmas Eve was a sight to behold. Emma realized, a few hours in, that she'd never spent a Christmas Eve anywhere but at home before. She hadn't even realized that pubs or restaurants were open, and if she had, she likely wouldn't have visited one. No, it had been a staple of Emma's childhood to spend Christmas Eve at one of her grandparents' homes, alternating between her mom and her dad's parents each year. Then, on Christmas Day, they'd spend the day with the opposite set of grandparents. It had worked for her family, and it seemed so normal to Emma that she couldn't imagine spending the holidays any other way.

But this, this was very different from what she was used to. And it wasn't half bad, either. The pub had been bustling with activity since Emma had arrived, with locals popping in to share a pint or drop off a plate of fruitcake for a friend. The carols had been playing on the stereo, with patrons chiming in for a verse or two when the mood struck.

Emma had been sitting at the bar, nursing a mug of mulled wine. Connor and Patrick had both insisted that they didn't need her help, that her only responsibility was to enjoy herself. And she had been doing a fine job of that, too. She'd met all of Connor's neighbors and nearly everyone who had popped into the pub stopped to shake her hand and say hello. Emma had been surprised by how friendly they all were, only half of it explainable by the holiday spirit.

Finally, one of the older gentlemen she'd met pulled up a stool and sat at her elbow. It was Sean, the doctor she'd met on her first day on Inishmore.

"We're all really glad to see Connor so happy, lass," he said.

Emma smiled. "I'm glad he's happy, too. I'm happy with him as well, and it's nice to be here for Christmas."

Sean shook his head sadly. "It's not just that. Of course, we're all glad to be happy. It's just been a long time for Connor, that's all. It's nice he's finally met someone good."

"What do you mean?" Emma asked.

"Since he and Christina ended, I mean. He hasn't exactly been a barrel of laughs. It wasn't easy for him."

"I'm sorry? I'm not sure what you mean."

"He didn't tell you about Christina?" Off her head shake, Sean sighed. "Just like the old boy, keeping all his cards close to his chest. He was miserable when they parted ways. A total bear to be around for at least the first month he was back here."

"Did they...did they break up because he was moving back here? Or did he move back here because they broke up?"

"That's something you'd have to ask him, I'm pretty sure. I'm a bit hazy on all the details, to be honest. It seems to me like they were still going together when he moved back here, but then pretty soon after that, they just couldn't stand being so far apart and it all ended. The main thing, as far as I'm concerned, is that our Connor lad has a nice gal in his life now, and I imagine he's got no intention of letting you go, at least not if he's half as smart as I think he is."

Emma smiled, though her thoughts had already flown away with Sean's words. Connor had been in a long-distance relationship before, and it hadn't worked. That wasn't exactly a good omen for the two of them.

She put on a brave face as she continued to talk with Sean. "Well, I *am* going to have to go back home to the US, eventually. But I have no intention of parting ways with Connor, even when that happens."

Sean was shaking his head ruefully again. "It's no good, lass. Connor might be too nice to say this to you, but I'm an old man without anyone to impress. If you leave, it'll be just like Christina all over again. It's only a matter of time, you know."

"Only a matter of time...?"

"Jaysus, lass, how are you not following this? It'll all be fun and games for a while, with you over there in America and Connor here on Inishmore. But his last girlfriend, she was in Dublin, for crying out loud. And *they* couldn't make the distance work. If you expect things to be so much different and better with you all the way in bleeding New York, you're more deluded than even I could imagine."

"Wow. Um, thanks?"

"There there, now. I didn't mean to ruin your night." Sean patted her on the shoulder. "It was just a dose of Christmas honesty, but what do I know? I'm just an old man who never fell in love with an American myself. How could I know the first thing about what's going to happen between the two of you kids?" He nodded towards her prehistoric phone on the table. "You all have those fancy intelligent phones now anyway. I'm sure they make it a whole lot easier for couples all over the world to stay in touch with each other. You two will figure it out. If you're meant to be, you'll find a way to make it work."

"Thanks, Sean." Emma forced a smile at the older man as she stood up and excused herself. She'd had enough honesty for one evening, and she didn't want to admit how much his words had riled up her inner turmoil. "I appreciate the honesty, and I'll think about it all. Have a merry Christmas."

As she approached the end of the bar, Connor reached across and laid a hand on her arm. "Everything okay, Emma? I saw you talking with Sean and you looked a bit too serious for Christmas Eve."

Emma shook her head. "It was nothing. He made me think, but that's not necessarily a bad thing, is it?"

"It can be. What did he make you think about?"

Emma was waging an internal war with herself. Part of her wished she could just stuff all these fears and anxieties down and put on a brave face like nothing was wrong...but a bigger part of her knew she couldn't keep it to herself. And as uncomfortable as it was to have to wear her heart—and her anxieties—on her sleeve, it was a hell of a lot more authentic than any pretending she could do, and for that she had to be thankful.

That still didn't mean it was a pretty process.

"He was talking about Christina, who I gathered from context was your ex-girlfriend. But more than that, he was basically saying a long distance relationship is a death sentence and that I should just stay here and we've only been together for, like, a week, and it's all just…too much."

Connor stepped around the bar, encircling Emma in his arms and pressing a kiss to the top of her head. "There there. It's okay."

But Emma couldn't stop. "I don't even know how to be in a relationship with someone who lives in the same city as me, so how could I possibly make it work with someone who's on the other side of the world? I might be too busy altogether to actually be a good partner to another person. You don't even know me when I'm not on vacation. When I'm not this chill, relaxed version of myself. And *why* in the world are you laughing at me right now? This isn't funny, Connor!"

Connor chuckled. "I'm not laughing *at* you, love. It's just hard not to see the humor when someone refers to themselves as being chill and relaxed while they're literally out of breath listing all their worries."

"Ha ha. It's definitely hilarious, that's why I'm enjoying this so much."

Connor pulled her closer, squeezing her tighter, and Emma felt her tense muscles brace against him for just a moment before surrendering to the comfort he provided.

She melted into his embrace, letting him take the weight off her shoulders and into his own arms for just a moment.

"Connor?" she whispered, unsure if he'd even be able to hear her. "Is this even going to work? I don't want to cause us both needless pain..."

He was silent for a moment, and Emma took solace in the idea that maybe her inner vulnerable thoughts had been drowned in a sea of celebratory noise. But then he spoke, his words rumbling in his chest against her ear.

"I can't see the future, so I can't make you any promises about what will happen. But I know that it's worth doing this, even if there's some pain. I can't stand the thought of you just leaving, of this ending before we've even had a chance to see what it could be."

"But what about Christina? Sean made it sound like that was just about distance, and she was only in Dublin. I mean—"

Connor stopped her with another kiss, this one on the tip of her nose. "When did Sean become the love doctor, for crying out loud? The man knows his way around a medical examination, sure, but he's no expert on relationships. No, what happened with me and Christina was never about the distance. If anything, the distance was just an excuse. One that hurt less and created less work for both of us than the truth."

"What was the truth?" She pulled back enough that his arms still encircled her but she could see his face.

Connor grimaced. "Her work was her world, and, unfortunately, it was a world I'd lost all interest in. I'd lost interest in most things, I guess, with the depression. I tried, I really did. And it took a lot out of me, considering how low I was. Once I moved here, she didn't have time to come and see me—or even time for me to come see her—and I resented her and the work for it. But instead of talking about her work-life balance and my need to not be so black and white in my thinking, we just blamed it on the distance and ended it."

"Ah." Emma smiled weakly. "So...nothing that could become a factor in our relationship then, huh?"

There was pain in Connor's eyes as he reacted to her words. "I can't speak for your part, for how much you might put your work before your own happiness or health or our relationship." He lifted a hand to her cheek, peering deeply into her eyes. "But I can work on the part I played in all of that. I'm taking care of myself now, better than I knew how to do then. I'd never resent you for loving what you do or blame the job for keeping us apart. I've learned plenty about my happiness in these last years, and about how it's my responsibility to find it and not anyone I might be partnered up with. It's not your job to make me happy, and it's not my job to make you happy. If we can somehow find a way to be happy when we're together, that's enough."

"I can't promise that I'll be as available as I want to be. I...I wish I had a clearer head about this. I wish I knew what I needed to do next. Do I need to quit my job? Scale back?"

Connor shook his head. "No. Nothing rash. You're getting ahead of yourself, I think. I don't need a promise from you that you'll be back in a week or that you'll visit every month or talk on the phone every night." He gestured to the room around him. "I'm here. With these people. I'm not going anywhere, and you don't have to worry about me meeting someone new and leaving you for her. I'll wait for as long as it takes. I just...I just think your priority, when you get back, has to be finding your happiness. Not putting pressure on yourself to figure things out with me. Can you try that? Just...eating proper meals and sleeping every night and doing something just because it makes you happy and not because it might make you money?"

Emma was silent, flabbergasted. "Can you believe there's no one else in my life who's ever suggested that?"

Connor shook his head. "That can't be true. You've got parents, right? What about Claire?"

Emma winced. "You're right. I should have said, there's no one in my professional life who's ever suggested that my health matters. Or that anything but SLICE matters, if I'm being brutally honest."

"That's worth noticing then, eh?" Connor asked. "Both points, I mean. Both that the folks you work with don't seem to care about you as a person...and also that you don't necessarily consider anyone outside of your professional life when you're reflecting on who has influence in your world.

"Touche, good sir. Touche. Okay, I think that's enough harsh truth for one night. Let's have some fun, okay?"

Connor pulled her in for one more squeeze, dropping yet another kiss on the center of her head. "You've got it, gorgeous. As you wish."

# Seventeen

Christmas at the Ryan family house started early—likely because, as Connor had already informed her, the cooking was a family affair. So if there was a duck to roast, then by golly, they were all going to be roasting it together.

Emma and Connor arrived at his parents' house just after eight o'clock in the morning. It had been a late night at the pub, with one too many drinks for both of them, but they'd still managed to get a few solid hours of sleep. Combined with some extra strong caffeine this morning—coffee for her, tea for him—they were both feeling pretty fine, all things considered.

"So, we really show up in your mom's kitchen on Christmas morning with empty stomachs?" Emma asked as they piled into the truck, Lady jumping in between them. "It just seems like having hungry humans to deal with this early in the day is going to be the last thing anyone preparing a big meal wants to deal with."

"Trust me," Connor was shaking his head. "A Ryan family gathering, for any holiday or even just for a random Sunday roast, is an all-day affair. Ma will be expecting to feed us at least two or three times today, and who are we to deprive her of that?"

"You make a pretty good point," Emma admitted. "Plus, I forgot about the whole thing where we're all cooking together. So no one is really feeding anyone, right?"

"That's where you're wrong. We might all like to help out in the kitchen...but this is still Ma's day. And none of us would dare to take that away from her. So if she wants to feed you or serve you mulled wine far earlier than you think anyone should consume alcohol, well...it's Christmas, Em. Are you really going to deprive the poor woman of her one Christmas wish?" He had started the truck and was slowly pulling away from the front of the cottage.

Emma reached over and smacked him on the knee. "Thanks for the guilt trip, you goober. But even for your lovely mother, I won't ignore logic and reason...or my inner compass. So if some intuitive wisdom tells me to eat a piece of toast before I chug a mug of mulled wine, I'm not really going to worry about hurting anyone's feelings."

"Dang, girl. It looks like you're taking my warnings about looking out for yourself to heart. Are you going to take that new attitude back to SLICE with you?"

Emma felt her cheeks burn as a grin split her face. "Admittedly, that was a little uncomfy to say just then. So we'll see what happens at SLICE. I promise to try my absolute best, though."

Connor took his hand off the gear shift and settled it on Emma's knee. "That's all I could ask. I'm proud of you...even if it's uncomfortable. *Especially* if it's uncomfortable, actually."

"Thanks, Con." She looked out the window, enjoying the passing scenery as the coast went by them. It still felt like a dream, this reality she was living in. She could hardly believe that thousands of miles across that cold, salty water was her home country. Come to think of it, she couldn't wrap her head around the fact that this island, unlike the one she lived on back in New York, had ancient ruins, that everyone around her spoke with an accent—or spoke Irish, even—or that she was spending Christmas with a man she'd only met a week and a half ago.

Emma leaned into the oddness of the moment. If she didn't embrace it, she'd probably want to run...but where could she run? There was no ferry today, nowhere to go but Connor's house or his family's celebration. That left her only option for the day to be present, to enjoy it as much as she could, and to not worry—as much as possible, at least—about what the future held. Where her work was going, or where her relationship with Connor was going, either. Today, she had a job that paid the bills, and she had the company of a handsome man who made her feel things she'd never felt before. What more could she ask for?

❤ • ❤ • ❤ • ❤ • ❤

Christmas lunch was unlike anything Emma had ever experienced. Here, she'd thought that since she had some Irish ancestry in her family and since they all spoke the same language, that this day would be more or less the same as any Christmas she'd ever spent back home.

But she'd been wrong about that. For one thing, the weather was all wrong. *Different, not wrong,* she reminded herself. *Just because it's not what I'm used to doesn't mean it's bad, somehow.* But semantics aside, there wasn't a snowflake in sight, and a few times Emma ran outside to get something out of the truck without even bothering to put on her coat. *Definitely different.*

Then there was the meal. The delicious, delicious meal. Back in New York, Emma's family usually opted for a Christmas ham, but the duck that Connor's family prepared was out-of-this-world delicious. It had been roasted in a pan with onions and potatoes around it, and they'd had an assortment of side dishes to go along with it. Gone were the stuffing and green bean casserole she was accustomed to, replaced with a vegetable soup blended into a uniform consistency with an immersion blender. They had boiled potatoes and cabbage, and a tray of roasted turnips and parsnips. The whole Ryan family had been equal parts amused and horrified that Emma had never eaten either of those root vegetables before, and she had been thrilled to discover that they were, in fact, delicious.

There was a fruitcake and Christmas crackers to pop at the end of the meal, to top off the new experiences for Emma. As she was sitting back in her seat, hands gently holding her too-full belly, she felt warm and cozy, surrounded by this affectionate and wisecracking family who had embraced her as one of their own for the day. She fought off a twinge of sadness at the thought of leaving them, reminding herself yet again to enjoy the day. That it wasn't over yet.

After all, they still had gifts to exchange. After the table had been cleared, they all moved into the living room to sit around the Christmas tree. Iris sat on the couch, with Patrick and Nora on either side of her. That left two armchairs, one of which George promptly claimed. Emma hung back, unsure of herself. The room was so perfectly set up for this family, with a spot for each of the five of them. She couldn't help but feel like an outsider, a burden even. She didn't want to be in the way, to act like she belonged more than she did. This was a family, after all, and intruding on their Christmas didn't make her one of them.

Connor's hand patting the seat of the vacant armchair broke her reverie. "Come on, sit down," he said. As if to convince her it really was okay, he perched on the armrest of the same chair. "We can share, it's alright."

"He's right, love," Iris interjected. "For crying out loud, you've been staying at his house. I think we can handle seeing the two of you sit near each other."

"Speak for yourself," said Patrick. "It's liable to make me vomit, all this PDA." His playful tone combined with a conspiratorial wink in her direction let Emma know he was—probably—kidding, but she still scooched a little further away from Connor. As far away as the chair would allow, anyway.

"That's enough of that, now," said Nora. "Let's get into the gifts already." Getting up from her spot on the couch, she went to the tree to disperse the packages under it.

Emma settled back into the sofa, soaking up the warmth of the moment. She watched the affection fly between everyone in the room, as they shared their inside jokes and memories of years past, unwrapped the gifts they had been dropping hints about for months, and clearly enjoyed each other's company.

There was nothing awkward about it. Emma didn't feel like a fifth wheel or an outsider...the joy she felt at seeing Iris receive a beautiful piece of handmade jewelry from Nora, or Connor's genuine laughter at the sweatshirt his brother had given him, it all came from a real place. She had been in situations before where she had to micromanage her facial expressions, pasting on a smile so that no one would know how out-of-place she felt. Or worse, trying to become invisible or not attract any attention to herself.

But it wasn't like that with the Ryan family. They were more than happy to bring her in on the memories that made them laugh, regaling her with stories from Connor's childhood. They opened the gifts she and Connor had bought them in Galway, thanking both of them with hugs and kisses on the cheek, even though Emma was sure they knew every single item had been Connor's idea.

In her turn, Emma opened the packages that were placed in front of her. The earrings Nora had made were a beautiful combination of teal and gold beads, and the scarf from Iris was as cozy and soft as it was gorgeous. She'd wear it all winter long and think of her every time she put it on. George and Patrick each gave her edible gifts to remember Ireland by, a lovely box of Guinness-infused chocolates, and from Patrick...

"...a bag of potatoes?" Emma asked, laughing so hard there were tears streaming from her eyes.

"What?" Patrick looked affronted. "Don't tell me you don't like them!"

She pulled him into a quick hug, rubbing her knuckles across his scalp in a classic noogie. "Of course I like potatoes. You have to know this is, like, the weirdest gift one human has ever given another. But I'll definitely eat them all. Maybe even share them with my friends and family back home."

She sat back down and looked up at Connor, who was still perched on the arm of the chair. His smile mirrored her own. "They're pretty great, aren't they?" he asked under his breath.

"Totally wonderful," she agreed. Then, to the room as a whole, she said, "Thank you all for letting me spend Christmas with you. It's been just what I needed, I think. And you've all been absolutely delightful. So welcoming and warm, making me feel like I belong here, rather than a stray who got separated from her family over the holidays." She brushed a drop of moisture away from her eye, surprised by the emotion she felt.

"There there, dear," said Iris, leaning over the arm of the couch to rest her hand on Emma's. "We're more than happy to have you, and you're welcome again anytime."

"Thank you, Iris." Emma smiled at her as her face got blurry. She blinked rapidly and turned back to Connor, who put his arm around her shoulders, anchoring her back in the moment just when she needed it most.

Connor jumped to his feet just then. "Well, Emma and I need to be going."

"What?" asked George. "It's too early for that. We've got to find a Christmas film on the telly and fall asleep on the couches together."

"That does sound like fun," Connor smiled at Emma, his cheeks flushing pink. "But as you may have noticed, I didn't give Emma her gift yet, so—"

"Oh gross!" interjected Nora. "We don't need you to hint around at what sort of gift you've got waiting for her back home."

The pink in Connor's cheeks turned fire engine red. "Nora, I swear to you I'm not hinting around at that. Jaysus, do you not know me at all?"

Nora's eyes were twinkling mischievously as she shrugged. "Well, you didn't give your 'gift' to her in front of everyone else, so...you know...I just put two and two together."

"Yeah, and you clearly stink at math," said Connor. "Anyway, we're going to head back. Sound good, Em?"

She nodded up at him, getting to her feet. "It does. Thank you all again, and Merry Christmas. You're all going to have a special place in my heart for this. I've never spent Christmas with anyone's family but my own."

After all the hugs were exchanged, Connor, Emma, and Lady made their way back out to the truck. Once they were inside and they'd started moving down the road, Emma shifted in her seat and turned towards Connor.

"So...I've got to ask," she said, barely restraining the teasing in her voice. "Was your sister right? Was 'Christmas gift' a euphemism for something sexy, or...?"

Connor shook his head, huffing out a laugh. "You're just going to have to find out."

"Looking forward to it. I've got a gift for you at home, too, so it'll be nice to have a little gift exchange of our own without everyone watching." She felt Connor's eyes on her. "Watch the road, love. You'll find out what it is soon enough."

As it turned out, both Emma and Connor had been talking about the kind of gifts that came in wrapping paper. Not that the other kind of Christmas gift wasn't on the table for the evening, too, but when Emma emerged from the bedroom with a small wrapped box, she was pleasantly surprised to see Connor holding something similar. She'd entertained the possibility that he'd be waiting for her in his boxers with a red bow stuck to his chest, but instead he had a small box wrapped in paper with tiny Christmas trees and stars on it.

He nodded to the box in her hands. "I've no idea how you pulled that one off. We've been together nearly every hour of every day. How is it I don't have the first idea what you've got in your hands right now?"

Emma shrugged. "I guess you weren't paying attention that well. Or I'm just very sneaky. Do you want to find out what's inside it?"

"You know I do," said Connor, taking her hand and pulling her down next to him on the couch. He handed the small wrapped box to her. "And this is for you."

"You go first," said Emma, handing him the rectangular package in her hands. As he ripped into it, she felt her nerves rise. What if it was wrong, somehow? What if it was too much? For a first Christmas together, shouldn't they have set some ground rules, like how much they could spend on each other? Well, it was too late for that now.

Connor had opened the package and was staring at what was inside—a voucher for a round-trip flight from Galway to New York. His jaw dropped nearly down to his chest. "Emma, this..."

"I know, I'm sorry. It's too much. Presumptuous. I can—"

He cut her off with a kiss. "It just surprised me, that's all. If you want me to come to New York, I mean...I'd love that. I've never been there."

"Really? You're not mad? It feels like a plane ticket is a very serious gift to give someone, especially this early in a relationship. I don't know what I was thinking..."

"Why would I be mad? Don't forget, I know how you tech people operate. This is a perfect gift—hell, it's practically a guarantee that we'll be seeing each other again soon."

"I used my airline miles to pay for it," Emma explained. She nodded to the box in her lap. "I just didn't want you to think I'd spent some exorbitant amount of money."

"Honey, a plane ticket is a plane ticket. It's a big gift however you slice it. Ha! SLICE. I didn't even mean to make a pun."

Emma stuck her tongue out at him. "Don't remind me of my job, how about that? I just didn't want you to freak out about the size of the gift, that's all."

"Emma Emma Emma. When will you learn? It's not the size of the gift that matters, it's how you use it."

"Ahh, right. And how will you use it? To come visit me in New York or to go sight seeing when I'm out of town?"

"Hmm, that's a great question," said Connor. "I'll think about it and get back to you. Now why don't you go ahead and open yours?"

Emma slipped her finger underneath the tape of the neatly wrapped package. Inside, there was a box, which looked like it would contain a piece of jewelry. Mercifully, it wasn't shaped like a ring box, or else she really would have freaked out then and there. Instead, it was square in shape, like there might be a bracelet inside.

She slipped off the lid and inside she found...a keychain. One of those souvenir keychains you could find at any number of the shops they'd walked past together in Galway.

She raised a questioning eyebrow at Connor as she held it up. "I...?" she started to ask, but he cut her off.

"Oh, right!" He reached forward and grabbed the keyring from her hand. "This is missing the most important part, isn't it? I just got it from Patrick this morning, but I'd already wrapped the box like some kind of muppet." He pulled a shiny silver key out of his pocket and worked it onto the keyring in his hand before handing both back to her.

"Is this...?" Emma nodded to the room surrounding them. "Did you just give me a house key?"

"It's just that you don't have a great track record with getting stranded on Inishmore, you know? And if you're ever stranded here again, I don't want you to worry that you won't have a roof over your head. So, whether or not I'm here, you'll always have a place to stay."

"I see." Emma slid closer to Connor, letting him wrap his arm around her shoulders. "And where would you be if you weren't here, anyway?"

"Oh, I'd definitely be in New York sightseeing." He kissed her then, squarely on the mouth. "Merry Christmas, love."

Emma relaxed into him, sighing. "Merry Christmas."

# Eighteen

The world looked a little brighter the next morning. After a late night enjoying each others' company, Emma and Connor had settled into a glorious deep sleep. Lady had even let them stay in bed later than any other morning of Emma's stay, and for that she got an extra treat with her breakfast.

There was a level of security that came from Emma having a key to Connor's cottage in her purse and knowing that he had a round-trip flight to New York with his name on it that settled all the little voices that had been gnawing at her the last few days. They were going to see each other again. It was practically a guarantee at this point. Knowing that, the thought of Emma returning to the States and getting back to work was no longer such a scary idea.

Emma and Connor were starting the day like most of the previous ones they'd spent together—slowly, quietly, with caffeine and reading material. Iris had encouraged Emma to pick up a novel or two from her bookshelf for her flight home, and Emma was indulging herself already. There was nothing worse than getting on a plane only to realize you didn't actually care about any of the characters in the one book you'd brought. It was a far better strategy to start reading now, hoping that by the time her plane took off, she'd be so engrossed she'd barely notice the ground slipping away beneath her.

Connor was at the other end of the couch, flipping through a magazine he'd brought back from Galway. At the sound of a beep, he reached to the end table, picked up Emma's phone—the battery had finally died last night—and slid it across the couch to her. "I think it's charged now," he said. "Keeps beeping though, so I'm guessing there's a message or something on it."

Emma flipped the phone open, her stomach dropping as she saw six missed calls from Dean and another ten from Beth. *What in the—?*

"Something wrong?" Connor asked her, noticing her sudden pallor and the cold sweat beading up on her forehead.

Emma shook her head. "It's just work. It looks like they were trying to get in contact with me all night, but my phone was dead. I'd better call and see what's going on."

"Are you sure? It's so early in New York, I think most people would still consider it night."

"I'm sure. Dean won't appreciate me waiting, and he's probably already going to be upset that it's taken this long to get me on the phone."

Emma pressed the send button on Dean's contact entry, then lifted the phone to her ear. Her heart was pounding, whether from the possibility of impending disapproval from an authority figure or from that second cup of coffee, she'd never know. No, that wasn't true. It was definitely about the first thing, though the second thing wasn't making it any easier.

Dean answered on the second ring. "Emma! About time. I've been trying to get in contact with you for hours."

"I'm sorry about that, Dean. My phone died, but it didn't seem like a crisis since it was Christmas. Did something happen?"

Dean laughed humorlessly. "Yes, you could say that. You haven't been following the news? Checking the SLICE social media accounts?"

Emma bit back a retort. "No, I haven't been able to. I'm not sure if I told you, but I don't have internet access here, so..."

"Still? I'm surprised at you, Emma. I know your friend 'took away' your smartphone as some kind of cute trick to make you relax or something, but you know they sell phones and laptops and all sorts of other technology in Ireland too, right?"

Emma was incredulous. "Really? That hardly seems necessary. If I remember correctly, you and Beth assured me you didn't need my help...that things would, in fact, be better, easier even if I weren't involved. Is that no longer the case?"

"It certainly isn't. This whole mess with Chad Bradley has blown up. You can't believe the attention that clown is still getting. And SLICE is floundering. We need you here, being the face of the company. I thought you'd be back by now, but here it is, after Christmas, and you're still on some island in the middle of nowhere. It's more than a little disconcerting for those of us who invested so much of our own capital into your little company, if you get my drift."

She got his drift, all right. Dean was losing confidence in her, and if that happened, the others would follow along soon after. If she couldn't manage to keep him on her team, SLICE would be out of investors and advisors before she could even get off the phone.

"Dean, I assure you, I'm doing everything I can to get back as soon as I can. My flight was canceled because of the weather, but I'm sure I'll be able to fly out in the next day or two. In the meantime, let me see what I can do from here."

"It's not enough, Emma. Not anymore. We've been floundering here, and there's been no leadership from the founder of the app. We need to do something meaningful, and we need to do it fast."

"Okay." Emma could feel Connor's eyes on her, offering support and asking if she was okay, but she didn't dare look in his direction. "I'll find a way out today. I'll be in the air before the sun sets."

"You're not hearing me, Emma. It's not enough. Your absence and your radio silence have already damaged the perception of SLICE beyond what you can repair. We need to make a change."

"Alright, then why don't we—"

Dean cut her off. "I didn't mean you and I, Emma. I meant 'we' as in the actual owners of the company. The ones who provided all the capital to get it up and running and who stand to lose the most if it tanks. We need to change the public face of SLICE."

"You mean get influencers on the app? I was thinking about that, too. They're so much more—"

"Of course we need influencers on the app. But we need a new face of SLICE, too. I'm sorry, Emma, but we need to talk about your future at SLICE."

Emma was silent. It couldn't be happening...could it? This was her idea. How could anyone possibly fire her from it?

"Emma? Are you still there? Say something."

"Dean, I..." Emma's mouth was dry, her face growing hotter by the moment. "I don't understand. How is this even possible? SLICE is my app. You can't replace me!"

"This was in the contract you and I both signed when I made my initial investment, Emma. There's a clause in there about sharing the responsibility to make decisions in the best interest of the company, and—"

"It certainly doesn't feel like you're sharing this decision with me," Emma interjected.

"You didn't let me finish. Decisions are shared among the investors and the founder, but if any one stakeholder is deemed incapacitated by the remaining others, then those others reserve the right to make decisions on behalf of the whole."

"Incapacitated? I'm in Ireland, not in a coma! I can't believe this is even a possibility!" Emma stood and started pacing in front of the fire. She could feel Connor's eyes following her, but her gaze remained locked in the middle distance. If she turned to him, she'd either fall apart or direct her frustration in his direction, neither of which would help her through this phone call.

"You've been unreachable, and you've been unresponsive to the emails that have been sent. Your social presence has been nonexistent, even as media outlets and app users have been tweeting directly at you and going viral in the process. You've been truly 'off the grid,' as they say. And that's all well and good if you need a mental health staycation, but for God's sakes, Emma, you're running a company."

Emma couldn't believe what she was hearing. They couldn't let her go...replace her...could they?

"Dean, I'm sorry, I truly am. I was under the impression we were all on the same page about this—you and Beth were the capable hands I was leaving the company in. What changed? How did we end up here, having this completely unbelievable conversation?"

"Because things got real, Emma. It was one thing when Chad Bradley seemed like a flash in the pan, getting his fifteen minutes of fame. But it's been two weeks. And honestly, none of us really thought you'd be offline the whole time. We thought we could send you away, you'd get a bit of rest, but you'd be working with us remotely the entire time. It's like you ghosted us, Emma. And frankly, the fact that you were able to check out this much says something alarming to the rest of us."

"What do you mean?"

"Come on, Emma, let's get real. It's one thing for a coffee shop owner to leave work at work. To go home and not think about all the lattes he made that day. Or to go on vacation for a week, leave someone else in charge, and not check in every fifteen minutes."

"Right...and in contrast to those coffee shop owners, I would say on-call doctors have the opposite experience. They probably shouldn't even go to the bathroom without bringing their phones or pagers with them, just in case."

Dean sighed. "And folks in the tech world, too, Emma. You might be right that no one's life is depending on you doing your job...but this app and the livelihood of everyone attached to it depends on you being reachable. All the time, honestly. Things move too fast in this realm for you to take an entire week off and expect everything to be just the same when you come back to work. I can tell you that, at all the other big apps, no one's ever really taking a vacation. They're checking in, they're working from the beach, and they're leaving a highly capable team of people behind to run the show back home."

"Which is just what I did. I still don't get what changed, why this has to be such a big deal."

"...it's that, Emma. Right there. It's hard to believe your heart is in it when you can walk away from it. And the other investors and I...we need more than that. We need the assurance that our money was well spent and it's going to find its way back to us. I'm sorry to say it, but we no longer have that assurance with you."

"What...what's going to happen? What do I do now?"

"We need you to come back as soon as possible. This is serious, Emma. I can't offer you any assurance that it's not too late to save your position at SLICE, but the sooner you come back...well, the better it will be for all of us."

As soon as Emma hung up the phone, she was stomping down the hall towards Connor's bedroom, with him hot on her heels.

"Emma, what happened? That sounded bad."

She wheeled around to face him. "You think? I might be losing my job. My *job*, Connor! For being here. For not being available to them by email or text message or social media. Connor, I *founded* the damn thing. I...I didn't even think this was possible. I don't know what's happening."

Connor stepped forward, approaching her like the wild animal she felt she was possessed by in that moment. "What are you doing? Where are you going?"

"I have to be there, Connor. I can't fix this from here. Not over the phone."

"Can you fix it there?"

Emma was quiet as Dean's words raced through her mind, his tone of disappointment like she'd never heard it before. "Honestly? It doesn't sound like it. I think they're done with me."

"I'm sorry, Emma. I really am. Even as critical as I've been of the whole industry, I never would have wanted this for you."

"I just keep thinking over what I could have done differently. How I could have prevented this colossal mess from happening."

Connor stopped her words with a kiss on the nose. "You couldn't have changed it, Emma. And what difference would the last few days have made? It was Christmas yesterday, for crying out loud."

Emma laughed humorlessly. "Apparently, in the tech world, there are no off days. Not even for Christmas. And apparently that was my problem, how easily I was able to step away."

Connor shook his head. "If that's the case, then good riddance to them. You need a job, a life where you can take a day off. Or, for God's sake, take a vacation once a year. Emma, this is no way to live—"

She held up her hand to stop him. "I'm pretty sure you're right about all of that...but I can't hear it right now. I just lost my job, Connor. My job at the company *that I founded*. I don't need to hear about the silver linings of it right now."

He nodded. "You're right. What do you need from me?"

Emma forced a smile. "You're sweet to ask. Sorry, I'm just...kind of all over the place right now. Can I use your phone to look for flights?"

"Of course. I'll make you a cup of tea."

"Thanks. You're a gem." Emma kissed him on the cheek, already feeling the strain this new dynamic was putting on their relationship. She didn't have time to worry about that right now, though. One crisis at a time was more than enough to manage, thank you very much. A career she'd spent nearly the last decade of her life building disintegrating before her very eyes had to take priority over a relationship that was barely two weeks old.

Even as she thought it, she felt a pang. Between her career and Connor, only one of those things filled up her heart. Sure, SLICE had been full of dopamine hits, from the first time she saw her name trending on Twitter to the first time she was asked to be a keynote speaker. But, like all dopamine baths, the effect never lasted long. Even in the midst of one ego-boosting opportunity, she'd be daydreaming and scheming about how to secure the next one.

Connor, though...this was different. *And that's why it's all too good to be true. Why it's all about to crumble before your very eyes,* Emma's cynical brain chimed in. *Just because one area of your life is falling apart doesn't suddenly mean another area is fantastic. That's just how contrast works. If anything, maybe avoiding this whole "relationship" mess would have kept you from losing your job.*

"I can't go there right now," Emma muttered to herself under her breath. She might not be a relationship guru with 10,000 hours of experience being in a couple, but even she knew that blaming Connor's existence in her life for something bad happening thousands of miles away wasn't the way to go.

She sat down at the kitchen table, where Connor had placed his phone for her. He was bustling around in the kitchen, filling the kettle and finding the good biscuits in the pantry, so she got to work on searching for a flight.

"Dang...Connor, what time does the last boat leave?" she called over her shoulder.

"In about an hour. Why?"

She still wasn't facing him, engrossed in scrolling through the phone in front of her. "There's a flight tonight. I'm wondering if I can make it to the airport in time."

Connor had come closer, looking over her shoulder. "*Tonight* tonight?" Emma looked up at him, reading in his tone what was written all over his face. He ran his hand through his hair. "Wow, this is really happening, I guess. That soon." He rallied, pasting a smile over the downcast expression too late for Emma not to notice it. "We can get you there in time," he said. "Are you all packed up?"

Emma didn't have time right now to worry about his feelings and what they meant. If they made it to the boat in time, there would be a few minutes to say meaningful things to each other there.

She jumped to her feet. "Not yet, but I will be. Wait—" She pivoted back to the table, picking up the phone she had so unceremoniously dropped on its surface. "I should actually book this flight. Where is my head?"

While she went through the checkout process, Connor stood quietly next to her, offering his strength without smothering her with affection. She wanted to be wrapped in his arms, in that moment and plenty of future moments to come. But if he held her right now, she might crumble, and she might not get the things done that needed to happen if she was going to salvage any semblance of a professional reputation.

It was good that Connor picked up on her need for distance and strength, even if his doing so felt strange and foreign. She kept telling herself that, over and over again, as she left the room alone and packed her things, preparing to leave Inishmore.

# Nineteen

Connor had insisted on joining Emma to the airport. "It's not really up for discussion," he'd said. "If you're only going to be in my country for a few more hours, you'd best believe I'll be spending every minute that I can by your side."

It was hard to argue with that, even if his words had stirred up something that Emma didn't particularly care to think about. She'd been so focused on straightening out the mess that was her career that she hadn't had a moment to think about what was about to happen with Connor.

They were going their separate ways, after a week and a half that had changed everything. It was so overwhelming to think about what the future held for them that Emma wondered if it wouldn't be safer just to focus all of her attention on work.

*That's it,* she thought. *A to-do list. That's what I need. Let's see, I'll need to have meetings with each of the investors,*

*talk with Beth about booking some media appearances, tap
into my network to see what opportunities are out there...*

"Everything okay?" Connor had poked his head into
the bedroom, where Emma was packing up the last of her
things.

"Great," she said, forcing a smile. "I'm just about ready
to go."

Connor's smile mirrored her own. "Terrific. I'll take that
suitcase for you when you're ready. And I called the dock
already, just to make sure there's room for us on the boat.
We're all set."

"Thanks, Connor. I really appreciate it."

"Of course." He shifted his weight as if he was about
to leave, then leaned back on the door frame. "If there's
anything I can do, you'll tell me, right? I want to help, I
just don't know—"

Emma cut in. "I will. But honestly, I think it's all pretty
much a waiting game at this point. There are a lot of things
I need to figure out that I won't be able to delve into until
I'm back home and talking with people face to face. The
irony of working in tech and social media is that direct
human interaction still prevails above all else." She laughed
without humor. "Though I might have to stop saying I
work in tech and social media soon, huh?" She looked up
from the suitcase she was zipping, her eyes finding Connor's. "I think I'm about to be unemployed. It just hit me.
And I have no idea what I'm going to do next."

At the desperation in her eyes, Connor pushed himself
off the doorframe and crossed the room, encircling Emma
in his arms. "I remember how scary that feeling was."

She looked up at him, scrutinizing his face. "You do? I thought you wanted to leave your job? That it was your idea?"

He nodded. "It was. But that doesn't mean I was smart about it, that I had a plan before I left. I found myself back here on the island, sleeping in my childhood bedroom, with no clue what I was going to do next."

"How long did it take before you started working at the pub?"

"Oh, that happened pretty soon, actually. But it was never meant to be long term. Just a means to an end, helping out my family and earning a bit of money. It's still a bit of a shock to the system some mornings, realizing that I'm still here, still working at the pub, even though it's literal years since I started."

Emma shook her head. "No offense, but that's what I'm afraid of for myself, too." Noticing the look on Connor's face, she hurried to explain. "I don't mean about the pub, specifically. Or about Inishmore, either. I think I'd love to be here, and the pub might be one of the most fun places there is to work. I'm just afraid I'm going to find something temporary and it's going to become my whole future. I don't want my next job to be the one I retire from unless it's, like, *perfect*. You know? But if I end up doing tech support at a high school...well, there's nothing wrong with it, but let's just say it's not my dream."

Connor was quiet for a moment as he pulled her tighter and rested his chin on top of her head.

Finally, he spoke. "Do you know where your worth comes from, Emma?"

She pulled back so that she could look into his eyes, trying to find his meaning as if it were written across his irises. "What do you mean? What worth? Like how much the next company I work for is going to pay me?"

Connor shook his head. "I probably shouldn't have started this conversation when you had work on the brain this much. But no, that's not what I meant. I mean, your worth as a human being. What's your value to this planet? To the people in your life? Where does it come from?"

"I already know it doesn't come from my work or from how much money I make, so you don't have to patronize me with that particular lesson."

"I'm not trying to patronize you. This is the lesson I learned when I left Dublin, and it wasn't an easy one. It was a real kick to my ego, working in the pub. And every single person who came in, for at least the first month, every single one of them asked me what happened to my big fancy job, why I had come back. It was like I had to relive my failure with each one of them, over and over again."

"I'm sorry, I didn't realize..."

"And at first, I got defensive. I tried to justify myself, to convince both them and me that I was going to do something bigger and better. Because on some level, I still believed that my worth came from how much I achieved."

"How did you get past that?" Emma asked.

Connor shook his head. "I think being asked the same questions day after day just finally broke me. I realized there was nothing wrong with working at the pub. With serving people and putting a smile on their faces. I realized none of them actually cared if I got rich and famous;

they just wanted to see me, to know that I was happy and healthy and up for a chat. Things got a lot simpler then."

"Is that it, then? The answer?"

"What do you mean?"

Emma was exasperated. "I mean, do I have to let go of all of my ambition in order to be happy? Is that the big secret that I can't figure out, for some unknown reason? Do I need to spend the rest of my life scrubbing toilets to realize that there's more to life than magazine covers and TV interviews?"

Connor's jaw tensed and his cheeks flushed. "There's no shame in serving others, Emma. Remember that before you start to shame any particular professions. I've scrubbed my fair share of toilets, and that's done a lot more good for the people that use them than any magazine cover ever did."

Emma shook her head. "I don't really need this right now, Connor. If you've got something to say, then go ahead and say it. Otherwise, save the profound wisdom nuggets for another time, please."

"That's just it, though. When is there going to be 'another time?' Your work pops in to demand your attention, and you're just...gone. Faster than I can even keep up with what's going on, to be honest. You're out of here, and it feels a bit like you're blaming me for what happened. But you're forgetting that you chose to be here, Emma. I wasn't the one that took your phone away, I wasn't the one that made you miss your boat back, and I sure wasn't the one to make the weather too bad for you to fly back. So if there's something that you feel like I've done to ruin all of this, then please feel free to let me know what it is so I don't do it again. Because right now it feels like you're about to walk out of my life forever and not even look back."

Emma stopped in her tracks, floored by Connor's vulnerability. How was it possible to feel so frustrated with someone and so...drawn to them at the same time?

She reached her hands up, caressing his face as she searched his eyes. "I...I'm not blaming you, Connor. I'm just frustrated with what's happening, and...well, you're the only person here. Who else am I supposed to take it out on?"

He scoffed, shaking his head. "What if, instead of taking it out on *anyone*, you talked through it with me? What if you were here with me, for just a few hours longer, instead of already back in New York in your mind?"

"You're right." She laughed at herself, exhaling audibly through her nose. "It feels productive to me, somehow, to obsess and overthink about what's waiting for me on the other end of my flight. But that's not going to make the journey go by any faster, and I don't want to get all the way to JFK before I realize that I've said goodbye to you." She kissed him then, slowly and tenderly. "I'm sorry. Thank you for bringing me back to you, even if it's just for a few more moments."

He smiled. "I'm a greedy bastard, what can I say? I want all the moments you can possibly give me, and I'll fight anyone—even you—who tries to take them away from me."

"That's fair, especially considering the circumstances. What do you suggest we do with the remaining moments we have?"

Connor's eyes glittered mischievously. "I've got a few ideas."

The boat ride back to Galway went by too quickly, even with all the seasick passengers on board. When the third person near them asked for a motion sickness bag, Connor had taken Emma by the elbow and led her to the far less crowded upper deck of the boat.

"Just keep your eyes on the horizon," he told her. "It may not be a totally foolproof way of avoiding barfing in a bag, but it's always worked for me."

Looking out at the horizon, Emma sighed. "It's going too fast, and I hate it."

"What, the boat?"

She turned to face him. "No, the time. I thought, you know...'time flies when you're having fun.' So, I figured maybe if we were feeling absolutely nauseous and terrible, then it would feel like we had all the time in the world together."

"Ah," said Connor, his eyes focused ahead of them. "But the clock is still ticking."

Emma leaned into his side, enjoying the feeling of being anchored to this man, this man she'd so recently brought into her life but who she already couldn't imagine being without, gazing out at a common goal together. "I'm really going to miss you," she said, her voice surprising her with how small and vulnerable it sounded.

He put his arm around her then. "I'm going to miss you, too. But I'm hoping you'll come back so you can use your Christmas present."

She smiled, reaching into her pocket to touch the key he'd given her. "I'll be carrying the key with me at all times, just in case. And you'd better use your Christmas present, too."

Connor nodded once. "I most certainly will. I'll give you some time to get settled back in the States...and time to *really* start missing me. Then I'll talk to Da and Patrick, leave the pub and Lady to them, and come crash on your couch."

Emma sputtered in surprise. "Not only are you depriving me of Lady, but you're going to sleep on my *couch*? On second thought..."

"Lady doesn't have a passport." He winked at her. "But I was only kidding about the couch."

"I figured as much—"

"If I'm flying over an ocean to see you, I'll be sleeping in a bed, thank you very much. The couch is all yours."

Laughing and shaking her head at him, Emma settled back into Connor's side, taking in the view of the Cliffs of Moher one last time as the tour boat made its way back to Galway. She hadn't known what she was getting herself into, that day she'd taken off for the Aran Islands tour and slipped and fallen in a cemetery, but with this good man at her side, she was confident it had all been worth it.

Time didn't move any slower as the boat docked in Galway, or as Emma and Connor secured themselves a taxi to go to the airport. They sat in the backseat together, her hand in his as he stroked his thumb across her knuckles and made small talk with the driver about Galway traffic.

Too soon, they were at the airport, standing outside facing each other, Emma with her luggage in hand and her heart in her throat.

"I— Thank you, Connor. For everything."

He looked at her like she had two heads. "Do you really think I'm saying goodbye to you out here? Don't be daft, woman." He winked. "There's a cafe inside. We'll check your bags, then go sit and have a coffee together."

"Oh. Great! I didn't realize." It wasn't getting any easier, the idea of the impending goodbye, with all the postpone-ments. There was a part of Emma that wanted to rip this sadness off like a bandage, just get it over with and begin the process of putting herself together.

But there was also a large part of her that was happy to live in denial, nearly convincing herself with every delay that the inevitable goodbye wasn't actually coming.

No doubt misreading the expression on her face, Con-nor spoke up. "Don't worry your pretty head. I'll have you to the security gate in plenty of time to catch your flight." He wiggled his eyebrows at her. "I know you were just trying to think of a nice way to excuse yourself because you want to be sitting at your gate at least three hours before your flight departs. As tempting as it is to try to make you miss it, I swear I won't do it. Cross my heart."

Emma could play along. There was no need to get too real just yet—that was still coming...later. "Good," she said, smiling at him. "You read my mind."

Inside the airport, they waited together to check Emma's bags. She couldn't help but imagine what it might be like if they were waiting in this line to fly some place together. It was already a nice change of pace to have someone in the line with her, to not be waiting by herself for a journey she would take alone.

*Don't get too excited,* her thoughts reminded her. *You're still boarding that plane alone, and no matter who you're sitting next to, they will not want you to rest your head on their shoulder.*

She sighed, both of them stepping forward as the line moved around them.

"You alright?" Connor asked, raising an eyebrow.

"Mm hmm." She nodded. "Just anxious about flying—but what am I *not* anxious about these days?"

Connor put an arm around her shoulders. "It does seem like an awful lot is happening, all at once. I'd say you need a vacation, but..."

"But that's what got me here in the first place?" She tried to keep the bitterness from her voice and failed, judging by the wounded expression on his face.

"Come on, then. It hasn't been all bad, has it?"

Emma shook her head, leaning into Connor. "No. Of course not. You...you've been wonderful. I think it's just that leaving you feels so crappy and that's all I can think about right now."

"It's not my favorite, either. I stopped myself from asking you to move in with me, by the way. It seemed like maybe giving you a key was enough, but...anyway, I would have happily kept you. It's a shame you've got friends and family waiting for you back in New York."

"I notice you didn't say I've got a job waiting for me there." She shook her head at herself. "Sorry. I missed the point of what you were saying by having yet another pity party for my dead or dying career." She looked into his eyes, her hand rising of its own accord to his cheek. "In my dream world, I'd still be here. I don't know what I'd do about the friends, the family, everything I left back in New York. But even though it's probably way too soon to say it, I'd rather be with you than pretty much anyone else."

"Same here. I hate that you're leaving, and I am confused every moment by that fact. Ever since I left Dublin, I've frankly been a bit of a loner."

"Oh really? The fact that you moved to a remote island with hardly any people on it would *never* have clued me in to that."

He gave her another tighter squeeze around the shoulders. "As I was saying..."

"Right. Sorry. Continue." The two of them continued to inch their way forward, getting closer with every moment to the check-in counter.

"Well, I kept waiting for you to wear out your welcome. You know, for me to wake up one morning ready to have my space back to myself. To think, 'sure, it's been nice having the company, but I'm ready to have my own space again. Just me and Lady.'"

"Uh huh...and did that happen?"

His expression was earnest. "I think you already know the answer to that question." He shook his head. "Not even close. There wasn't a single moment I wished you weren't around, and I think my little cottage is going to feel a lot sadder and emptier without you in it."

Emma sighed, releasing her suitcase handle to wrap both arms around Connor's waist. "I hadn't even thought of that," she said. "My apartment is going to be so cold. So empty. No you, no Lady...I'm not even excited to get back home, not the way I usually am." She looked up at Connor, but without releasing her grip from the hug, all she could see was his chin. "Darn you, Mr. Ryan. Did you just ruin my apartment for me?"

Connor shrugged. "It wasn't my intention, I swear. But if it makes you want to turn right around and come back to me, I won't complain."

Emma was silent then, wishing that was a possibility. Sadly, considering the mess that was waiting for her in New York, it was unlikely she'd be able to go anywhere outside the city for quite a while.

Connor exhaled, his warm, minty breath blowing her hair into her face. "I know, I know. It's not going to happen like that. Maybe I'll be visiting you in The Big Apple before you even know it."

"I'm counting on it." Emma pulled back enough that she could see his whole face, trying to read his eyes to see if he meant it. "You'd better not be kidding me. And you'd also better not call it that when you visit."

His expression was sincere. "Who knows how long I'll make it without having you in my arms? I know travel's going to be kind of off the table for you for a while, but maybe it's about time I ventured a little further than Galway."

Emma jumped up and down, squealing with joy and surprising herself in the process. "That would be..."

"Amazing, I know." He smiled at her. "And the thought of facing a big city again, no matter how much I dislike them, is worth it just for that reaction. That settles it, my dear. I'll be there."

"Is that a promise?"

He nodded. "You can count on me."

# Twenty

There wasn't enough time before Emma's flight left. Buoyed by the promise of a visit from Connor, the day lost some of its sting—*some*, but not all.

The couple had sipped their beverages at the airport cafe, Emma anxiously checking the time more often than she would have liked. Even when she didn't really want to leave, the thought of making that foolish of a mistake—of missing her flight while she was already in the airport—was unbearable. Thankfully, Connor knew her well enough to know that she needed to be through security far earlier than he would have opted for if he were the one in the air today.

Their goodbye at the security gate had been warm and cozy, arms wrapped around each other and mouths finding their match for just one more kiss time after time. Every time sadness threatened to rear its head, Emma had tamped it back down with an excited reminder they would soon be reunited in New York.

"You know it's alright to be a bit sad, don't you?" Connor had asked her.

Emma shook her head. "That can happen later...and preferably not when I'm going to be surrounded by strangers on the plane. Anyway, what's there to be sad about? You'll be in New York before I even know it!"

"That I will." He kissed her again, patting her lightly on the bottom. "Now, don't you think you'd best be getting through that security gate? We wouldn't want anyone else to be the first in line to board your plane, now would we?"

"Shush," Emma laughed. "But yeah, I probably should. I'll miss you." She kissed him. "I'm glad I met you, I really, *really* like you, and I can't wait to see you again."

She felt Connor's smile against her lips. "I, too, am glad I met you, really, *really* like you, and can't wait to see you again."

After they parted, Emma made her way to the line, where she handed her passport and boarding pass over to the agent waiting to inspect them. As she continued towards the x-ray machines, she kept glancing back over her shoulder, her eyes finding Connor where he was waiting and watching. He didn't leave the whole time she was within sight, and she wished once again that she had her regular cell phone so she could at least text him and tell him to go home.

Instead, just as she arrived at her departure gate and deposited her backpack on an empty seat, she was surprised by a ringing from her jacket pocket. She pulled out the

ancient brick of a cell phone and smiled when she saw the
name on its pixelated display.

It was Connor, proving to her once and for all that just
because she was out of his sight didn't mean she was out
of his life.

Emma's arrival back in New York was a whirlwind. She'd
slept terribly on the plane, force-feeding her brain all the
new release movies the airline had to offer, just to keep her
mind off of what she was leaving behind in Ireland...and
what was waiting for her at home in New York.

Claire had picked her up at the airport and brought
her back to her apartment, where her dear friend had
stocked the fridge with a few essentials and also left her
(fully charged) smartphone. Claire ran out to pick up
some of Emma's favorite Thai takeout, placing the bag on
the counter and kissing Emma's forehead before excusing
herself.

"I know," she said, holding up a hand to stop Emma
from getting her first word out. "You've got lots to tell
me, and I have so many questions I want to ask you. But
I also know, based on those dark circles under your eyes,
that you're facing levels of exhaustion that are not that
different from being majorly wasted." She nodded towards
the takeout bag. "Eat some food, drink some water—a
*lot* of water, actually—take a hot shower, and go to bed.
We'll talk when we talk." She stuck out her tongue. "Just
messing with you. We'll talk tomorrow. As soon as you
wake up, I'm guessing."

Emma hugged her friend, grateful that her tired brain didn't need to string together any thoughts into sentences just yet. It seemed unlikely that she'd be able to operate a coffee machine or order a meal right now, never mind tell a story that actually made sense. And to her *author* best friend, no less. No, it was better to wait until she'd slept off some of her exhaustion and processed a few of the tangled mess of emotions she was feeling right now.

"I'll call you in the morning?" she asked Claire, who nodded back at her.

"Anytime, love. Welcome back."

When Claire was gone, Emma set about getting as comfortable as possible, as quickly as possible. She wrestled with whether she should shower first or eat first—she was both starving for non-airplane food and also *very* aware of just how travel-stinky she was. Ultimately, efficiency won out. She ran water for a bath while eating her drunken noodles in her undies. She poured a glass of wine and a bigger glass of water to take with her into the bath, grabbing her phone at the last minute before she closed the bathroom door.

Staring down at the unfamiliar piece of technology in her hand, she was surprised at how foreign it felt after such a short time apart.

"Hello there," she greeted it, holding down the power button to fire it up again for the first time in over two weeks. "I'm not entirely sure I missed you, but I guess it's nice to see you again, old friend."

Her phone responded with a slew of notifications, eliciting a groan from Emma. There were hundreds of text messages, unread emails, and assorted other pieces of communication, all fighting for her attention.

"Nope," she said to herself, locking the screen again. "Nope nope nope." If Claire was discouraging her from even having a conversation right now, there was no way that diving into her work inbox was a good idea right now.

But there was one thing that couldn't wait. She fired off a quick message to Dean.

"I'm back in NYC," she wrote. "Do you have time tomorrow to meet and talk things through?"

His response came quickly and was brief and to the point. "Not tomorrow. Monday morning at 10 am. Coffee Bean Cafe."

Ugh. Emma would have to wait a whole day to have the conversation she was dreading. It was a good thing Claire was already intending to spend Sunday with her.

The phone vibrated in her hand, indicating the arrival of a new message, no doubt coming to join all of its brothers, sisters, and cousins in vying for her attention. A quick glance at the screen, however, told her that this one was different, as a smile spread over her face.

For starters, it didn't have a name attached to it, just a slew of numbers that started with +353. If her travel-addled brain remembered correctly, that was the country code for Ireland.

"Ms. Kells, this is a courtesy message from the Eyre Square Hotel. We hope you arrived home safely, but we regret to inform you that you left your hurling shirt behind in your hotel room when you left. Please forward us your address at your earliest convenience, as it would truly be a tragedy if we were not able to return this shirt to its rightful home."

Emma tipped her head back against the edge of the bath, her grin breaking her face in two. Obviously, this was a joke, and obviously Connor was the one sending it. After all, she'd checked her bag twice to make sure the hurling shirt was packed, and there was no way she would have left it behind.

Before she could respond, another message came through.

"Just kidding, it's Connor. I wanted to make sure you gave me the right number, so, instead of playing it cool like the kids do these days, I texted. Was it right? Is this you? Lady misses you, btw."

Emma could play along with this game. "Sorry, Connor. Looks like she gave you a fake number," she wrote. "For what it's worth, I, a perfect stranger you just happened to text, am also a fan of hurling and of not playing it cool. Give Lady some extra pats from me, please."

Then she fired off another text. "Just kidding, it's me. I'm too tired to know if that joke was actually funny, and I didn't want you to think you got catfished."

Connor's response was immediate. "Well, it couldn't possibly be catfishing since I've actually met you in person and know that you're a real human. Either way, I'm very relieved to have your correct number and to be texting you right now. How was the flight?"

Emma wrote, "Long and tiring, and not in the good way. I'm taking a bath now, probably going to be heading to bed at about the same time as you, even though it's 5 hours earlier."

"That bad, huh?" read Connor's response. "I'd be happy to give you a back rub and sing you a lullaby if you were here, but alas..."

"Whoa whoa whoa. Lullabies were on the table? How am I just finding this out now? You, sir, owe me a lullaby."

"Duly noted. You can come and collect on it any time you'd like."

They continued to text—and Emma continued to smile—until her bath water had run cold and her fingers were turning into prunes. With promises to chat more soon, they said good night, and she brushed her teeth and tucked herself into bed. The exhaustion brought on sleep faster than she expected, but not before she had time to touch the empty side of her bed, feeling a twinge of loneliness for the first time in this apartment she'd always loved. What had once felt like the ultimate symbol of her success and independence now felt emptier than she would have wanted. Determined to make the most of it, Emma spread out like a starfish in the middle of the bed, remarking at the strangeness of not sharing the space with Connor before she passed into a deep, deep sleep.

Claire joined Emma for breakfast the following morning for Sunday brunch, the two friends catching up for hours over pastries and coffee. Claire had entered, holding out the bag of baked goods as if it were a peace offering, her expression contrite.

"Now that you're a little more back to yourself, I feel like I need to apologize," she said. "It seems like it's my fault this whole SLICE thing blew up. If I hadn't taken your phone..."

Emma dismissed her with a wave of her hand. "Please. I mean, yeah, it was super inconvenient not to have a phone that could do things besides make a simple phone call. But it's not your fault. You couldn't have predicted something like this happening."

"I really couldn't. I thought they were the ones to tell you to take the vacation in the first place." Her voice raised at the end of her sentence in question, eliciting a shrug from Emma.

"You and me both. Honestly, we should probably talk about this whole work mess after I've had a chance to talk with them. Process it a bit more. Surely there are more interesting things we can catch up on in the meantime." She wiggled her eyebrows at her friend, and Claire squealed with delight.

"Yes, please!" she cried. "I want to hear all about your Irishman."

Emma smiled. That sounded good, and surreal at the same time—*her* Irishman. At least it was less complicated than referring to him as her boyfriend...was that what he was? That seemed like a conversation they should have had face to face.

She shook off the unwelcome thoughts, smiling at her friend. "And I want to tell you all about him, too..."

The conversation went on for an hour, with Emma spilling all the details and Claire oohing and ahhing at just the right moments. When Emma was finally done, Claire sighed. "I'm a little jealous, I have to admit," she said.

Emma was shocked. "What? No! You could have just as much romantic excitement in your life if you just went out and met someone once in a while..."

Dismissing her with a wave, Claire shook her head. "I'm not jealous like *that*, you goofball. I know I'm a catch; I'm just not actually interested in all the work it takes to be in a relationship right now. No, I'm jealous of the *story*. I wish I'd written it, but I can't very well steal your actual life as inspiration for a novel."

Emma laughed. "Well, I'm sure you could pull some pieces from it if you wanted to. Names changed to protect the innocent, and all that, of course."

"Of course." Claire smiled. "I'm happy for you, Emma. He sounds like a great guy, and I've never seen you like this. I think it's beautiful that you met like this, that things got serious for you so naturally...and so quickly. It's nice to remind yourself that you believe in love and magic, isn't it?"

But Emma was hung up on something Claire had said. "Do you think it happened too quickly? That's what I was worried about, honestly. Like maybe it wasn't real, but we just got caught up in the emotions of it. The excitement of it. I may have let myself fall too hard, too fast, and now I'm going to get long-distance dumped and never get the closure I need."

"Whoa there," said Claire, placing a reassuring hand on Emma's thigh. "Don't get ahead of yourself. And that's not what I meant. I mean, yeah, it *was* quick. But not in a bad way, not at all." She shook her head, smoothing her blonde hair out of her eyes. "Anyway, now is not the time for a relationship freakout. No, if anything—" She reached into her bag and pulled out a stack of DVDs. "If anything, now is the time for our rain checked Christmas Eve Eve date."

Emma threw her head back, laughing out loud. Leave it to Claire to keep the tradition alive, even if Christmas had already passed. She thumbed through the pile of DVDs, pulling out a couple of her favorite holiday rom coms. "I can't believe you," she said. "I didn't even know you had all these DVDs." A thought occurred to her, making her frown. "Do I even have a DVD player anymore?"

"Correction: I *didn't* have all these DVDs until about a week ago. After you got stranded with Connor, I had a sneaking suspicion our Christmas Eve Eve was getting postponed, one way or another. I did a little online shopping, so we'd be prepared for it whenever it happened, even if it ended up being in the middle of July."

Emma laughed again. "You're exaggerating, right? There was no way I was going to stay there for months, not with only one season of my wardrobe to work with."

"Glad to hear it. Now, let's figure out what we're watching first. And to answer your question about the DVD player, I brought one of those, too." She reached into her bag again, pulling out the boxy device and blowing a layer of dust off of it. "Sorry about that. Probably should have cleaned it before I filled my purse and your coffee table with ancient basement dust." She shrugged. "Oh well, too late to change that now."

"Indeed." Emma picked up the DVD player, examining it like an ancient artifact. "It's crazy how quickly technology changes, isn't it? I remember how excited I was when my parents got their first DVD player, and now it seems bizarre and outdated, like why wouldn't you just stream a movie or buy it digitally? Not that I'm not grateful that you have this."

Claire winced. "Maybe bringing another piece of outdated tech to you wasn't the best idea...sorry for the reminder about that ancient phone."

Emma dismissed her concerns. "No need to apologize. There's a certain irony to it, you know? *Tech startup founder taken down by prehistoric cell phone.* Like I couldn't have seen that coming?" She shook her head in dismay. "Maybe on some level I *did* see it coming...and I just let it happen. I guess we'll never know." Things were getting too heavy; time for a change of subject. "Anyway, what should we watch first? I'll make another pot of coffee."

Two holiday rom coms later—one with a business-minded single woman moving to a small town and another with a business-minded single woman falling in love on a vacation abroad—and Emma needed a break.

"These movies get a little heavy handed with the whole 'work won't make you happy, but love just might' messaging," she said. "I mean, I knew that was the case, but it feels so much more obvious when it's, like, the story of my life right now."

"Hmm," murmured Claire, who was jotting down some notes in the notebook she always carried with her. "Sorry," she said, when she set down her pen between the pages and looked up. "I just had some novel inspiration and couldn't let it get away. What were you saying?"

"Nothing...I mean, it's just sort of weird how these movies feel like they're trying to give me a moral lesson about my own life, you know? And it's not like I was trying to choose the stories that were the most like my own." She picked up the remaining DVDs, scrutinizing the covers of each one. "I'm pretty sure all of these have some element of 'woman who thinks her career is the most important thing in her life finds out that it isn't.' That's a real theme right now, isn't it?" She eyed the notebook in Claire's lap. "I sure hope you didn't write an idea just like that down in your magic notebook..."

Claire shrugged. "I mean, if it's the story that keeps getting told over and over, then there must be some truth to it, right?" She put her hands up, no doubt in response to the reaction written all over Emma's face. "Relax, I'm not talking about some kind of sexist nonsense about how women are better off having families than building companies. It's more just the idea—and this is true for all of us—that lasting fulfillment doesn't come from work. It really is all about the people in our lives, and not just the ones who are there in a romantic capacity, either."

Emma raised an eyebrow. "Convince me, please. Because I don't see a lot of these kinds of stories directed at men, so..."

Claire shook her head. "Oh, they're there. And isn't there that cliche saying about how no one on their deathbed ever wished they spent more time at the office? Even for me, feminist slash over-worker that I am, that saying *still* conjures up an image of an old male CEO on his deathbed. But it's true for all of us. You...and me, too."

"But you love what you do," Emma protested. "And you're such a talented writer...maybe the world really does need your stories. Maybe you really are making it a better place."

Claire shrugged. "Maybe. But if it happens at the expense of my relationships or my health, then I'm not convinced it was worth it. No one is going to be handing out awards at the end of our lives, congratulating us for sacrificing sleep or never taking the time to be vulnerable with someone in a meaningful way so that we could write more novels or—no offense—somehow convince people to spend even more time on their cell phones."

Emma was quiet, lost in thought. "You're right," she said finally. "It's so easy to get caught up in the success, the accolades, the attention...but the truth is that I've given up more for my career than I've gained from it."

Claire leaned her head on her friend's shoulder, the two of them silent together.

When Emma spoke again, her tone was brighter. "I don't know what to do with this knowledge, not really. I don't think the lesson my conscience is telling me is that I need to retire and go retreat to some off-grid location...but I do need more balance, whatever that means."

Claire squeezed Emma's hand. "I'm glad to hear you say it." She sat up then, turning with a smile on her face to stare Emma down. "And if you could get that much wisdom out of just two Christmas movies, just think what's going to happen when we work our way through the rest of the stack!"

# Twenty-One

Emma had intended to talk with the SLICE investors during that first full day back in the city, but spending it with Claire, getting their Christmas Eve Eve tradition a few days late was just the balm her soul needed after two solid days of stress and exhaustion.

Still, when Sunday evening rolled around and her meeting with Dean was hanging over her Monday morning like an executioner's axe, she felt a pit in her stomach. She shouldn't feel nervous about the meeting; it wasn't as if there was anything *new* in the bad news department that could be sprung on her, was there? She already knew her career was on the line—the only uncertainty that remained was whether things would end on good terms, or whether it would be a dumpster fire. Either way, she resigned herself to accepting her fate.

It helped that she was due to have a video call with Connor after her meeting finished the following day. They'd already promised that he'd be available throughout the afternoon, so no matter what time her meeting finished, she should call. It was nice to have something to look forward to when the day was due to start in a less than stellar manner.

Emma put on her comfiest pajamas, made herself a cup of hot chocolate—the good kind, with milk heated in a pot on the stove and not just water boiled in the kettle—and scrounged around for a pretty journal and a pen that wrote smoothly. As silly as it might seem to someone who didn't get what was so great about the analog world, the aesthetic appeal of her notebook and the pressure and flow of her writing instrument were very important factors for what she was about to do.

Settling in with her steaming mug, Emma opened the journal to the first blank page and began to write. The words flowed out of her in a stream-of-consciousness manner, and she did her best to shut off the part of her brain that wanted to judge what was flowing for not being perfect. She reminded herself to keep the pen moving, not to read or criticize what was coming out of it.

Twenty minutes later, she had written this:

*Everything that happened with SLICE is such a mess...but maybe this is for the best? Have I ever been truly happy there? Or have I just enjoyed the relative levels of fame and success I've achieved? I think I rediscovered a part of myself in Ireland, and I don't just mean the romantic (ahem, and bedroom) parts of my-*

*self that I tapped into with Connor. There was
something so powerful about actually being
unplugged, for the first time in I don't want
to think about how long. It made me question what we're even doing in the social media
world...is any of it done in the best interest of
the users? Or is it all just to earn the next dollar
for ourselves? If there is a way to use tech for
good...that's what I would want to do. And
I would want to do it in a way that didn't
require me to give up so much of myself. I don't
want to be the face of a brand or to have to be
accessible 24/7 just because "that's how it works
in this industry." I don't know how this is going to look, but I think I'm getting a clearer
picture of who I want to be in this next version
of myself.*

"Wow," Emma said to herself, as she sat back to sip her
cocoa and reread what she had written. It was true what
they said—"they" being Claire, naturally—that writing
really did help you process what you were feeling in a way
that thinking just couldn't. Case in point, Emma had been
thinking about her SLICE problem ever since she'd spoken
to Dean on the phone, but it was only when she wrote
about it she got the first clue of what she might want to
do next.

"But," she reminded herself, speaking out loud for extra
emphasis, "I can't fall into that old trap again. The one
where I think my work is the most interesting and only

important thing about me. If I'm going to do this, I can't give myself away to it completely. I need to find a healthy way to do it. With balance." She scoffed. "Whatever that even looks like..."

She felt...excited, for the first time in a long time. Or maybe it was just a nervous feeling, but she told herself it was excitement anyway. Excited for the potential of what she could build professionally—assuming she was about to *have* to build something new professionally—and of the impact that she could have on those who most needed it.

Still, even without a clear picture of her next steps, Emma felt hopeful, confident that she was going to land on her feet. Maybe she was even going to do something that would have made her seven-year-old self proud, that idealistic little girl who thought kitten cuddles and puppy snuggles would be the best replacement for currency. That the world would be a better place if everyone just smiled more. That little girl may have learned a thing or two about how the world worked when she entered middle school, but Emma knew some of that idealism was still there, and she was ready to tap into it.

At ten o'clock sharp the next morning, Dean Fischer dropped into the seat across from Emma at Coffee Bean Cafe, travel thermos in hand. His lips smiled at her, but his eyes were cold and distant. "Sorry I'm late," he said. "I got caught in an interview that ran a little long this morning."

Emma checked the time on her phone. "You're right on time, Dean. No need to apologize." She smiled back at him, outmatching his sincerity by at least double.

"I guess that's right. I'm just so used to being the first one here that it seemed like something was wrong."

Emma felt herself bristle but didn't let it show. Was this a power move, setting her up as some sort of flaky, perpetually late employee right before he let her go? Or did he just like the feeling of authority you got from being the first one at the table, choosing the best seat, and sitting back and waiting while the person you were meeting fell into their own inferior position across from you? Either way, it left a bad taste in her mouth.

"So Dean," she said, forcing her grimace into a smile so that she wasn't just baring her teeth at him. "I imagine we've got quite a bit to talk about. Would you like to dive in?"

Dean nodded. "Yes, no need to waste any time with small talk; we can do that another time. I presume you're all up to date on the Chad Bradley drama?"

"I think so," said Emma. "I read everything I could find last night, but I want to be sure I didn't miss anything important. It looks like he kept very busy on the talk show circuit."

"He did, though God only knows why they kept giving him airtime. It's clearly a classic case of having a great idea, not acting on it, and then getting your panties in a twist when someone else takes the initiative first."

"I didn't read it that way at all," said Emma. "I think Mr. Bradley never had the idea in the first place; he just saw a young woman getting attention for something he figured anyone of average intelligence could do, so he challenged my integrity on the national stage. It wouldn't be the first time a woman's abilities in the tech arena have been doubted, and it won't be the last."

"You may be right," said Dean, his tone conveying he neither thought she was right nor cared if she was. "Either way, we've done our best to discredit him by ignoring him, diverting our efforts to building SLICE's platform with key influencers, and making it clear when we're asked on record about Chad Bradley that we find it laughable. Behind the scenes, of course, we've done everything possible to cover our butts. Including scouring your old emails for the history of SLICE—when you first started talking about it, sharing your ideas with others. Our legal team has all those documents, and they can easily be used to prove it's our intellectual property if it comes to that."

Emma's jaw dropped. "Sorry, what? You really went through my old emails? And you have the nerve to talk about SLICE being *our* intellectual property? If we ignore the fact that you violated my privacy, we still have to confront the reality that it's my name and my name alone on those old emails."

Dean was shaking his head. "Emma, we've been over this. It's all in the contracts we signed when we came on as investors. In exchange for the capital we gave you, we retained ownership of SLICE. All of this is above board."

"Even going through my emails? How did you all manage that one?"

Dean had the decency to look sheepish. "Ah...that. Beth helped us out. Naturally, she has access to your accounts in order to manage your inbox and socials when you need help, so we just..."

"Unbelievable," said Emma. "Really. I guess I shouldn't be surprised, but I still am. Somehow, someone combing through my inbox feels nearly as invasive as reading my old journals. Or pawing through my drawers." She shook her head, her hands idly spinning her coffee cup on the table in front of her. "So what happens next?"

"I think you already know, Emma. We need a clean break, a fresh start. And I don't believe we can really get that if we keep you in your current position."

"I've got to hand it to you, Dean. You're making it a lot easier for me to let SLICE go. I thought it would be hard...heck, I was crushed after you called me. But the more space I've had to think about it, the more obvious it becomes that this is not the best environment for me. For my physical health, my mental health...all of it."

For the first time since he'd sat down, Dean's expression relaxed. "I'm glad to hear you say that, Emma. I really am. I want us to part ways on good terms, no matter how it may seem. Fundamentally, our differences come down to work ethic, work-life balance, boundaries...whatever you want to call it. It seems like you're trying to have healthy ones, and I respect that as a person, but as an investor, a business partner..." He trailed off, the meaningful look in his eyes speaking volumes.

"As a business partner, you want a workaholic," said Emma. "I get it." She looked at him then, taking in the slump of his shoulders, the tiredness in his eyes. "We were friends too, Dean. And as a friend, I hope you find whatever it is that you're looking for. I'm not sure it can be found in a business or an app...but you deserve to rest, too. To enjoy time with your family. To take a vacation once in a while. Can you try to do that before you retire or burn out on the job?"

"No promises." He smiled weakly. "But I trust you'll do such a good job of living an actual life that you'll make us all jealous." His eyes were sheepish when they found hers. "Are you ready to talk about next steps? How this transition is going to work?"

Emma nodded. "Bring it on."

By the time Emma got back to her apartment, she was practically vibrating with ideas and excitement. Despite its frosty start, the meeting with Dean had gone better than she could have anticipated. She had accepted an advisory role with SLICE, paying a minimal salary, but enough to keep the lights on (assuming she lived some place with a lower cost of living than New York City) while she figured out her next steps. She had looked over the profiles of the top candidates they were considering bringing on as SLICE's new CEO, and as much as Emma hated the fact that they were most likely only considering female candidates out of a desire to retain access to grants they'd be unqualified for with a male CEO, she'd been thrilled to see who'd made the top of the list. As she read through the accomplishments of the top three CEO candidates, a mean case of imposter syndrome threatened to rear its ugly head before Emma reminded herself that they were, in fact, vying to replace *her*. She didn't need to prove herself worthy of being in their presence, and that thought was like a breath of fresh air.

Arrangements had been made for Emma to join in on an upcoming press conference, and, once the new CEO was announced, for the two of them to do a small PR tour together. It would mainly be a tour of the New York-based talk shows, and Emma was looking forward to it as the end of an era.

She was feeling lighter and freer than she had since she'd first spoken to Dean on the phone. In fact, she was feeling lighter and freer than she had ever since she'd taken on investors for SLICE. Being responsible for other people's money and not wanting to let them down had caused more than a few sleepless nights, and it had turned her decision-making process from a streamlined gut check into the Second Guessing Myself Olympics. She wouldn't miss that.

She opened her phone screen, swiping through the social apps displayed there. Soon, after she'd made her last posts as SLICE's CEO, she'd delete them. In the new life that was waiting for her, no one needed a minute-by-minute update on her thoughts, meals, likes, or dislikes. And what a relief that was.

The ideas for the Next Big Thing were swirling something fierce. Emma had always enjoyed the creative part of her job more than the public relations part of it, and getting to start fresh with something new and exciting was making her fingers itchy.

But she had promised Connor she would call him, so she did that before she could lose herself for hours in her brainstorming mode. Emma plopped down onto her couch, put her feet up on the coffee table, and started a video call. While she waited for him to answer, she ran a hand through her hair, wondering briefly what it looked like before remembering that he was the last person who was going to comment unfavorably on her appearance.

"Hey, Em!" Connor's face filled her screen, his grin covering the bottom third of it. It was the first time she'd seen his face since she'd left him at the airport, and she was surprised at how emotional she felt, just seeing him again.

"Hi," she said, unable to stop a smile that mirrored his from spreading across her face. "Oh my gosh, it's so good to see you. I can't believe how much I missed your face."

"You and me both, gorgeous. How are you? Are you okay? Did things go alright today with that Dean guy?"

She nodded. "They did. Oh gosh, Connor, there's so much to tell you. It's hard to believe it's only been a few days since I saw you; I feel like I have a month's worth of news to catch you up on."

"Trust me, I get it. I've got some rather exciting news for you, too." His eyes were twinkling, a sure sign that he was up to something. And as much as Emma wanted to share her every thought and feeling with him, a wave of curiosity crashed over her, pushing it all out of her mind.

"You have to go first," she said. "I'm so curious what's got you smiling like that."

"That's fair," he grinned. "I'd tell you to guess, but you'll never get it."

"Out with it then," she prompted.

"I'm going to be coming to visit you very soon. Does next week work for you?"

If Emma had been drinking something, she would have done a spit take just then. "You...what? Really? Connor Ryan, are you messing with me right now? Don't tell me you're coming to New York if this is just one of your jokes..."

"I'm not messing, I swear. I really am coming to New York in a week." He scratched his head. "The flights are all booked, actually."

"The flight I gave you?"

"No, I'm saving that one...this one was paid for."

"Spill it! Who paid for a flight for you? Please don't say your secret New York girlfriend and three children are flying you out for a visit."

"Nah, there's only two kids." He laughed, his eyes wrinkling at the corners. "I'm only messing. I got an interview for a job and they're flying me out. I just decided to extend the stay a bit. Maybe spend the whole week with you?"

"...in New York?"

"Yes, of course I'm going to stay with you in New York. Where else would I do that? Unless you want to go to Miami, in which case I would definitely be up for some sunshine..."

"No, I mean the job. It's in New York?" Emma was dumbfounded, a conflicting mix of thoughts and feelings washing over her like so many waves.

He grinned. "It is. I hadn't even considered looking for jobs in the tech field again, not until you came and then left. It made me realize that maybe there's a way of getting back out there, off the island..." His voice trailed off as a pink tinge crept onto his cheeks. "It doesn't hurt that this particular job happens to be in New York."

As much as Emma was about ready herself to flee from this city, saying good riddance to SLICE and all of its associated stress to start over somewhere new, there was something about the fact that Connor was considering moving there that filled her with warmth instead of dread. If he wanted to come here, maybe she'd feel differently about living here. "Is it because I'm here?" she asked.

"Yes, of course it is. I'm a huge fan of the Statue of Liberty, of course, but I wouldn't consider moving countries just to be near her."

"I'll be sure not to let her know. Something like that could break her heart, you know, and that's the last thing any of us want."

"True." He gave her an easy smile then, some tension that she hadn't noticed before dissipating from his shoulders. "That's enough about me, now. Why don't you tell me what happened with Dean this morning?"

Emma blew out the air in her lungs through her lips. "Where to even start... well, I can tell you it all went well."

"That's great! Are they keeping you on, then?"

Emma shook her head, enjoying Connor's confused look. "They set me free, actually. No, it's good, I swear. I think I needed this. And I'm actually feeling pretty positive about what I'm going to do next."

"What's that, then?"

"I haven't quite nailed it down yet," she said, "but I know it would be something in the area of enhancing people's lives with tech rather than just making them addicted to yet another social app."

"Ahh yes, that old gemstone."

"And I want boundaries. I want a life like the one I got a taste of with you on the island. With time for lazy mornings...and the reminder that there's so much more to experience than just work. That lets me have relationships and prioritize my health, rather than always being caught up in the next opportunity for success or recognition. I just...I want to feel more human again. I want to relax, to do work I believe in, and to take a freaking vacation once in a while without feeling like I need to be glued to my phone."

"Amen," said Connor, his eyebrows sky high. "Well said, all of that. I'm proud of you. You figured all of this out, and you look so peaceful, so confident in yourself."

"I am," said Emma, smiling widely. That was enough sharing for one call. There was still the fact that she was thinking about leaving New York to discuss...but that could wait until Connor was there, thinking about taking a job in New York himself.

# Twenty-Two

"To life, and actually getting to live one," said Claire, raising her glass to clink it against Emma's. The two of them were sipping champagne on Emma's couch, after Claire had insisted that a big revelation like Emma had had about her career could only be acknowledged with a champagne toast.

"Cheers to that," agreed Emma. "I feel like I've got some catching up to do, for the years that I spent consumed by my work...but I'm up to the challenge."

"Heck yes you are," said Claire. "And I'm here to help you in any way I can."

"Thanks," said Emma, smiling. "If you happen to have any great ideas for tech inventions that could enhance relationships rather than taking away from them, I'm all ears. The only thing my brilliant plan is missing is a concept to build it around."

"Details, details," said Claire. "You're great at that kind of stuff. I'm sure you'll figure it out. Didn't you think of SLICE, like, in the shower?"

Emma nodded. "Most great ideas come at times like that, when your subconscious actually has a moment to breathe."

"Really? Is that why I always do my best writing right after I've woken up from a nap?"

Emma chuckled. "I imagine there's some truth to it. It's not easy to train that part of yourself to be creative, though. It's hard wired in most of us—in me, for sure—to try to think a problem to death. You know, like right now...with this new concept I want to come up with. I'm so tempted to just sit in front of my computer and write words and do research and tell myself that I'm not going to bed until I have a grand new idea."

"...but...?" Claire prompted.

"But when has that ever worked? The 'eureka' moments come in the shower, or out on a walk, or right after you've woken up from a nap."

"So you're telling me I need to keep you busy doing all sorts of fun things until you come up with a million dollar idea? Geez, twist my arm, why don't you?"

"What are you thinking?" Emma asked.

"Oh. *So* many things," said Claire, pulling out her idea notebook and scribbling furiously in it. "Walking around in a new neighborhood, taking the ferry to Ellis Island, going to a concert..." She paused, pen in the air. "You said something about making relationships better, right?"

Emma nodded. "Yeah, I've narrowed it down a bit. At first, I was just thinking it had to be tech that 'helped make the world a better place,' but that's *way* too broad. I'd never come up with an idea if I had expectations that big for it. But then I realized that it's all about the personal revelation I've had. That I want to prioritize my relationships and my health and not just be so singularly focused on my career."

"So that's it!" said Claire.

"What's it?"

"That's the first, most important thing—your why. The moral of your story, if you will. You want to help people prioritize relationships and health, at least as much as their careers."

"Yeah..."

Claire grabbed Emma by the shoulders, shaking her with excitement. "Emma, this is huge! With your focus narrowed down like that, you're going to come up with something soon, I just know it. Don't stress about it, don't try to force it...just relax, and let it come."

"I can try that, but..."

"But relaxing has never really been your strong suit?" Claire grinned. "My friend, this is what I'm here for!" She got to her feet, walking decisively into the kitchen to get her coat off the coat rack. "Come on!" she called back to Emma. "Let's go for a walk!"

Emma laughed. Leave it to Claire to know how to power her way through a creative block—it probably came with the territory of being a writer. But if it worked for Claire and the novels she churned out like clockwork, then maybe it could work for Emma, too.

❦ · ❦ · ❦ · ❦ · ❦

It hadn't taken long—only long enough for Claire and Emma to get turned around after too many sips of champagne, find themselves in front of a Vietnamese restaurant they'd never seen before, and return home with a loaded bag of takeout—for Emma to have her first inklings of an idea.

"I've got it!" She turned to Claire with fire in her eyes and a wildness coursing through her.

Claire held up her finger to Emma's mouth to silence her, while at the same time pointing her towards the coffee table. "I left the notebook there," she said. "Write it down. If you talk to me, I'll get confused if you get all technical, and I don't want my lack of a left brain to make you lose faith in whatever this brilliant idea is that you're having."

Emma chuckled to herself, shaking her head. "Leave it to you to have a system for capturing ideas. I should take your advice more often."

"Yes, you definitely should," agreed Claire. "It's done a lot of good for you lately, from your handsome Irishman to this idea that's going to be the next big app. I'm confident of it."

Emma rolled her eyes at her friend. "No pressure or anything." Hurrying into the living room, she flopped on the couch and picked up the notebook, writing so furiously her handwriting looked like a doctor's prescription pad.

*Relationships and health, combined with social media somehow. Regular social media thrives on comparison, making us feel like everyone else is living a more exciting life than we are. But are people fed up enough with it to try something different? What if there's a way to encourage and inspire people to...call their parents, meet up with their friends more often, sleep for a decent amount of hours, and eat a vegetable or two...without turning it into a competition?*

*What if the interface just looks like a social media site, but it's not that at all? So there are no likes or comments to make people keep coming back to the app over and over again? In fact...maybe the app can only be opened twice a day, once in the morning to set intentions for the day, and once in the evening to check off the boxes and reflect on what they've done. A gratitude list, even.*

*Nothing to keep them coming back to the app; just a gentle reminder in the morning and a notification in the evening. Suggestions for self care items to add to their list for the day—no work stuff, just things that will benefit their health, wellbeing, and most treasured rela-*

*tionships. Still the "highlight reel effect" we see on other social sites, but it'll just be their own highlights. Because they can upload photos at the end of the day, and those will come back to remind them at randomized times.*

*How do we keep it free? Sponsors? TBD.*

"Are you back in the land of the living?" asked Claire, topping off Emma's champagne glass. "You were seriously in the zone there. I don't think you even heard me come into the room."

"Yeah, I...didn't, actually." She waved the notebook in her hand. "I think I've got something here. It's not all figured out yet—what is?—but I think it's off to a great start."

"Excellent!" said Claire. She had brought their food into the living room and was unloading the containers onto the coffee table. "Want to tell me while we eat, or let it marinate a little longer?"

"Oh shoot!" Emma jolted up in a moment of revelation. "I want to tell you about Connor coming here next week. I can't believe I haven't told you that yet!"

Claire scowled. "And neither can I!" Her face softened into a smile. "Though obviously all of this—" She gestured vaguely towards Emma and the notebook she was holding. "—is important, too. But spill! Tell me what's going on with sexy Mr. Connor. Why's he coming so soon? Did he miss you that much already? Trick question. Of course he missed you the moment you left. But really, why is he coming this soon?"

"It's...weirdly complicated, actually. He has a job interview in New York." Emma picked up a container of pho, inhaling the intricate combination of flavors, her eyelashes fluttering with anticipation.

"New York, New York?" Claire asked, indignant. "The same city that you're talking about leaving behind?"

Emma nodded, digging into the soup she was holding. "The very same one."

"And did you not think to tell him you're not planning on sticking around here much longer?"

"I didn't want to discourage him from coming here." Emma shrugged. "He seemed like he was almost excited about the job interview, and he should at least see it through, right? It's not like the job is a sure thing, and it's not like that's the only reason he's coming to the city."

"No, but it's a pretty significant one."

"I'll talk with him about it when he's here. Who knows, maybe he'll get the job and we'll both enjoy being here so much together that I'll decide to stay. And he'll move in here, and we'll live happily ever after."

"Uh huh, maybe..." Claire didn't look convinced.

"What does that look mean?"

"Nothing. It's just..." Claire sighed, as if she were gathering her strength for what she was about to say next. "It's just that I've never heard you that excited about something unknown. When you called me after your meeting with Dean and said you were thinking about leaving New York, that they were giving you the kind of salary you could live off of in so many other places just not right here on this expensive, expensive island...I felt excited for you. Like this was the beginning of a really interesting character arc."

"And now?"

"And now it makes me wonder how much of it is about you and how much of it is about Connor, to be honest. Were you just talking about leaving because you wanted to go be near him? And are you just thinking about staying for the same reason?"

Emma sobered up quickly. "My gosh, Claire, that's some major conclusion jumping you're doing there. I haven't figured *any* of this stuff out yet, so there's no need to jump down my throat over it, okay?"

"You're right, I'm sorry."

"Until today, I had no idea there was even a chance of a salary from SLICE. And sure it's small, but it's not nothing. It just got me thinking, that's all. That money might not be enough to live here in the city, but it would be enough to get me on my feet someplace else. And until today, I also didn't know that Connor was looking for jobs in tech again, so I certainly didn't know he was thinking of taking one here. Just...just let me figure this out, okay? You can't expect me to make sense all the time. Especially not when I'm jet lagged and you're feeding me champagne."

Claire shook her head. "I got a little intense there, sorry about that. I think it's just that you're so brilliant...not just as a company founder, but, like, as a human. And I don't know Connor, apart from the fact that he's a sexy man with an attractive accent, so I got a little freaked out that he was going to be the new SLICE in your life, that's all."

"What do you mean, the new SLICE?"

Claire had the decency to look sheepish. "I mean...well, SLICE ran your whole life, you know? It took you away from me, away from your family...and we all saw your stress level increase the longer you were running it. Me confiscating your phone at the airport, that was my feeble attempt at an intervention."

"Yeah, I figured that part out."

"But you breaking free from SLICE? That's going to be such a good thing for you, you know? And the more you talk about this new work that you want to do, the more I can see that it's going to be something meaningful...and that maybe you'll even be able to take a dose of your own medicine and not let it take over your life."

"That's the plan. I'd be a major hypocrite if I spent all this time promoting self care and nurturing our relationships while being a total workaholic myself."

"That's just all really good, really inspiring stuff, Emma. And I got scared when you started talking about Connor that he was going to derail it. That you would do anything to be with him, while forgetting that there are other people in your life who want to spend time with you, too."

Emma was quiet. She could admit that things had gotten intense rather quickly with Connor, but this was all unexpected.

"It's not about romantic partners versus work, you know?" Claire continued. "It's about having work life balance so you can talk to your mom on the phone, spend Christmas Eve Eve with your best friend, and...yes...cuddle in bed for hours with your hunky new boyfriend. It's all of it."

Emma slid closer to Claire, her pho long abandoned on the coffee table. "Is that what it felt like to you? That I was abandoning you...myself...to this new relationship?"

Claire shrugged, looking down at her lap. "Not exactly. I mean, I was...*am*...happy for you, too. And it's been a long time since you were really *in* a relationship, you know? So I know this honeymoon phase intensity isn't the way it's always going to be. I'm just afraid to lose you to Connor after I *just* got you back from SLICE."

Emma hugged her friend, pulling her close. "I am so...*so* grateful for the intervention, Claire. You saved me the first time around, forcing me to take a break from the things that were consuming my life. But you're right...I *am* intense, throwing myself into whatever—or whoever—is consuming my thoughts." She shook her head. "This, right here, is the reminder I needed about balance. Balance in all things, yes? Not just work...but life. Love. All of it." She sighed, pulling away from Claire and slumping back against the sofa. "This is all way more complicated than I ever thought it was."

Claire slumped back next to her. "None of us have it figured out, you know? This app you're making...it's going to help a lot of people. I really believe that. But there's no perfect solution that works for everyone, and none of us is growing in a linear way. I mean...one step forward, three steps back, right?"

"Ugh. Yeah, I guess. I mean...this kind of feels like a kick in the pants, you know? Like there's no way I can win, with my work or with Connor." She put her hands over her face. "I just want to give up. Retreat into a blanket fort and never come out again. It's too hard...all of it."

"Hey now," Claire pulled Emma's hands off her face, staring down into her eyes. "Weren't we toasting and celebrating just a couple hours ago? What happened? Don't tell me you let a little bit of real talk from me scare you off of...well...everything."

Emma groaned. "Maybe I did. I don't know. It's scary to make changes, especially when you're not sure if you're making them in the right way. I miss doing things I'm good at."

Claire raised an eyebrow. "You mean like SLICE? Didn't that cause you a metric ton of stress?"

"Who cares? At least I knew what I was doing, even if I *was* working too many hours. Those hours were spent on problems I knew how to solve. Now I'm starting over from nothing, and at the same time I'm trying to figure out how to be in a relationship—a long distance one, no less—for the first time since..." Her voice trailed off.

"...since ever?" Claire finished for her. "Come on, I've been your friend long enough to know you aren't exactly the queen of domestic bliss."

"Then yeah, you're right. Since ever. And what kind of total noob makes their first real attempt at a relationship with someone who lives thousands of miles away on a freaking remote island?" She pointed her thumbs at her face, where she knew her expression was bordering on panic. "*This* overachiever right here. What was I thinking?"

"Well, for one thing, if anyone can jump from skill level zero to skill level ninety fresh out of the gate, it's you. I have faith in you," said Claire, her hand on Emma's upper arm. "And as far as what you were thinking...maybe you

were actually *feeling*? And letting yourself be led by that?"
As her voice raised at the end of each of her questions, her
eyebrow did too, as if she were waiting for Emma to scoff
at her.

Emma let out an exasperated sigh. "A lot of good that
did. Remind me to restore my factory settings as soon as
possible. Feeling makes things complicated...at least with
thinking there's a clear, logical next step forward. Look at
me, for crying out loud. A week of feeling and I lose my
job and nearly lose myself to a relationship I'm not sure I
have any business being in."

"I know it won't help if I say this..." Claire began.

"Then don't," Emma warned.

Claire winced. "I have to. I think you might be over-
reacting a teeny tiny bit. Connor is a great guy, and he
makes you happy. He's coming here—yay!" She waved
her hands next to her head in exaggerated celebration.
"It's okay to be happy about seeing him *and also* to not
know what's going to happen next for the two of you."
Her expression sobered as she leaned forward, closer to
Emma. "Just promise me you'll talk openly with him
about the whole New York thing. Too many relationships
get needlessly dramatic—especially in fiction, and trust
me, I should know—because people don't tell each other
the basic things that they need to know."

Emma made a face. "So what, I need to just come right
out and ask him if he's thinking of moving to New York
for me?"

"...yep."

"And I also need to tell him I'm thinking of leaving New York and that...um...maybe I'd be open to coming back to Inishmore for a while?"

"Ding ding ding."

"Ugh!" Emma groaned, picking up a pillow and burying her face in it. "Those are such real, vulnerable things to say! Can't we just do the 'does he really like me that much? Is he as serious about this as I am?' dance for like 6 months until we inevitably break up over the phone?"

"If that's how you want it to end, then by all means, go ahead." Claire's expression was stony when Emma lifted her face from the pillow.

"Of course I don't want to break up over the phone."

"Good. Then keep that in mind as you do the brave thing and, you know...talk about your feelings. Maybe even put yourself out there first, rather than waiting for him to take the first step."

Emma rallied the strength in her bones, her will, and her heart under one common goal, finally nodding when it all felt aligned. "I can do that. I may need another pep talk right before it happens...but I can do that."

Claire grinned, her pearly whites beaming like high beams at Emma's eyes. "Great. I'd love to meet Connor, of course, so if you time it right, I can pull you into the bathroom for a quick pep talk right before you go get your dude."

"You can't just have this conversation with him for me? You're the one who's a wordsmith, after all."

Claire rolled her eyes. "No way. That's been done to death."

# Twenty-Three

With a week to prepare for Connor's visit, Emma busied herself brainstorming and researching her new business venture. The more she kept herself busy, the easier it was not to stress about the conversation she needed to have with Connor.

Happily, there was plenty to do with her new app idea—and with SLICE, too. They had chosen a new CEO, a woman named Athena Owen who couldn't have been a better fit if Emma had chosen her herself. Athena was the first in her family to attend university, and she had risen to the top of her Ivy League business program. She had taken a few computer engineering courses—"just for fun," she'd told Emma at their first meeting—so even though her primary responsibility would be to serve as the public face of SLICE and to make business decisions, she also had a solid understanding of how the app actually worked.

Since their first meeting, Emma and Athena had met two more times, ostensibly so that Emma could pass on all of her CEO wisdom, but the reality was that the two women had quickly realized the potential for a friendship forming between them. Emma was relieved to know that her upcoming publicity tour with Athena wasn't going to be a chore, but rather that it would give her the opportunity to spend even more time with this powerhouse CEO-to-be.

As far as Emma's new idea, that was developing at a far better rate than she could have hoped. She'd been collecting research on the importance of boundaries, the addictive nature of social media, and anything else that supported her motivation for building this new project. She'd even sketched out the simple screens that would display on the app. Emma's background was in programming, not design, so that was the one part she intended to contract out. As far as the rest of it, the more time went on, the more convinced she was that at the beginning, at least, she needed to do this alone. No investors calling shots and increasing her anxiety. No one else to have an opinion that needed to be taken into consideration.

No, she would build the app—with the help of a designer—and then she would be the tech support team, updating the app with each new update to the platforms it would exist on. There would be room to hire customer support in the future, but Emma's role would primarily be in response to the reviews left on the app platforms. Of course, she would need a group of influential people—she hated the word "influencers," but it *did* describe what she was looking for—to direct traffic towards the app once it launched.

That was one area where Athena had already proved their relationship was pivoting from a professional one to a friendship.

"Are you kidding?" she'd said when Emma had shared her desire to grow this new app without ever actually getting back on social media herself. "Emma, you invented SLICE! You don't think we'd be more than happy to promote your new endeavor? Throw some traffic your way?" She shook her head. "Look, I shouldn't have to tell you that you deserve *at least* that level of support from us. Ask for what you need, Emma. Everyone cares about you—even me, and I'm still just getting to know you—and we all want to see you happy and successful."

The two of them were sitting at a table at Coffee Bean Cafe, the same place Dean and Emma had had a career defining conversation just a handful of days ago. Emma put her hand on Athena's, smiling at her new friend. "Thank you, Athena," she said. "It just feels so strange to be leaving like this...I think I forget that we're not actually parting ways on bad terms."

Athena raised an eyebrow. "Or some of us aren't parting ways at all. You know I'm not going to stop texting you just because I've gleaned all of your SLICE-related wisdom, don't you?" She raised her eyebrows, nodding towards the plate of pastries between them. "I don't have a lot of boss babes in my life—and yes, I hate that phrase as much as you do, don't even say it—so I'm not letting go of one when I get my paws on them. Got it?"

Emma laughed. "Got it. And I know what you mean. It can be a little isolating sometimes, talking about CEO stuff while your friends are complaining about their bosses. It's not super relatable."

Athena took a sip of her drink. "Good thing I'm not trying to be relatable, then. Are you?"

"I guess not," said Emma.

Between Emma's technical skills and her professional network, things were moving forward with this new app at an impressive rate. She'd even come up with a name for it already—LIMIT{less}. The image of setting limits and spending less time online, combining to suggest the app's users were truly limitless in what they could accomplish and who they could become? *It was \*chef's kiss\* perfect*, Emma thought to herself.

Because the production of the new app was moving faster than Emma could have anticipated, it was a very good thing she had Claire and now Athena to help keep her grounded. Between the emotions she was feeling about stepping away from SLICE, the excitement of the unknown, and the anticipation of Connor's arrival in a few short days, she was feeling the pressure.

The press conference announcing Athena's new role as SLICE's CEO had gone well. Athena and Emma had taken the stage together, in front of camera crews from all the major news networks, and the two women had each shared their prepared remarks.

Emma had gone first. "Thank you all for coming here today," she began. "SLICE has been getting a lot of attention in the news lately, and we are here today to address all of that head-on. Though there was some controversy about intellectual property, I can assure you that has all been laid to rest thanks to our documentation archive and the round-the-clock work of our legal team. On the advice of our leadership team, I stepped out of the spotlight while all of this was happening, and during the time I spent away from SLICE, some things became clear about our next steps moving forward."

Emma adjusted her stance, making eye contact with reporters in the room in turn. "In this day and age, it's rare that many of us have the chance to do what I did, to step away from our devices and apps and reconnect with ourselves." She chuckled. "I can tell you with confidence that it's not as easy as it looks, and it can bring up some uncomfortable truths." She turned her head towards Athena and smiled. "But not all of it was uncomfortable. Together with the leadership team, I've decided to step down as the CEO of SLICE after acknowledging that my strengths lie on the technical side of app development and not on the public-facing business side. It gives me great pleasure to introduce you to our new CEO today, after a long and thorough search in which I can confidently say we have found the best woman for the job. Please join me in congratulating Ms. Athena Owen on her new position at SLICE. I look forward to many years of friendship and collaboration with this incredible mind and force."

Emma stepped back from the microphone, clapping and smiling at Athena as she made her way to the mic for her own speech. Athena looked back at Emma, nodding and smiling as she spoke.

"Thank you for that warm welcome, Emma. I'm thrilled to accept this position at SLICE and eager to get to work continuing the efforts of Ms. Kells. I'd also like to mention, though, a few things that she may have overlooked sharing with you."

Emma tried her best to hide the confusion she was feeling. Athena was deviating from her prepared remarks, and Emma had no idea what was about to happen.

"For one thing, Emma will be staying on in an advisory role. Everything that *is* SLICE exists thanks to her, and we couldn't possibly keep it going without her. And I'd also like to share—" She looked at Emma again, winking with an impish glint in her eye. "—that Emma's revelations about the importance of stepping away from your phone once in a while are in the process of becoming...something special. Another app, perhaps?" She shrugged playfully. "Who's to say? As the brand new CEO of a social media company, it's not in my best interest to encourage anyone to develop healthy boundaries. But as someone who has benefitted from Emma's friendship in the short time I've known her and who is simultaneously preparing for the massive task of filling her shoes...I'll just encourage you to stay tuned. Whatever she's cooking up, it's going to be special."

When the two of them left the stage, Emma pulled Athena into an embrace. "Thank you," she said. "You really didn't have to do that, you know?" She glanced over Athena's shoulder to where Dean was heading their way. "In fact, maybe you shouldn't have. The investors might not appreciate your comments about developing healthy boundaries with social media..."

Athena stepped back, her expression and arm waving dismissive of everything Emma had just said. "Please. If that was all it took for people to put down their phones and go for a walk outside, we wouldn't be in business in the first place." She shook her head. "No, everyone knows we shouldn't be spending so much time glued to our screens; the problem is just that most of us don't have the sheer willpower to actually do what needs to be done. I'm very hopeful that whatever you're creating is going to help those of us who want to be helped."

Emma raised an eyebrow. "Are you including yourself in that number?"

"Of course! Just because I'm getting paid to figure out ways to keep people clicking back to our app doesn't mean I want to see my screen time keep creeping higher day after day."

"Don't we all?"

Emma said her goodbyes to Athena and Dean, shaking a few hands on her way out of the venue. It felt surprisingly light to be walking away from SLICE, like the rare occasion when she wasn't carrying her wallet, keys, phone, and laptop bag. Like she had forgotten something, but also like she had regained some freedom. It felt good. And in that moment, sinking into place, she knew she was ready to move on. This season had been good, but it was, without a doubt, over.

❥ · ❥ · ❥ · ❥ · ❥

"Cheers to your new freedom and good riddance to SLICE, et cetera, et cetera!" Claire raised her beer bottle and nodded in Emma's direction. "How does it feel?"

"Surreal," Emma admitted. "I had forgotten how it felt not to have responsibilities, obligations, and the hopes and fears of a team of investors hanging over my head."

Claire shook her head. "I can't imagine. Are you stressing about money?"

"Surprisingly, I'm not." Emma shook her head, peeling at the label on her beer bottle. "I've got some savings and the money from SLICE. They'll get me by for a few months, especially..." Her voice trailed off as she thought about how to say her next words to Claire.

"Especially what?"

"Especially if I'm not in New York," she said.

Claire sighed. "So you've made your mind up then? You're really leaving."

"I have to," said Emma. "It just doesn't make any sense to stay here, not when there's a laundry list of places I could live for maybe a year on the savings that would last me a month in New York City."

"That makes sense then, I guess. You know you could always stay with me, don't you?"

Emma smiled. "I do, and I just might take you up on that. Maybe in between finding a sub-leaser for my apartment and figuring out where the hell I'm going next, I can crash on your couch?"

"Do you even have to ask?"

Emma's grin broadened. "No, I guess not. Thank you, though."

Claire scoffed. "Yes, because it's such a chore to spend time with my best friend. You'd *better* thank me." A beat passed before her expression changed to one of concern. "Have you told Connor yet? Or thought about what you're going to say to him?"

Emma winced. "I...no. Not really. He's going to be here in two days, and it seems like the kind of conversation we should have face to face."

"I agree. But you're definitely leaving, right? No matter what he decides?"

"I have to. This is the right decision for me, and even if he decides he wants to move to New York, I still can't stay. That's too much pressure on a new relationship, you know? What, would we live together? Paying rent together is a whole hell of a lot different from me crashing at his cottage for a week. And even if I could find another job here, just something to pay the bills while I'm building LIMIT{less}...I think I'm done with this place."

"I respect that...I really do. I know it's tempting to tell him you'll go wherever he is, but...well, that's what was worrying me before. That you'd lose your own inner compass and just follow him wherever he leads."

"There's a time and a place for making all your decisions together with someone else, and that is, I'm pretty sure, after you've known each other for longer than a couple weeks. Probably after you're married."

"Agreed. And even then, the emphasis is on making those decisions *together*, not one of you deciding for both of you."

"Exactly."

Claire's eyes were warm as she smiled at Emma. "So much growth and change these days, Emma. It's hard to keep up with you."

Emma laughed. "That seems to be the season of life I'm in right now, doesn't it?"

"It's just you finding and following your own true north. So cheers to that."

The two friends clinked their glasses. As Emma took a sip, she felt a bubble of uncertainty rising in her stomach. No matter how good it felt to be taking control of her life like this, she couldn't help but wonder what was about to happen with her and Connor. If this was going to be the end, she'd accept it like she'd accepted the end of her relationship with SLICE. But this one...this one would be a lot harder to get over.

# Twenty-Four

I t was finally the day Connor was due to arrive, and Emma was buzzing with excitement.

"*'Finally?'* Is that really what you said?" Claire was teasing her. "Emma, you've been apart from the man for nearly as long as you were with him in the first place, so I'm not really sure you're allowed to say he's *finally* arriving."

Emma rolled her eyes, glad to be talking to Claire on the phone so that her friend couldn't see her facial expression. "You're right," she said, deadpan. "I'm not even sure it's worth being excited at all."

Claire groaned. "Ugh, fine. I guess it's cute that you're happy to see him, and I'd probably be alarmed if you weren't excited at all. I'm just always here to play my role as Debbie Downer in your relationship, should you need me to provide you with that service."

"Gee, thanks! I'm not sure where I could get such a valuable service, so it's awfully kind of you to provide it for me for free."

"I'm not sure I said anything about it being free..."

Emma laughed. "Tell me something new. I've got a few hours to kill before I need to head to the airport, and I'm getting a little stir crazy over here. I've already cleaned the apartment way more thoroughly than I would normally do..."

"Ooh, then I'm sure Connor will be happy with his visit. You know what they say, the way to a man's heart is through a tidy kitchen and clean sheets."

"Okay, I'm seriously regretting calling you," said Emma, though she was laughing despite herself. "As your penance for giving me such a hard time, you definitely owe me an amusing anecdote."

"Hmm...amusing? Let me see what I can do." Claire paused. "Ooh!" she exclaimed at last, "Did I tell you about the real life meet cute I witnessed in the laundry room?"

Emma sat down, making herself comfortable as she settled in for Story Time with Claire. "You most certainly did not! Now spill..."

"Oh, this was some 'straight out of a movie' stuff. Our heroine had detergent but had forgotten to bring dryer sheets. Our hero had fabric softener but no detergent. Now, naturally, I was there too, and I had all the laundry-doing materials one could possibly need. But no, these two were already eyeballing each other well before they realized they held the key to clean clothes heaven between them. Now, naturally, you'd expect the dude without detergent to be the first one to realize the problem, since, you know, you usually wash your clothes before you dry them."

"Let me guess," said Emma. "He was just about to pour fabric softener all over his clothes when she swooped in and saved the day?"

"Ding ding ding!" crowed Claire. "It was adorable. Just before he was about to do it, she placed her hand ever so gently on his forearm and said—I assume, since I couldn't actually hear them—'I don't think you want to do that.' Then there was this whole misunderstanding because he thought she was saying men shouldn't do laundry or something like that...I'm not really sure, honestly, since I'm still writing the dialogue for this part. I need a more compelling misunderstanding, but I'm sure it will come with time."

"Does the story have a happily ever after?"

"The story I'm writing about it definitely does. For those two...I'm hopeful. It definitely has a happily ever after for their clothes, since everybody got to take a bath in both detergent *and* fabric softener. And when I came back to get my clothes out of the dryer, the two of them were there with matching to-go coffee cups, looking a little friendlier than they had when I left. If nothing else, they each got a laundry buddy out of the deal."

"Is that a thing? A laundry buddy?"

"Totally! Wouldn't you look forward to washing your clothes more if there was an attractive person you got to flirt with while doing it?"

"Are you asking if I would literally want to air my dirty laundry with someone I think is hot?" Emma asked. "No! Of course not! That's what audiobooks and podcasts exist for. Leave the flirting for a time when the possibility of encountering period panties isn't so high, thank you very much."

"You make a good point. Okay, I might have to change that in my story. Maybe they're...washing someone else's clothes? Like a nanny washing kids' clothes or an assistant washing their boss's laundry?"

"I think you're grasping, Claire. But keep writing it. If anyone can make that story entertaining, it's you."

It wasn't until Emma was already at the airport, waiting for Connor's arrival, that she noticed something was wrong. On the flight tracking app she used, the path for his plane hadn't ended in New York, but it had turned towards Washington, D.C., and it seemed to be holding steady there, for some reason.

She refreshed the screen a few times, hoping the mistake would correct itself and dismayed to see that everything stayed the same. She texted Connor to double check if what she was seeing was actually what was happening.

Emma: Are you in Washington, D.C. right now?

As soon as she sent the message, she started doubting herself. If Connor was on the plane, it was entirely possible he still had to have his phone switched on airplane mode. Was there another way to find out what was going on?

Thankfully, her questions were answered when her phone dinged a moment later with a new message.

Connor: Yep. We got rerouted. Circled NYC a few times waiting to be able to land (something about the president being in the city and the airspace being secured?) but didn't get permission. Flew to DC to refuel, I guess?

Emma: Wow, that's bizarre. At least it's a short flight from there to here. Any idea when they're going to let you take off?

Connor: We're all still waiting for more information, but I'll let you know when I know something. I hope we make it there in time for my interview.

*Wait...what?* Emma's thoughts were racing. Connor's interview was *today*? The same day he was arriving on an international flight, likely jet-lagged and sleep deprived? What was the man thinking?

Emma: I didn't realize that was today! I'm sure they'll understand if you need to reschedule, but we'll do our best to get you there on time.

Emma put her car back in gear and made her way to the short term parking lot. If she was going to be waiting for Connor for an hour or more, the least she could do was leave her car in an appropriate place and go get a cup of coffee to pass the time. She sensed there was already a security guard or two ready to tell her she needed to move on if she wasn't going to be picking someone up, and she pulled away with a victorious feeling before they could tell her to.

Once her car was parked and she'd found her way into the airport, Emma scanned the directory for the best place to sit this side of security. A coffee chain was a better option than a fast-food restaurant, though she doubted she needed any caffeine right now, as tense as she was feeling both with Connor's delay and his news about the interview.

Why hadn't he told her it was today? Or *had* he told her the date, and she hadn't realized it was today? It didn't matter either way. The fact was, the interview was happening this afternoon—*if* Connor could get here in time. She shuddered at the thought. City driving wasn't her favorite thing to do in the first place—the mere fact that she'd offered to pick Connor up today suggested just how much she actually liked him—but city driving with a time crunch was The Worst.

*It's fine*, she thought to herself. *Whatever happens, I'll just stay cool. I drove here today, didn't I? It's not like I don't know how to drive in the city...* She'd already entered the coffee shop, but she stopped in her tracks before getting into the line as a thought occurred to her. *Am I hoping that his interview will be rescheduled because I don't want to be the one to drive him downtown* or *because I don't want him to get a job in New York in the first place?*

"Great question, me," she muttered under her breath, sliding into the back of the line. It was a question that wouldn't be answered while she waited for Connor, so she resigned herself to sipping on a chai latte while reading a book on her phone.

In between turning digital pages of her novel and sipping on her chai, Emma checked the status of Connor's flight. In the end, the plane stayed on the tarmac in Washington, D.C., for another half an hour after she'd first texted Connor and then headed to New York.

By the time she'd verified—checking and double checking that it was really happening—that his flight was actually coming, Emma wasn't sure how to feel. She wanted to get excited about seeing Connor in such a short time...and yet she was still having a hard time believing that he was going to land this time. What if the plane just circled and circled again before rerouting the flight, this time to...South Dakota?

"It could happen," she grumbled to herself, as she made her way to the meeting point where she'd told Connor she'd be waiting.

But despite her lack of faith, it happened. Twenty minutes later, the airport doors opened, and there, walking towards her like a character from the best kind of dream...was Connor Ryan.

All the stress Emma had been feeling vanished, evaporating from her body like sweat on a hot day, leaving behind only the joy and anticipation of seeing this man, who had somehow gotten even more attractive to her in the time they'd been apart.

His face had split into a broad grin as soon as his eyes had landed on her, and his pace had quickened, too. He closed the distance between them, while Emma got as close to the exit as she could without attracting the attention of another security guard.

When they were within earshot, Emma called out to him. "Hey you," she said, grinning wider than she'd ever done in public. Joy of this level had always been reserved for the privacy of her own room, where no one would see her being too happy and think she was showing off or asking for trouble. But with Connor only an arm's reach away, she didn't care who saw how she felt.

He extended his arms as he took his last few strides, and Emma leaped into them, wrapping her arms around him and nuzzling into his neck. He smelled *good*...better even than she remembered, which seemed incredibly unfair after he'd been on a plane for hours longer than his already long flight. Even more than the smell, though, he felt good. Being in his arms felt like being wrapped in a weighted blanket of comfort and sexiness, and Emma never wanted to let go.

But he did let go at some point, long enough to kiss her and then step back, taking her in from head to toe. "My God, I can't believe how much I've missed you," he said. "It's alarming, frankly." He glanced at his watch and winced. "Ah shite. I'm sorry to do this, Em, but I've got an hour until my interview. Can we catch up on the way there?"

Emma shoved down the emotions that bubbled up as soon as he'd mentioned the interview. Whatever stress she'd thought had vanished like a fart in the breeze was suddenly back in full force. "Sure," she said, forcing a smile onto her face. "You have the address, right? I just need to enter it in my GPS, and we'll cross our fingers that traffic won't be too bad and we'll make it there in time."

"I hadn't thought of that," said Connor. "Here I figured since I'd made it to New York already, there was nothing more to worry about." His brow furrowed in thought. "Do you think I should reschedule?"

Emma was tempted to say yes, to spend the next few hours convincing him the interview wasn't worth taking in the first place...but she reminded herself that this was *his* path to decide, and not hers. "No," she finally said. "We can still make it downtown. Text me the exact address?" She picked up the pace as they left the airport and strode across the street to the parking lot, offering up a silent wish to the traffic fairies to be kind to them today.

Once they had loaded up Connor's things in the trunk of the car, Emma pulled out of the airport and back onto the main road. She kept her eyes focused on the road, but she could feel Connor's gaze turn from the view of the skyline to her profile. He reached over, his hand resting gently on her knee.

"Hi," he said. "Did I actually say that to you?"

Emma smiled. "Maybe not in words, but yeah. You greeted me just perfectly."

"How have you been? I know we've talked and we've texted, but...it still feels like there's a lot to catch up on."

Emma nodded. There *was* a lot to catch up on, but she wasn't about to share all of her revelations while she was trying to stay safe in the highway traffic and keep Connor in good spirits for his interview. She'd try a different approach, for now at least.

"There is!" she agreed brightly. "For example...since the last time I saw you, apparently you've started looking for jobs in the States." She snuck the quickest of glances over at Connor, his eyes darting away and out the window.

"Maybe," he said. "And what about it? Did that make you feel some kind of feelings?"

"Surprise, mostly," she admitted. "I mean, I haven't known you long enough to say I know all your plans for the entire length of your career. I guess it's mostly about the things we talked about...Dublin and the work you did there." She shrugged, keeping her eyes on the road. "It just didn't seem like you missed it. It seemed like you were happy on Inishmore and there wasn't a bone in your body that wanted to get back into the tech field."

"Hmm," Connor murmured, still not turning back from the window. "I can see how that would be confusing. But you're right." He turned his head, his gaze on her profile again. "I suppose it's in part because of the time we spent together. It got me thinking about my career, about the opportunities that might be available...about all that I might be missing by staying on Inishmore, so cut off from the world around me."

The temptation to feel crushed that this was about his career and not about his desire to be near her threatened to overtake Emma like a tidal wave. For all the effort she had put into not making all of her decisions based on this man, she still wanted him to do exactly that for her. What a mess.

Best to keep it light, for now at least. "Ahh, so talking with me about the mess I made of my career made you realize you could do it better?" she teased. "I'm glad to see from the address I'm taking you to that at least you aren't interviewing for my old job at SLICE."

Connor touched her shoulder then, so gently she wondered if he was brushing off a spider. "Emma...no. Nothing like that." He paused, as if he were hesitating to say his next words. "If anything, you inspired me. Your passion, your dedication...I know it's caused you grief, focusing too much on your work at the cost of everything else. But it made me realize I never really gave my all to anything that I did. So maybe I should give it another try?"

So that was it then. She had dared to dream that she had inspired him to love...to let someone into his life and to face the future bravely together, holding hands and supporting each other. But no…as far as he was concerned, the role she had played in his life was to wake him up to his own career potential and nothing more. For a brief bitter moment, she wondered if he even wanted to see her while he was in New York or if he was just being economical by staying with her instead of in a hotel.

*Do not say that out loud*, she warned herself. *Unless you're trying to start major drama. Remember the way he hugged you, that ease that you felt in his arms?*

But it didn't help. Emma couldn't shake the terrible feeling that her heart was about to be broken into a million tiny pieces, and so she did what she would always do in a situation like that. She built her defenses up stronger than they had ever been before, walls and walls of reinforcement around her heart to keep it safe from whatever Connor was about to do.

The rest of the drive was a blur, Emma's attention focused on the road and her responses to Connor coming as if she were operating on autopilot. She had pasted a smile on her face, and she was enthusiastically agreeing with whatever he told her about the job he was interviewing for. The protective wall around her heart was being built brick by brick, and even though she knew she shouldn't, Emma felt proud of herself for how strong it was becoming. Even with someone she cared about as much as Connor, she was still in control. And even if it hurt her in the process, being strong was something she would always be proud of herself for.

When they arrived in front of the office building, Emma pulled over to drop Connor off. "Good luck," she said, smiling. "Do you want me to wait for you?"

Connor shook his head. "I don't know how long it'll be, and I can't ask you to wait. Why don't you go on home, text me the address, and I'll take a cab there?"

Inside, Emma withered even farther. He didn't even want her to wait. With every passing moment, she felt more and more like a friend whose apartment he was crashing at than a partner who was on this journey with him. "Sure," she said, putting the car back in drive. "I'll see you there." As soon as he closed the door, she drove away, refusing to look back at him in the rearview mirror.

# Twenty-Five

**B**ack in her apartment, Emma was pacing. It wasn't going to be easy, having Connor here for a week, and her mind was racing with options. Should she fake an urgent meeting out of town—ooh, or a family emergency?—and leave him the keys to her apartment, only returning after he was gone? No, lying wasn't the way to go, and involving her family in her lie felt wrong on too many levels. Should she make up a bed on the couch and insist that he sleep there? Or sleep there herself, with some excuse about how early she needed to get up in the morning?

No, no matter which way she sliced it, it seemed like Emma was going to have to talk to Connor about this. She groaned, picking up her phone to call Claire.

As soon as she touched her phone, however, she realized there was a notification on the screen that she had missed. A text from Connor.

Connor: I got the job! Picking up a bottle of champagne to celebrate. Anything else you want?

Emma groaned, head in her hands. This was happening then. She had been holding out hope that maybe the job wouldn't pan out, and he'd reveal he didn't actually want it in the first place, and then the two of them would live happily ever after, like in one of Claire's stories.

Speaking of Claire, she'd better get her on the phone quickly, because Connor was on his way already. Unless...

Emma: That's great, congrats! I think this calls for cake, too. Don't you?

Connor responded with a thumbs up emoji, buying Emma at least enough time for her best friend to talk some sense into her.

She called Claire in a panic, her frayed nerves bathed in relief when she answered on the second ring. "Emma! You're supposed to be with Connor, aren't you? What's going on?" Claire asked.

The words rushed out of Emma faster than she could contain them. "He got the job, and he's on his way here now. Claire, I'm freaking out!"

"Whoa whoa. Okay there...I guess his interview was today, huh? Dang, that's soon."

"You're not joking. I took him straight there from the airport."

"Wow. You drove downtown for him? You must really like this guy, Emma."

"I do, but that's not the point!" Emma was exasperated. "The point is that he got a job here and I...I'm leaving. I can't stay in New York any longer. I'm putting up a listing for a sub-leaser as soon as I can, and I'm getting out of here.

But of course I haven't told Connor any of that, and now I'm going to totally ruin his celebration by springing it on him..."

"Emma," Claire cut her off. "You're spiraling. Life is like this, isn't it? Great things and terrible things happen at the same time, and sometimes something that's really awesome news for one person is a heartbreaking mess for another one. It's okay that life is still going to go on, even on the day that he got offered a job. Don't work yourself up into a froth, okay? You don't even know if he wants to take the job."

"Of course he's going to, Claire. Are you kidding? He'd be insane not to. I looked up the salary for that role online, and he would be doing really well there. Like...living in Manhattan well."

Claire whistled. "Wow, good for him. I'm still not convinced, though. The man already left one 'really good' job in Dublin for the simple life on Inishmore. I think it's going to take more than a fat salary to convince him."

Emma groaned. "Why are you so optimistic? Are you trying to convince me to get my hopes up just so I get crushed when he tells me the truth? It's not happening, friend. I'm preparing for the worst without hoping for the best. You're welcome to hope, but it's never served me particularly well."

"I get that," said Claire. "Still, if there's a way you can stay at least *kind of* neutral until you know all the information, that would be the ideal way to go, now wouldn't it?"

"Sure," agreed Emma. "But who can do that? If you were me...if we were talking about your future with someone you loved, would you be neutral?"

"Wow," said Claire.

"I know. I bet you hadn't thought about it like that, had you?"

Emma could practically hear Claire shaking her head through the phone. "You don't even know what you said, do you? You said *love*, Emma. That's huge. I knew you liked him a lot...I knew you were making plans for a future together, even. But for you to drop a love bomb...I get it. I get that this is hard for you."

Emma was stunned into silence. Sure, she had used the word "love," but she'd been talking about Claire and the hypothetical love of her hypothetical life...right? "Th...thanks?" she said to Claire. "Listen, I'm a mess. Can you come over?"

"No way. Maybe tomorrow after the two of you have talked. As much as this would probably be great material for my next novel, you have to realize it would be a whole new level of awkward if I were there with the two of you today."

"I guess you're right," admitted Emma.

"Of course I am! You can do this, Emma. They're just words. It's just your heart. Things might be wonderful or they might be terrible, but no matter what, they won't be boring. Aren't you grateful for that?"

Emma croaked out a humorless laugh. "That's one way of looking at it. I'll talk to you later about tomorrow. Either it will be a fun time with me and Connor, an awkward time with me and Connor, or a 'tears in your mimosa' time with just me."

"Either way, I wouldn't miss it. Love you, friend."

"Love you, too."

♥ • ♥ • ♥ • ♥ • ♥

Once she was off the phone with Claire, Emma went into full Rocky mode preparing herself for Connor's return. There were no stairs for her to sprint up or punching bags for her to box, but between the pacing, the bookshelf straightening, and the checking-out-the-window, she was expending probably the same amount of energy as Rocky had done.

Finally, on one of her glances out the window, she caught sight of Connor getting out of a taxi, shopping bags in hand. Emma's heart caught in her throat. This was it. The calm before the storm, the last few moments of peace before everything changed. For right now, watching him get out of the taxi, looking up at the buildings around him to spot which one was hers, she could imagine that this was their life. That he would have a key to her apartment, let himself in, prepare meals together, sleep in on the weekends...that life here could be as good as the life they'd shared during that dream they'd spent together on Inishmore.

As it became clearer from the way he was looking around and glancing down at the phone in his hand that Connor did not know where she lived, Emma pulled herself out of her reverie. As tempting as it was to let him stay down there indefinitely, to have the awkward conversation by default instead of face to face, she opened the window and waved. "I'm pretty sure breaking up with someone by letting them stand out in the street lost until they eventually go away is the lowest of the low," she told herself, as she put on a smile for Connor. His face had nearly cracked in two, so large was the grin on it when he finally spotted her. She gestured to the door down below her window, then went to the intercom in the kitchen to buzz him in.

Emma left the door ajar as she busied herself again. This time it was the top shelf of the dishwasher that needed rearranging.

The door squeaked on its hinges as Connor pushed it the rest of the way open. With just his head peeking in the door, he asked, "Emma? Is this the right apartment? This is New York City, after all...I know better than to just waltz on in."

Despite herself, despite the stress threatening to spill out of her eyes and all over the floor, Emma chuckled. "It is, and I promise not to use all my extensive martial arts training on you. Not this time, at least."

He crossed the floor in a few long strides, pulling Emma into his arms and planting a kiss on her like they hadn't already reunited at the airport. Despite herself, she felt his presence come over her like a blanket, calming her and dulling the sensation of the rest of the world. *What stress? Who, me, stressed? Couldn't be.*

It wasn't until he stepped back, holding her at arm's length, that she snapped back to reality. "Let me look at you," Connor said, drinking her in with his eyes. "God, how I've missed that face."

Emma grimaced, hoping to pass it off as a smile, and pulled out of his reach, back to busying herself in the kitchen. "I've missed you, too," she said over her shoulder, as she rearranged everything she had just placed in the dishwasher. "So tell me about your interview today. Congratulations again!"

Connor came behind her, encircling her with his arms and stopping her hands from the arranging and rearranging they were doing. "Come on now, love. Can't these wait until later? Come sit with me. Talk with me." He pulled lightly on her wrist, taking her out of reaching distance from the dishwasher.

"You're right," said Emma, turning to the cabinet. "We need glasses for champagne, right?" She started pulling different glasses out of the cupboard. "I don't have champagne flutes because I'm not fancy like that, but take your pick. We've got wine glasses, coffee mugs..."

Connor was still standing pressed up against her back, and he reached a long arm around her, picking up two small tumblers in one large hand. "Honestly, we could drink it straight out of the bottle or pour it on the floor and lap it up like kittens. I just care about you." He tugged her gently out of the room. "Now let's skip the tour for now and why don't you just steer me towards a sofa and a coffee table?"

In the living room, Emma sat next to Connor on the couch while he unwrapped the foil at the end of the champagne bottle. He loosened the wire cage from the cork, pointing the bottle so that no breakables were in its line of attack and so that it wouldn't spill on her nice couch, Emma noted with a pang of bittersweet affection. He really was a good man, and not just for the way he opened a bottle and the fact that he had some foresight and a basic understanding of physics. It was everything...the complete package, if you will, but the closer their conversation about his new job came, the closer the end of *them* came.

Emma was lost in those thoughts, already mourning something she hadn't even lost yet, when Connor lifted her chin, directing her eyes to his and calling her out of the dark storm of sadness that had pulled her in. "Where are you? What's going on? Are you...are you angry with me?"

She shook her head quickly, desperate to reassure him. "No, Connor. I couldn't be. I'm just...tired, I think." She watched as he poured the champagne into two glasses, handing one to her and raising the other in her direction. "Why don't you tell me about the job?"

"Well, first of all, we definitely need a toast. You can't drink—" He checked the label of the champagne and made a face. "You can't drink *ChamPeach* without a toast." He turned the bottle around in his hand, checking the label. "Did I, in fact, buy the cheapest, most juvenile and furthest thing from champagne that actually exists?" Reading further, he nodded. "Yes. Yes, I definitely did do that." He shrugged. "Oh well. I'm here for the company, not for the drinks."

Emma smiled. At least they weren't drinking the finest champagne in the world, something that would make her sad later when she recalled the first time tasting it had been right before a painful heartbreak. She lifted her glass higher. "To your new job," she said.

A hint of an unidentifiable emotion passed over his face—was that disappointment? "We can do better than that. It's just a job offer, after all." He smiled at her again, as if he were taking a moment to drink in the very sight of her before he spoke again. "Here's to all the unexpected ways you and I find to be together. May they keep on coming."

"Cheers to that," said Emma, clinking her glass against his softly. She had serious doubts they'd be doing a lot of finding each other unexpectedly once Connor was in New York and she was in the cheapest, least New York City place she could find. She raised her eyes to his. "So, are you going to tell me about the job yet, or are you going to keep me in suspense forever?"

"I'll tell you," said Connor with a small smile. "It's not a big deal. I just started looking to see what positions were out there, sending CVs to the ones that seemed like a good fit for my qualifications and experience."

"Yeah," said Emma. "I still can't wrap my head around it, you wanting to return to the workforce, and in New York, of all places. What changed?"

Connor shrugged, but he wouldn't quite meet her eyes. "It just seemed like maybe I was a little too young to retire. Like there's still potential for me and I may as well build my resume now while I've only been out of the workforce for a spell. Too much longer, and everything I know might be irrelevant."

"That makes sense, I guess," said Emma. "So what is the position like? The one you were offered today?"

Connor took another drink from his tumbler. "It's pretty much exactly what I was doing in Dublin, to be honest."

That surprised Emma. Hadn't the work he'd been doing in Dublin caused his burnout? His total retreat from the city? "Is...is that a good fit for you?" she asked. "I thought..."

"I know," said Connor. "I thought so, too. When I read the job description and saw all the overlapping responsibilities, I nearly deleted it from my list immediately. But they've assured me the company culture is very different here...that people actually honor the weekends and use their vacation days. Plus, it gives me the chance to be in a new city, a new country even."

"That makes sense," Emma agreed. "I just wanted to make sure it was really what you wanted, but...yeah. I guess it makes sense." She smiled again, her facial muscles feeling even more forced every time she raised them into an approximation of a grin. "Well, if it's what you want, then I'm happy for you."

Connor moved closer to her on the couch, putting his arm around her and looking into her eyes. "It is. I've missed you so much, and it hardly seemed reasonable to sit and wait for you to find your way back to Inishmore." He looked down as if he were feeling embarrassed. "The truth is, I looked for jobs in New York because of you."

Emma gulped down the rest of her champagne—or ChamPeach—and pulled away from Connor. "That's really sweet of you, but please don't feel like you need to make a big life change because of me."

Connor shook his head. "No, don't take it like that. I'm not trying to scare you off, Emma. I just...I don't know. I thought this was the only way of giving us a fair chance at being a couple. Flying back and forth just to spend a few weeks together hardly seems like the best place to begin a relationship, does it?"

"It doesn't, but..." Emma trailed off, biting her lip. *Rip it off like a bandage,* she told herself. *Stop teasing the man and tell him the truth.* "Well, it might still end up being long distance," she finally said. "I'm not staying in New York."

"You...what?" Connor's face was the picture of puzzlement. "Why not? Where are you going? What happened? Is this about me? Did I scare you away?"

"It's not you." Emma shook her head. "Without my job at SLICE and without even the nominal salary they were talking about paying me...there's just nothing for me here and this city is so damn expensive. I'm honestly kind of done with it here."

Connor was silent, his eyes not fully focusing as he looked through her, it seemed. "Do you know where you're moving?"

Emma shook her head. "Not yet. It just happened...losing my salary, I mean. I've got savings to live on while I figure things out, but they'll last me a lot longer if I'm someplace other than here."

"That's probably true." Connor was nodding. "Huh. Wow. Okay."

"I'm sorry for not telling you sooner," said Emma. "I didn't think it would be a great thing to spit out in the car while we were on the way to your interview."

Connor shrugged. "I get it, I do. It makes sense. I just...I'm not really sure what to do now, to be honest."

Emma grabbed both of his hands, staring him down with imploring eyes. "You can't...don't change your mind because of me, Connor. You've got to do what's best for you and for your career. I just didn't want you to make the decision to move here because of me. I was kind of afraid of that, actually," she admitted.

Connor was quick to shake his head. "No, no. It wasn't because of you. I mean, sure. I was aware that you lived in New York, but it's a big city, so it's not like I thought we'd see each other every day or anything like that. I meant what I said about getting back into the business and sharpening my skills. And I'm sure there are all sorts of things New York has to offer that I couldn't get on Inishmore."

"Good then," said Emma, smiling weakly. "It seems like that's settled, then." A thought occurred to her, brightening her spirits a fraction. "We could still see each other, you know. It doesn't have to be over just because I'm not here. I've still got friends in the city, and wherever I go, I'm sure there will be flights to New York...or cars to drive here if I'm closer."

Connor shrugged again, but he wasn't speaking.

Emma plowed ahead. "And I'd do anything I can to help you settle in." She looked around the living room of her apartment. "You could even sub-lease this apartment from me if you wanted to. It's really hard to find places to live in New York, as I'm sure you know, so..."

"Thanks," said Connor, though it was obvious from his tone that he didn't mean it. *Here it comes,* thought Emma. *The end. The bubble has burst. The fire has burned out. There will be no survivors. There will be no long distance love for us, just memories of the beautiful and short time we shared.*

"I just want you to be happy," she told him, squeezing his arm. "That's more important to me than anything else. Be happy with your job, live somewhere nice, and...oh my

God!" She squeezed his arm tighter as a thought occurred to her. "What about Lady? Connor, I don't think this apartment allows dogs. Is she moving to New York with you? What is she going to do if you leave her behind? You couldn't do that, could you?"

Connor took a deep breath, closing his eyes as if drawing the strength for his next words from deep within. "If I move to New York..." His blue eyes found Emma's, piercing deep into her being as he continued. "And the key word there is *if*. But if I move to New York, Lady will be coming with me. But maybe now we should talk about why you seem so determined to cut me out of your life?" His gaze turned sad, his expression vacant. "What's going on, Emma? Did I do something wrong? I'm trying to make a grand gesture here, but it seems like everything I do is wrong."

# Twenty-Six

Emma put her head in her hands. "Honestly, Connor, I'm so confused. What are you even talking about, grand gesturing? I just...I'm just so freaking tired. This is all really overwhelming, and it's honestly been hard enough to figure out what the hell I'm doing with my career without even beginning to think about us. Sorry. It's just the truth, though. It's not like I don't care about you a lot...I'm just trying not to run out of money in this city and end up on the street."

Connor moved closer to her. "Is it that bad, really?"

Emma nodded. "Yes...no. I don't know. I might be over-reacting. I've just...I've never been here before, you know? I always had something lined up, from university to my internship right to my own business. Now, it's all opening up in front of me and I don't have the first clue what I'm supposed to do next."

"I get that," said Connor. "I think that's similar to how I felt when I left Dublin. Like I had the whole world of options open up in front of me and it was exciting...but at the same time, it was too much. Like I had all these choices, but none of them would ever be as good as the one I had given up."

Emma laughed. "Yeah, there's that, too. There's this part of me that's consumed with regret, thinking this would all be so much easier if I hadn't blown things at SLICE...if I still had a job."

"But would you be happy? Were you happy when you worked there?"

Emma shook her head fervently. "No. I know this is for the best. I know it deep in my bones, but there's still this part of me, closer to the surface, I guess, that hasn't gotten the memo. It's the part of me that craves certainty, or that at least wants to know where my next paycheck is coming from."

Connor sat silently with her, his arm still around her shoulders, his hand stroking up and down her upper arm. "What a mess of a time for us to meet then, hey?"

Emma turned to him, startled by something she heard in his voice. "I don't regret that, not at all. I hope you know that." She gazed up into his eyes, her hand finding its way to his cheek of its own accord. "None of this is about regretting you."

He placed his hand over hers, smiling gently but sadly. "I know that, I really do. But it would make sense to regret meeting me when you did. Especially when I show up here with the grand gesture while you're still trying to figure things out."

Emma shook her head. "It's not regret, but there's some sadness there. It feels inevitable to me that this whole mess of time and space and geography is going to tear us apart or never let us be together in the first place, and that feels awful."

"Is that why it felt like you were trying to push me away?" Connor asked, his eyes dropping from hers as he waited for her answer.

"Yeah. Definitely," said Emma. "It would be easier to say goodbye if we weren't that attached, so I tried to convince both of us that we weren't, I guess." She chuckled timidly. "Um...did it work?"

His eyes flew back up to hers. "Not at all. I'm definitely still attached." He shook his head. "But I can't be the cause of nothing but stress in your life. So just for the next few minutes, I want you to do a little thought experiment with me, okay?"

"Okay..." Emma was hesitant, but she trusted him.

"Okay." Connor took a deep breath. "Just...imagine this with me, okay? Close your eyes if it helps. And maybe try to forget that it's me talking to you."

Emma laughed out loud at that. "And who should I imagine is talking to me, if not you? I don't exactly have a wealth of men with Irish accents talking to me on a daily basis."

"That's fair." Connor thought for a moment. "Let's say it's Colin Farrell then. Does that work for you?"

"Oh, that definitely works for me." She closed her eyes and settled back on the sofa. "Carry on, then."

She could practically hear Connor shaking his head at her. "Okay, then. You're free. The job that was stifling your life, your health and your creativity...it's gone. Poof! Plucked out of your life like an errant weed in a beautiful garden. You can go anywhere. You can do anything you want to do. There's nothing holding you back...no commitments, no attachments. You're free. The whole world is stretching in front of you like the cereal aisle at an American grocery store. You can pick anything you want, no consequences. Well, I suppose that's not true of the cereal, unless you're particularly fond of jacking up your blood sugar, but I digress. What do you want? With all the options out there, what do you want to choose?"

Emma was silent. By some miracle, she'd actually been able to go on that journey in her mind, probably even further than Connor had intended. She was in a blank white room, like the loading screen in The Matrix movies, with places and jobs and people filing before her without end. There were so many places, the whole world in fact, that she could explore. And she had skills, she knew that. She could throw away the whole LIMIT{less} idea and get a job within a week. But she also had a really good feeling about the app, and more than that, she really *wanted* to see what it could become. She felt herself smiling. This was an exciting reality, not a scary one. She could do work she believed in, without any sense of dread hanging over her, reminding her she needed to pay her sky high rent or live up to the expectations anyone had for her.

It felt like freedom, and Emma was surprised and relieved to find she could still remember what that felt like.

"You're smiling," said Connor. "I guess that's a good thing?"

His voice brought Emma back to the moment, asking her another question. In this vision of her new future, was she alone, living her best empowered single lady life? Or was there someone by her side? Without even realizing she had asked herself the question, she already had her answer. She wanted Connor. The time they had spent together on Inishmore had been the catalyst for all the growth that was currently happening, and she knew there was further the two of them could go together.

And it wasn't just that. She loved him. She loved being with him, feeling safe in his arms, laughing with him, and being inspired by the person he was. He was brave, leaving the known and stable career in Dublin behind for a simple life without any glamor, flare, or fame. He was good and kind and humble, working behind a bar, helping his family, and taking care of his dog like she was the most noble being on the planet. And wasn't she? Didn't Emma miss Lady enough to justify flying back to Ireland right this very moment?

Emma blinked her eyes open to find Connor giving her space. He wasn't staring at her face like his future hung in the balance. No, he was sitting back, hands in his lap, studying them while he waited for her to come back into the room.

"Wow," she said. "That was...amazing. Where did you learn to do that?"

Connor shrugged. "I'm not convinced I ever did. I just talked you through my own decision-making process, and I'm glad it sounds like it worked." His face was sheepish, his eyes on his lap. "I had to do something like that with myself to figure out I needed to leave Dublin. It wasn't until I figured out what I wanted...and could actually be honest with myself about it that I knew I had to go. But that was after spending months and months in denial."

Emma sighed. "I probably should have made a change months and months ago, too." She looked at him, waiting for him to meet her eyes. "Where were you then? I could have used an exercise like this...or *all* the pep talks you've given me in the short time I've known you, if I'm being honest."

He gave her a small smile. "I've been around."

Emma picked up a pillow and tossed it at him playfully. "You've been on a remote island off the coast of Ireland, you goofball. You didn't exactly make it easy to find you."

He caught the pillow and tossed it back. "But you did, didn't you?"

Emma sobered up at his words. "I did. And I'm really glad I did." She fell silent, unsure how to tell him what she had realized about herself, her future, and his role in it.

Finally, he broke the silence. "So, what did you learn? If you want to share, of course. I just...I noticed you were smiling, so I figured it was something good." He grinned at her. "Tell me, then. What does the future hold for Emma Kells?"

"Well." Where to even begin? "For one thing, I'm happy about leaving SLICE. No regret, just relief. And..." She examined Connor's face to see his reaction to her next words. "I'm happy to be leaving New York, too. This city isn't for me anymore and I couldn't stay here, not even for you."

Connor nodded, resigning himself to what was coming, no doubt. The other shoe falling.

"But." Emma reached over, taking his hands in her own, her thumbs rubbing the backs of his hands. "But that doesn't mean I don't appreciate the grand gesture. Maybe...maybe it could just look different."

Connor perked up at that. "What do you mean?"

Emma shrugged. "I'm honestly not sure. When I was visualizing that ideal future that made me happy, there were so many beautiful places I could be. They were swirling past me like someone was flipping through a photo album at vertigo-inducing speeds."

"Any of them jump out at you? If it's not too intense, I'd pretty much go anywhere to be with you." He pulled a face as he heard the words come out of his mouth. "Too much?"

"Almost," said Emma. "And it would definitely be too much if I weren't about to ask something just as crazy."

"Oh yeah? What's that?"

"What if Ireland was the place that jumped out at me? The one I wanted to spend more time getting to know?"

Connor's grin was blinding. "Really? And why is that?" He put on a serious face, but it didn't succeed in hiding his playfulness. "Is this about reconnecting with your ancestors? Because I don't know much about that, but..."

"Yes, it's 100 percent about that and nothing else." Emma rolled her eyes. "No, of course I think the old Emerald Isle is magical, but it's a lot more about the people I met there, you know? It just feels like we're not done yet."

"It's about Lady, isn't it? I tell her every day that she's the best dog out there, but I just don't think she believes me. Now, if you move across an ocean just to be near her, I think she might finally get the message."

"It's *definitely* about Lady." Emma let Connor pull her into an embrace, their kisses ending any further playful banter between them. When she needed a breath, Emma pulled back. "You know it's about you, too, right? I mean...no offense to Lady, but it's mostly about you."

Shock and affront covered Connor's face. "Really? Wow, she'll be crushed." He smiled then, kissing her once more. "No, in all seriousness, that's the sweetest thing I've ever heard. And I'm glad to hear you're just as crazy about me as I am about you."

"No, but seriously," said Emma. "Moving to New York for me? That was almost certifiable."

Connor raised an eyebrow. "But you moving to Ireland is different?"

Emma nodded. "Of course! Have you seen how beautiful Ireland is?" A sideways smile crossed her face. "I'm sorry to tell you this, sir, but this move is not only about being near you. Getting to explore Ireland is also a major perk."

"I respect your opinion," said Connor. "And for what it's worth, I would have found things to enjoy in New York besides you."

"I'm sure you would have," agreed Emma. "But I think it would have been more of a challenge for you. Nothing against New York, but you don't exactly seem like a big city kind of guy."

Connor shivered as he shook his head. "Is it that obvious? For you, though, I could have made the best of it."

♥ · ♥ · ♥ · ♥ · ♥

It wasn't until a few hours later that the topic of what Emma was going to do for work in Ireland came up. They were lying in bed, tangled up in the sheets and basking in the sleepiness that had overtaken them both after a handful of very stressful days.

"You know," said Connor, stroking Emma's hair. "I hate to break the moment and all its peace and wonderfulness, but at some point we'll have to think about what we're going to do, career-wise, I mean."

"Hmm," agreed Emma, her eyes drifting closed. "That's a good point. You don't mind if I crash at your cottage, do you? I'm guessing there aren't a lot of places for rent on Inishmore."

"I gave you a key already, didn't I? It'd be pretty strange if I told you not to use it now."

"That's true." Emma pursed her lips in thought. "I still didn't want to assume."

He kissed her on the head. "While I do love that about you, I assure you it's not necessary. What's mine is yours, and all that."

"Especially that hurling shirt," Emma teased. "Though I'm pretty sure that's just mine now."

"We'll see. I might wear it again one of these days. I reserve the right to do so, you know."

"Indeed," agreed Emma. "You can think that all you want, but let's see how it actually works out for you."

Connor placed another kiss on her forehead. "Are we really doing this? You, me, and Lady? What are you going to do for work?" He sputtered, stumbling over his words. "Not that you have to work, I mean. I won't charge you rent or anything like that. I just figured, you know...it might be a bit hard for a—no offense—workaholic like yourself to quit cold turkey. Do you have something in mind?"

Emma grinned broadly. "I can't believe we haven't talked about this yet! Oh my gosh, yes, I have the perfect thing in mind. I'm already working on it, actually." She had been talking about LIMIT{less} a lot lately, it was true, but getting the chance to explain the whole concept—and to someone who was as interested as Connor seemed to be—was a real treat.

When she finished, he was silent for a moment. Finally, he shook his head and murmured a soft, "Wow." Peering into her eyes, he continued. "You amaze me, you know that? When you lost your job, you were knocked down for...what...a day? I mean, you practically embody the whole 'when life gives you lemons, make lemonade' idea. When I left my job in Dublin, you don't even want to know how long I wallowed and felt sorry for myself."

"A long time?"

He nodded. "I might still be wallowing, if not for you."

"How do you mean?"

"Oh, I mean...I was going through the motions just fine, you know? I'm sure you saw it in my stellar bartending the first time we met. I was doing everything that needed doing, but I wasn't exactly the picture of happiness, domestic bliss, and having actual ambitions in life."

She elbowed him lightly in the ribs. "You could have fooled me. That pep talk you gave me the first night?"

"The night we slept side by side, holding hands in my bed?"

"That's the one. That pep talk is at least part of the reason I bounced back as quickly as I did. If not for all the things we shared, and the life you introduced me to...I might still think my work was the most important thing about me."

Connor pulled her close, nuzzling into her next with soft kisses. "That would be a real shame, you know that?"

"Mmm," Emma murmured. "I do now." She pulled back far enough that she could see both of his eyes. "So tell me what you think about LIMIT{less}. Other than that I'm brilliant, I mean. Your professional opinion, if you will."

"If I were a gambling man, I would not have placed any amount of money on you asking me for my professional opinion. Not today, and probably not ever."

"Why not? You were the one taking a job interview, if you can recall that far back."

"Five hours ago? Believe it or not, I think I can." He shook his head, clearing his mind. "No, it's just strange, that's all. I dusted off that old professional identity of mine for the job search. Very begrudgingly, I might add, doing it only because I thought of it as a means to an end." He lifted her hand to his mouth, placing kisses across her knuckles. "That end being spending more time with you, of course."

"Of course."

"And I'm relieved that a corporate job in New York City isn't in my near future. Definitely."

"I sense there's a 'but' coming..."

He smiled. "Good intuition, that one." Staring her down, his eyes got serious. "But how would you feel about having some help in the inbound marketing department for LIMIT{less}?"

"Are you joking? I can't tell. You know, you really make way too many jokes, especially during serious moments."

"I'll note that down on my to-do list for future self improvements. But I'm actually serious this time. All the work I did in the tech field, all of it was to do with search engines and directing traffic to the best possible places. I could help you set up a strategy for search engine optimization, content marketing, email campaigns..."

Emma was dumbfounded. "And you would do that?"

"Of course. In a heartbeat."

"I mean, you would do that without feeling icky about getting back into this field you so happily left?"

Connor chuckled. "Well, I've *never* described my feelings as being 'icky' so I'm pretty sure I could continue not to. But no, really. For you, I would do this gladly. Without a single ounce of regret or frustration or ickiness about working in front of a computer again." He winked at her with a cheeky grin. "I'm pretty sure I'd even enjoy it."

"Really? Why?"

"Is it really that hard for you to believe you've come up with an idea that's that inspiring? Because that's a huge part of it. I love what you're doing, and it's a mission I can get on board with, unlike the mission of that company from earlier today, which we shall never speak about again. But it's you, too. You have to know that. If there's anything I can do to help you, I'm all yours. I'm not holding out any of my skills from you, not even the ones that are a little rusty and under-used these days."

Emma pulled him closer, wiggling her eyebrows. "Not *any* of your skills?"

He laughed, pressing his smile against hers in the first of many kisses. "Not a single one."

# Twenty-Seven

"**A**re you sure you want to come to the pub today?" Connor asked Emma at the door of the cottage. It was one year to the day since she had first arrived on Inishmore. "I know you wanted to get some things done around here before Claire arrives tomorrow. You can take the day off."

Emma pushed past him out the door. "I already told you it's a done deal. You really think I'm going to stay at home and sit in front of my laptop all day?" She scoffed. "You don't know me as well as you claim to if you think that's what's happening."

"Fair enough then, suit yourself." Connor put his arm around her shoulders as they walked away from the cottage. "It's still strange to me not to see you working any chance you get."

She elbowed him in the ribs. "Come on, now. You knew that version of me for, what...a couple of weeks? I've been *so* much better about the whole work life balance thing in these last months."

"Mmm hmm, sure. If you say so." Connor's lips were pulled into a straight line, his eyes shining mischievously. "I mean, yes, I can readily admit that you're much better about boundaries when it comes to *your* work..."

Emma rolled her eyes. "Oh, come on. So I like helping out at the pub. Is that really so terrible?"

"Not at all." He pulled her in and kissed her on the head before they went to opposite sides of the truck to climb into the cab. "But I *was* thinking we should take an actual weekend off soon. Let Patrick run the place for a few days."

"Oh, really?" Emma raised her eyebrows at her boyfriend. "What did you have in mind?"

Putting the truck in gear, he pulled away from the cottage and began ambling toward the town. "Galway, if that sounds good to you. Or what about a weekend in Dublin? You still haven't been there, have you?"

"Really? I thought that would be the last place you'd want to go."

Connor shrugged. "I'm open to the possibility that just because I didn't like the job I had in Dublin doesn't mean the entire city is a lost cause."

"Wow. I mean...wow." She stuck out her tongue at him. "That's some real progress. Seriously."

"So does that settle it, then? Dublin in January?"

Emma smiled at him, overcome by the bliss and peace of the moment, of every moment since she'd taken her one-way flight back to Ireland. "It does. Do you want me to ask Patrick? Lay on a little guilt trip?"

One side of Connor's mouth lifted in a smirk. "Why do you offer? Do you really think I can't guilt my own brother into covering the pub for me for a weekend?"

"I just think a feminine touch might go a little better than you putting him in a headlock. I'm sure he'll feel like it's his duty as an Irishman to make sure I get to see as much of the country as possible. He'll do it either way, if I know Patrick, but maybe this way he'll do it with a smile on his face." She shrugged.

Connor shook his head as a soft laugh escaped his lips. "If it's up to you, there'll be nothing but boring old peace in the Ryan family gatherings. Where's the excitement in that?"

"I'm sure you can think of other ways to make your life more exciting." She rolled her eyes. "Have you thought any more about opening another pub in Galway?"

Connor nodded. "I have. It's not a bad idea at all...it's definitely got me thinking. And don't think I didn't notice what you did there, bringing it up right after we were talking about adding excitement to our lives."

"It would certainly be a way of keeping things fresh, for you and for Patrick. The two of you could take turns working here or working in Galway..."

"And I'm sure you wouldn't mind spending more time in Galway, either." He raised an eyebrow in her direction.

"I'm happy on Inishmore, to be honest. Happier than I expected to be, that's for sure. But I do think I might need a little more city action in my life, you know?"

Connor nodded. "I was thinking exactly that. After New York, I know it's nice to have a break from all the hustle and bustle. But I sure don't want you to get bored and leave me because you can't handle life on the island."

Emma reached over and put a hand on his knee. "It would take a lot more than boredom to get me to leave you." She smiled, squeezing his kneecap playfully. "I mean, at the very least, I would let you know before something like that ever happened."

"Oh, would you?"

"Definitely. It would be all complaints about how there's no movie theater on the island or how you never take me out anywhere to dinner..."

"We had dinner at the pub twice this week!"

Emma rolled her eyes. "You know that's not what I mean, but good cover, lover boy. No, I think you're already tuned in. Wasn't Dublin your idea after all?"

Connor's mouth closed abruptly, like a fish gulping air. "Maybe," he mumbled.

"So have no fear, then. A weekend away here and there works just fine for now. And if we end up going to Galway regularly in the near future, well...I won't be complaining about that at all."

Connor squeezed her hand before moving his back to the gearshift. "That's why I suggested it, love. I'm just giving you a hard time."

At the pub, Patrick was already waiting for them. He'd prepped everything for the impending arrival of their first wave of customers, and he was back in the kitchen making a big pot of potato soup and getting an assembly-line style set-up prepared for the orders of fish and chips that would be coming in shortly.

He looked up from the lemon he was slicing wedges, then glanced pointedly at the clock on the wall. "About time the two of you showed up," he scowled. "If you want me to run the place myself, why don't you just say it?" He winked at Connor before turning his attention back down to the sharp knife in his hand.

"I'm pretty sure she's onto us, Patrick," said Connor. "You can drop the act. You're still working this weekend, right?"

"Of course. What else would I be doing?"

Emma frowned in confusion. "Wait, what? I thought you were just covering tomorrow, when we are picking up Claire and bringing her back here. The whole weekend?"

Patrick nodded. "Yep, I'm running the show for the next few days while you two—" He gestured towards them with the knife in his hand. "—pick up Claire and get tour boat things squared away in Galway and Connor gets ready for his big romantic gesture." He looked up abruptly, a devilish grin on his face. "Whoops. Have I said too much?"

Emma looked at Connor's face, but all she could find there was a glare directed at his brother. "Perhaps," he said through gritted teeth.

Patrick shrugged. "You're the one who told *me*, of all people. You should know by now I'm the world's worst secret keeper." He winked at Emma. "So, Emma...if there's anything you'd like to know..."

"That's enough," interjected Connor, steering Emma away from his brother and back to the front of the pub.

"The two of you don't need to be talking to each other again today, do you?" He continued speaking without giving Emma a chance to answer. "Good, that's settled then."

Emma's mind was racing a mile a minute. The fact that Connor and Patrick already had a plan in place wasn't inherently meaningful...maybe the two of them had actually just thought ahead for once in their lives. No, that wasn't true, and she knew she was lying to herself. Something big was happening this weekend. Bigger than Connor setting up a tour boat company? What was all that about? That was already huge, and she was only now realizing that she hadn't *exactly* known that was happening.

"Wait a minute," she said to Connor, turning around to face him. "The tour boat? That's really happening?"

Connor nodded sheepishly. "It is. I...I wanted to surprise you. It was sort of your idea, actually, and a damn good one at that. I love the boat trips—don't worry, you can stay on shore, I'm sure you'll find ways to pass the time in Galway. And we could use a tour company that's actually run by a local. No more false promises of gluten-free beer and all that. I thought it would be fun to just surprise you with it, and now, from the look on your face, I don't have the first idea why I thought that was wise. I...I should have told you. I'm sorry."

"No." Emma shook her head. "It's not that. Honestly, it's your decision. It's not like we're business partners. I'm flattered that you liked the idea, and I love that you and Patrick are working together and making decisions together. It would have been a great surprise." She squeezed his biceps playfully, smiling into his eyes. "I'll try to forget that I know anything. See if I can trick myself into being surprised."

"You don't have to do that," said Connor. "Patrick might be a surprise-ruining bastard, but at least I still have a few tricks up my sleeve."

"Do you?" She raised her eyebrows. "Ah, that's right. I seem to remember him saying something about a romantic gesture?"

Connor's jaw flexed, no doubt because he was gritting his teeth and grinding his molars down to dust. "Did he? I must have missed that. I can't imagine what he was going on about."

"You really can't?" Emma grinned. "I guess I'll have to actually be surprised about that one, then. Unless the surprise is that he made it all up and there's actually no grand surprise or gesture or anything romantic at all waiting for me." She frowned. "Um, actually, you should probably tell me if that's the case. Because I might be a good pretender..." Connor coughed pointedly. "Okay, I'm not good at pretending, and if I spend all weekend waiting for something special to happen and it doesn't, I might be a little bit of a sad panda."

"You'll get your surprise," said Connor, holding up his hand. "I won't say any more than that. No matter how many puppy dog eyes you make at me." He pointed towards the tables near the door. "Now go, make yourself useful. Fill the salt shakers or wipe up the sticky spots. Heck, take some honey and add some sticky spots if you think that will make things more interesting."

Emma turned towards the tables with a smile on her face. Whatever was coming, she didn't need to know any more. Connor had clearly gone to great lengths to plan something special for the weekend, and now it was up to her not to overthink it before it happened. Now if only there was something to help take her mind off it...

Eight hours later, Emma almost regretted wishing for something to help take her mind off Connor's romantic weekend plans. But only almost.

The day had been surprisingly busy, though there had only been one tour boat. The same one Emma had taken a year ago, if she remembered correctly, though today it had been packed to the gills.

Emma had served bowl after bowl of soup, and she'd barely seen Connor, for how busy he'd been in the back keeping a steady stream of fish and chips flowing out to the dining room.

Once the boat had left, the locals had come in. It was almost as if they'd been hanging back, peeking out of the blinds to make sure it was safe to come out. Emma doubted that, especially considering how friendly and chatty all the Irish people she'd met had been, but she still couldn't help but notice how many familiar faces turned up outside the pub just after the last boat disappeared over the horizon.

While Patrick filled the pint glasses and poured the shots, Emma disappeared into the kitchen to check on Connor. "How's it going back here?" she asked, eyeing the stovetop where he was stirring a massive pot. She raised an eyebrow at the pot. "No more fish and chips?"

Connor shuddered. "Not for at least another week. I can't handle the sight of another cod fillet or the smell of another potato wedge right now." He lifted a ladle from the pot, showing her what was inside. "It's stew tonight. It's just about done, too, and we can get out of here when it is."

"You don't want to stay for dinner and drinks?"

He shook his head. "I know that probably should sound appealing to me, but there's nothing I want more right now than to cuddle up with you and Lady and fall asleep on the couch." He rubbed a hand over his mouth, stifling a yawn. "Is that the trap of being in a happy relationship? No more late nights out on the town?"

Emma laughed. "Well, if you want to go out clubbing here, you know I wouldn't try to stop you." She placed her hand gently between his shoulder blades, rubbing lightly. "I think it's just that being happy at home means you're no longer wondering if you're missing out on something that's happening out in the real world. There's some kind of security in it, you know?"

Looking at her over his shoulder, his face softened into a warm grin. "I'd make a dumb joke, but you're absolutely right." He let go of the ladle and turned to her, pulling her against him and encircling her with his arms. "I love you, Emma Kells. And I'm happy every day that I get to share my life with you."

She pressed a soft kiss to his lips, pulling back to look into his eyes and meet his smile with her own. "I love you too, Connor Ryan. I still can't believe we were lucky enough to find each other."

A grimace crossed Connor's face just then, alarming Emma. "What? Did I say something wrong? Are you in pain?"

He shook his head. "No. It's just...damn it. This is what happens when I actually bother to make plans." His teeth were still bared when he looked her in the eyes again. "I don't want to not ask you this just because I already planned out some fancy romantic something or other."

Understanding washed over Emma, her worry replaced with amusement. "Don't let me stop you. I can still enjoy a romantic getaway even if there's no big surprise waiting for me there." She stepped back, crossing her arms and waiting to be entertained. "Go ahead, then."

But it wasn't entertaining, what happened next. It was tender and vulnerable and beautiful, and the laughter she thought would be bubbling out of her turned out to be lots and lots of happy tears as Connor untied his apron, placed it carefully on the counter, and then got down on one knee in front of her.

His eyes were wet and his chin was quivering as he reached up to take both of her hands in his own. "Emma, I can't wait any longer to ask you this. Ever since the day you walked into my life, I couldn't believe my good fortune that someone like you would even look my way. It's been the honor of my life to have been chosen by you, to be loved by you. You're already my partner. You're already the only person I want to see in the morning, the only one I want to fall asleep next to, and I never want to be away from you. I want to share everything with you, and not just my favorite hurling shirt. Everything I have and everything I am, it's all yours. So, if it's not too much to ask for one more mammothly big blessing in my life...Emma Kells, will you marry me?"

Emma pulled Connor to his feet, kissing him until they both needed to break for air. There was a question in his eyes still, and she realized she hadn't said her resounding yes out loud. "Of course," she said, choking the words out through the tears streaming down her cheeks. "I'll marry you tomorrow. Not probably the best plan since my friends and family are all a world away and would kill me if we eloped, but you get the idea. I love you so much, I pinch myself that I get to be with you, to be loved by you, and in every sense except the legal one, I feel like I'm already married to you." She wrapped her arms around him, squeezing as close as their bodies and propriety would allow. "Let's make it official."

Connor stroked her hair, his hand finding its way to the back of her neck and pulling her head against his chest while he kissed the top of her head. When she pulled back enough to see him, she saw his cheeks were wet with the tears that had spilled down them, matching her own. Love erupted out of her as a mess of laughter and even more tears as she stood up on her toes to kiss his salty cheeks. "So that's what was waiting for me in Galway?"

Connor smacked his forehead with his palm. "Aw shite. I forgot. Not just that..." He reached down into his pockets, as if to double check something, and pulled them out again, empty. "Your ring. I don't exactly have it on me."

"I hadn't noticed," Emma deadpanned.

"My grandmother's ring," he explained. "My da gave it to me, but it's in Galway having one of the stones reset. I was going to pick it up tomorrow and have it in time for the proposal...which was supposed to be *after* Claire's visit, preferably in January, on our romantic getaway to Dublin and Glendalough."

Emma laughed and kissed him again. "It's perfect like this, trust me. You and I, we don't exactly do things in the proper order, now do we? I slept over at your house the first night we met, met your parents the next day, and you gave me a key as a Christmas present."

"Really? You're not disappointed not to have the grand proposal story?"

"Are you kidding? I love it. This is *our* story, and it's just perfect."

# Author's Note

Thank you so much for reading this story of mine. I had a lot of fun writing it, traveling back to Inishmore in my mind over a decade after taking my first trip there.

I've spent a lot of holidays away from home (or in a new home away from home), and that is what has inspired this series. Whether it was Easter at a pub in Dublin or Thanksgiving in Turkey, the joy and celebration was (almost) always stronger than the homesickness. It is my hope that this series will provide both an escape for those longing to travel and a taste of comfort for those who find themselves thousands of miles from home during the holidays.

The "Home (Abroad) for the Holidays" theme will continue in 2023 with *Christmas at Terminal One*, Claire's story.

To stay updated on other works in progress, please visit my website at kcmccormickciftci.com and subscribe to my newsletter. I send out monthly updates on upcoming releases, books I'm loving, and other recommendations.

If you loved this book, please consider leaving a review, as that is one of the best ways to support indie authors like me. Reviews left on major retail sites (wherever you bought this book is a great start!), The StoryGraph, GoodReads, and BookBub will help other readers discover this book, too.

# Acknowledgments

This book would never have come into existence if not for the life-changing year I spent in Ireland and, in particular, one windy, cold day spent on Inishmore. I'm especially grateful to my Aunt Mary for braving the elements (and proud of both of us for not joining the seasick ranks on the journey), and to my housemates and their families for making it one big adventure. I never would have guessed that day would come back for inspiration just over a decade later, but I'm very glad that it did.

To Lucy, for taking my limited vision and breathing a whole new life into it with this gorgeous cover. Thank you for sharing your talent with me, and I can't wait to see what we come up with together for next year.

To Paula, for your real-time reactions and advice on how to refine the story into what it only had the potential for. I hope I've done you proud.

To my mom and to Sarah Daniel, for being two of the surest sources of encouragement and light in my life. I'm so grateful for both of you.

To Hüseyin, for everything. Meals cooked, litterboxes cleaned, emotional support provided. You listen intently even when I'm thinking out loud about marketing strategies, and if that isn't one very specific definition of love, then I don't know what is. I love you.

To everyone who has taken a chance on one of my books, left a review, shared it with a friend, or sent me a kind word. There's a lot of solitude in writing, but the connection that happens between the one who writes a story and the one who reads it is an otherworldly kind of magic. Thank you.

# About the Author

KC McCormick Çiftçi is an English teacher turned romance writer. She is from Michigan, but spent the majority of her twenties living and working abroad, collecting the experiences that inform the stories she tells. She enjoys telling multicultural and international love stories through sweet romance, romantic comedy, and women's fiction. She lives in Turkey with her husband and a herd of cats.

Prior to diving into the world of romance, KC published two self-help books for intercultural couples, *Lov-*

*ing Across Borders* and *The K-1 Visa Wedding Plan*. Both are available wherever books are sold.

For updates on upcoming releases, behind the scenes news, and book recommendations, visit kcmccormickci ftci.com (or just point your phone camera at the QR code below).

# Also By KC McCormick Çiftçi

## Austen in Turkey

Pride, Prejudice, & Turkish Delight

## Intercultural Relationship Self Help

Loving Across Borders

The K-1 Visa Wedding Plan

Lightning Source UK Ltd.
Milton Keynes UK
UKHW041806171122
412353UK00003B/39

9 781734 494068